The Stone's Secret

Ashlynn Carter

Copyright © 2024 by Ashlynn Carter

All rights reserved.

No part of this publication may be reproduced, distributed, or transmitted in any form or by any means, including photocopying, recording, or other electronic or mechanical methods, without the prior written permission of the publisher, except as permitted by U.S. copyright law. For permission requests, contact Ashlynn Carter at ashlynn.carter@proton.me.

The story, all names, characters, and incidents portrayed in this production are fictitious. No identification with actual persons (living or deceased), places, buildings, and products is intended or should be inferred.

Book Cover by Ashlynn Carter

First edition 2024

*For my family,
you are my greatest strength*

Chapter 1

"Again." Alice panted out.

"Seriously, Alice? We have been at this for hours." Matthew was bent over with his hands on his knees and breathing hard.

"I said again, Matt." Alice growled out. As she took up her fighting stance. "I can do this."

"I know you can. We all know you can. But working yourself to the point you can't stay awake at the dinner table is not going to make you better. You need rest." Matthew said as he watched her with a worried look on his face.

Alice lowered her guard and looked at him pleadingly. "It's the only way I can escape the dreams." She whispered.

"You are still having the dreams?" Matthew walked over to her.

About a month after Greyson disappeared, her dreams had begun. In these dreams, Greyson was either in a dark cell nursing recent injuries, whipped while tied to a post, or strapped down to a table as he was tortured in various ways.

What upset her more was that even though men yelled at him or taunted him, Greyson said nothing. He didn't even cry out when the whip would come down on his back. She could see the pain in his eyes and his jaw clenching, but he never let a sound escape his lips.

She felt a tear run down her cheek and she wiped it away quickly. She was past the tears, now she was just angry and wanted to tear apart everyone who had taken part in hurting Greyson. She refocused her attention on Matthew as he watched her carefully. "I had another one last night. It was the torture room again." Alice let out a tense breath.

"Alice, we will find out what happened to him." Matthew patted her shoulder. "If Grey found out that I trained you like we were trained, he would kill me. Come on, let's get something to eat."

Alice nodded and followed Matthew as he headed inside. "You're right, Matt." She let out a soft laugh. "Grey would kill you." He stopped walking and looked at her with wide eyes. "He had become so protective. He got so angry he shifted to his wolf when I talked about kissing guys to find out which one was my fated mate."

"I thought you said he was your fated mate?" Matthew stared at her as if in shock.

"He is, but he didn't realize it. He was pretty dense." A smile spread across her face as she thought back on how red his face had been and how he kept growling at her. She looked back at Matt to see him watching her with his mouth slightly open and his eyes as big as saucers. "Why are you looking at me like that?"

"You haven't smiled a real smile in the nine months you have been back. It just caught me off guard." Matthew blinked and continued walking. "It's good to see it again."

Once inside, Alice went up to her room and took a bath. After she was clean and dressed, she made her way to the library. Matthew and Rowan were already there with a tray of food set off to the side. Each one had a book and scratch paper they were taking notes on.

As she walked in, they both looked up at her. Rowan pulled a chair out for her, and she took it gratefully. He pushed the tray full of food in front of her and gave her a hard look.

Rowan had taken it upon himself to make sure she ate regularly after she passed out a week after her arrival from not eating. She learned it was more exhausting to argue with him, so she picked up the fork and put a bite in her mouth.

Seeing that she was eating, Rowan went back to his book. Alice could not express how grateful she was for Rowan and Matthew. Not only was Matthew continuing to train her, he and Rowan were also helping her figure out how to destroy the Guardian's Stone. The book Greyson retrieved from the hidden library was written in riddles and wasn't just about the Guardian's Stone.

It talked about several different powerful objects. The book never said the name of the different objects and didn't make it clear which one it was referring to.

There was an illustration of her necklace and the book told why the Stone was created. Greyson had been right. An Alpha named Tyson had sought for an audience with a prophetess named Mara. He wanted her to give him a prophecy of his future. After seeing her, Tyson fell in love with Mara and instead of asking for the prophecy, he asked if he could court her.

The two grew incredibly close over the next month. Mara had become distant once she realized the reason Tyson had first come to see her. She was afraid that he only wanted her to provide him with prophecies. Tyson swore his love was true, but Mara told him to bring her a token to prove his love.

As an Alpha, Tyson had the ability to issue commands to his people and they had no choice but to do as he said. His command seemed more powerful than a normal Alpha. A normal Alpha's command only affected those in his pack, but Tyson's affected all wolf Shifters.

He rarely used it, and his people respected him for not forcing them to follow him. To prove himself to his love, Tyson put his Alpha command into a token and presented it to Mara a week after she told him to prove his love. Mara was so moved that he was willing to give her complete control over him and his people that she accepted his offering, and they were married.

Because of the power within the Stone, Mara and Tyson built a safeguard into it so that only a blood descendant could activate the power of the Stone. Years later, the Stone was hidden within a castle. The knowledge of activating it could be found there.

Together with his fated mate, the descendant will be able to use the Alpha command that is within the token. Only an equal sacrifice given as proof of love between a fated pair can undo the magic of the stone.

Alice finished her plate of food and shoved it aside. "Any luck uncovering what could be considered better than handing over the ability to control yourself and thousands of others? Or found where the King and Queen's castle is located?"

"Sorry, sis. I can't seem to find any mention of a royal castle anywhere." Rowan sat back in his chair and shook his head.

"I haven't found anything either." Matt said. "But I had a thought. If the first token was given in love, wouldn't any token given between a fated pair that love each other be equally as good?"

Alice blinked in surprise. It made sense. Equal in value didn't necessarily mean equal in physical power. Now all they had to do is find the castle and Greyson so they can destroy the Stone. "Has there been any news on Greyson's whereabouts?" Alice asked.

Matthew became fidgety. She focused her attention on him, but he avoided making eye contact with her. After several tense minutes, Matthew broke the silence. "It's only rumors. There is no evidence to back up any of these claims." Alice raised an eyebrow at him as she waited for Matthew to continue. He let out a sigh and leaned forward so his arms rested on the table.

"There is talk about Sasha getting so mad about being unable to break or entice a prisoner, that she was forced to ship him to the Howling Meadows Pack in Valencia. Rumor has it, Sasha isn't the one in charge. She answers to an Alpha named Maddox, and he is getting frustrated over Sasha's inability to find one girl." Matthew glanced over at Rowan before looking back at Alice. "These are all rumors though. We have some men looking into Alpha Maddox and his dealings with Sasha. Hopefully they can find something to point us in the right direction."

Silence filled the room again as they took in the information. It would make sense. An Alpha wants more power and wants the Stone in order to have complete control over more than his own pack.

Greyson wouldn't break. He was too strong. He had lived through so much because of the Barnetts that he would never tell them anything. If he was still alive, he would be in Valencia at the Howling Meadows Pack. She looked between Rowan and Matthew.

"We need to find him in order to destroy the Stone. I will give your people two weeks Matthew, but then I am leaving for Valencia."

"Mom and dad will never let you go, Alice." Rowan said. "You would be putting yourself in danger by walking right into the den of the man looking for you."

"Mom and dad won't know I am gone until it's too late. They also will not know where I have gone." She gave Rowan a pointed look. "I think walking into the den is exactly what I need to do to get Greyson back. I need to find the Queen and King's castle to destroy the Stone. We all need to be there in order to activate the power of the Stone since the knowledge can only be found there. I need to activate the Stone in order to destroy it. I can use them to get me there."

"It's really risky, Alice. We don't even know if Greyson is alive or not. I don't think Grey would want you to do this." Matthew said.

Alice slammed her fist down on the table, causing everyone to jump. "You don't know what Greyson would do. That stupid man went and got himself shot and captured, leaving me no choice but to do this." She growled out. "Plus, I owe him something and I plan on delivering it."

Alice stood up and stormed out of the room. She needed to blow off some steam, so she headed back out to the training grounds. It didn't take Alice long after arriving back at her parents' house to realize that Greyson had intentionally made Bradley mad. He had gotten himself shot on purpose to protect her hiding place, and she was furious with him for doing it.

She had been assaulting the punching bag for an hour when she heard someone come up behind her. Taking a deep breath, she recognized her Uncle Isaac's scent. She continued throwing punches. She was just starting to feel calmer after what Rowan and Matt had said and she didn't want to get worked up again.

Ten minutes passed and she finally gave up on ignoring her uncle who waited patiently. It seemed he wasn't going anywhere until they spoke. She turned around and faced him.

"Is there something I can do for you, Uncle?" she asked while crossing her arms over her chest. Sweat coated her skin and she was breathing hard.

"You remind me of him. He would train like this when he needed to work things out in his head." Isaac said with a sad smile. Greyson's disappearance affected her uncle almost as much as it did Matthew and her. He always had a sad and painful look in his eyes when he spoke about Greyson.

"Well, he did train with me for several months. Maybe his habits rubbed off on me." Alice shrugged.

"Your mom sent me out here to talk to you. It seems they are worried about you." Isaac said while glancing back at the house. "Would you care to join me for a walk?"

Alice followed his glance and saw her mother watching from the window. "Sure." She said as Isaac started walking toward the gardens, and Alice fell into step beside him. "I know they mean well. It's just hard. They look at me like they expect me to crumple to the floor. I have caught them whispering about Greyson, but as soon as they see me, they stop talking."

"You have been distant since returning and they are just concerned about you. I'm not exactly sure what happened during those six months you and Greyson were in hiding, but everyone can see a huge change in you." She could feel his eyes on her.

The sting of tears began, and Alice blinked hard to clear them away. "I fell in love with him." Alice whispered with a small shrug and sad smile.

"You fell in love with him?" Isaac looked shocked for a brief moment as he stopped and turned to face her. The shock quickly changed to deep sadness.

"By the time I realized it, he was taken." Alice felt her anger rising again.

"Taken? What makes you think he is still alive?" Curiosity and hope filled his voice.

Alice told Isaac about her dreams, and after Matthew's report, she believed he was in Valencia. "I just know he is. I need him to be."

"Alice, one of my reasons for coming here was to talk with you about some information I have received from a contact of mine." He paused for a moment before continuing. "I'm glad that you think he is alive, because I was worried about upsetting you."

"What are you talking about, Uncle Isaac?" Alice asked. Hope started to bloom in her chest, and she desperately wanted to hear what he had to say.

"I have a contact in Valencia. She said that a friend of hers has seen a prisoner recently. The guards were interrogating the prisoner about a young woman that has visions. She said he didn't respond and, well, he ended up having to be carried back to his cell." Alice's heart felt like it was going to beat out of her chest. "The Pheonix has asked me to see if there is any way to extract the man before he is executed."

"The Pheonix? Executed?" Alice had never heard of anyone by that name. And Greyson couldn't be executed.

Isaac gave a firm nod. "The Phoenix is the one in charge of all the Hunters. Our family manages just a small branch of the organization. It is rare that The Pheonix reaches out and assigns specific assignments like this. Usually, The Pheonix gives us reports on Shifters to watch, or situations that we need to look into."

Alice furrowed her brow. "Who is The Phoenix?"

"No one knows. It's a bit of a complicated and long story, but The Phoenix has been instrumental in keeping Arlania safe." He began slowly walking again. "Whoever this young prisoner is, The Pheonix feels he is important enough to want him out of there. I came to tell you that I think Greyson might be alive, and to let you all know that I am going to be gone for several months."

"What? You're leaving? Now?" Alice was surprised that her uncle would be going there personally.

"The Phoenix wants him extracted immediately." Isaac pulled her into a tight hug. "I will send word as soon as I am able." Isaac stepped away and shifted into his falcon as he took flight. Alice watched until her uncle disappeared. She needed to talk with Matthew before she packed. No matter what anyone said, she was going to Valencia.

Chapter 2

"Matt?" Alice called as she reached the library.

Matthew looked up from the book he was studying. He was at the table where she had left him hours before. He had an apologetic look on his face. "Look, Alice, I'm sorry. I miss him too, but…"

"It's okay, Matt. You were right that we didn't know if Greyson was alive or not. Have you spoken to Uncle Isaac about his trip?" Alice asked as she took the seat next to him.

"What trip?" Matt asked with his brows furrowed.

Alice lowered her voice. "Someone called 'The Pheonix' asked him to go to Valencia. Apparently, there is a prisoner there that is being interrogated. They think he has information about the girl with the visions. Uncle Isaac is supposed to try to get him out of there."

Matthew's eyes widened in surprise. There was excitement shining in them for a second, before his gaze became more guarded. "We do not know it is him, Alice."

"You're right. We don't, but Matt…I need to know if it is. Uncle Isaac mentioned a possible execution. I cannot sit here waiting to find out if the prisoner is Grey, and if he has been executed or not." Alice felt the familiar sting in her eyes, warning her that tears were close to falling.

Matthew pulled her into a hug. "I love you like a sister. I really don't like to see you hurt. Let me go instead. I might even be better than Isaac at getting the prisoner out. I will send word once the identity of the prisoner is known."

"Matt, I need to go too. I have to know if it's Grey. I need him." Alice sniffled. She knew Matthew would do everything in his power to keep her here where she was safe.

"Alice, please. Stay here with Rowan and your parents. If it is Grey, then I will bring him back here as fast as I can." Matt pleaded with her as he pulled back and looked into her eyes.

Alice sat quietly for several minutes going over her options. She should reassure Matt that she would remain behind, but she hated to lie. Alice swallowed as she looked to the other side of the room in thought.

She could let Matt leave and then follow the next day. She would stay in the shadows and watch what happened from a safe distance. She could leave rescuing the prisoner to her uncle and Matt. But she wanted to be there if the prisoner ended up being Greyson. She needed to be there.

Alice looked back at Matt, who was watching her closely. "Okay, fine, but I am trusting you to keep me constantly updated." Matt continued to watch her with suspicion. "I promise I will be here when you leave. But promise me something."

"Anything, sis."

"Promise me that if it is Greyson, that you will bring him back to me." Alice blinked back tears. She had made Greyson promise her something similar before he left for the library.

"I promise, Alice. If I find Greyson, I will make sure he gets to you safely." Matt kissed her cheek before standing up. "I am going to get ready and leave within the hour."

Alice watched Matthew walk out of the library. She knew he was going to be mad at her when he found out that she followed him. She sat in the quiet of the library for several more minutes before getting up and heading for her room. She had lots of things to get ready if she was going to leave once everyone was asleep.

Alice finished putting her books, clothing and her daggers into her bag when she heard yelling down the hall. She quickly hid her bag under her bed before leaving her room. She followed the yelling down the stairs and out the front door. Rowan and Matthew were facing each other with her parents a few feet away.

"It's your job to guard her and you are leaving!" Rowan's face was red with anger.

"I need him to go." Alice stepped off the porch and walked calmly toward everyone. All eyes turned in her direction.

"What are you talking about?" Her father asked. "Matthew is your guard. You can't just dismiss him whenever you feel like it."

"There has been a new development. Matthew needs to go assist Uncle for a little while. Until he gets back, I can take care of myself." Alice crossed her arms over her chest. "You know it's true. Matt has been training both me and Rowan, and both of us have become very capable fighters."

Grudgingly, Alice's father and Rowan let Matthew leave. Alice let out the breath she had not realized she had been holding. Alice felt guilty knowing she was going to cause her family to worry even more about her when they woke the next morning to find her gone. Again.

Alice lay in bed as she listened to the household settle in for the night. She waited another hour before climbing from her bed and getting dressed. She grabbed her pack and quietly headed down the stairs. Ducking into her Uncle Marcus's office, she softly closed the door behind her.

A memory resurfaced of the night she and Greyson made their escape the year before. Shaking her head to clear it, Alice took a deep breath. She was determined to do this. She was done hiding. She was going to find Greyson and they were going to destroy the Stone. Alice moved to the window and climbed through. She followed the same path Greyson had led her on the last time.

As soon as she reached the tree line, Alice shifted to her wolf. She grabbed her bag with her mouth and took off into the night. She slowed as she passed the church, but then continued. She didn't have time to stop and say hello. She picked up her speed again. Maybe on their way back to her parents' house, she and Greyson could stop by to see the preacher and his wife.

Alice spent the rest of the night running. As the sky began to lighten, Alice found a cave to spend the day in. She did not bother shifting back to her human form, but instead settled down on the dirt floor. She missed the feeling of Grey's warmth next to her and his large head resting on her back. She closed her eyes and willed herself to sleep.

* * *

Alice had sat in a cave with a small fire for warmth and light throughout the day. She had been traveling for three days now. She mostly slept through the day and shifted to her wolf during the night to cover more ground.

She stared into the dying embers as memories of her and Greyson running away resurfaced. The night they nearly froze to death before finding the church. Their wedding. Greyson holding her as she cried herself to sleep. Alice poked the logs with a stick as she blinked back her tears.

She needed to concentrate on finding him. Whether Greyson was alive or dead, she needed to know what happened to him. But if Grey was the prisoner in Valencia, she had a feeling her nightmares were visions of what was happening to him.

Nine months. He had been enduring unspeakable amounts of pain for nine months. Alice's stomach twisted uncomfortably at the thought. She took a deep breath and wiped the tear that escaped onto her cheek. She sniffed and stood before kicking dirt over the remains of her fire.

Restless, Alice moved to the mouth of the cave. She let out a sigh of relief. It was finally dark enough for her to start out. Having to sit in the various caves left her with nothing to do but think or try to sleep. Both activities always brought thoughts of Greyson.

Alice shifted into her wolf and ran from the cave. Her next stop was the Finn's. Alice had missed them terribly over the last nine months. Asher, Avery, and Alisha had quickly become some of the most important people in her life. Then Greyson disappeared, and she had to go back to her parents' home. Not having Greyson with her had made leaving them so much harder for her.

The Finn's store was close to the Valencia border, and she was hoping to get her horse and stock up on supplies before setting out into the unfamiliar country. Alice planned on stopping by the home she and Greyson had shared before going to the Finn's store.

She had been running for hours when her wolf's sensitive nose started picking up familiar scents. Alice slowed her pace and looked around. She spotted the grove of trees that marked the tunnel that led to the hidden pocket where Greyson nearly died. She listened and sniffed the air for anything out of the ordinary. She shifted back to her human form and continued heading for their house.

The sun was beginning to lighten the sky as Alice came to the clearing. Their home looked just like it had the day they left. She carefully worked her way toward the door. So much time had passed since they were forced to leave, but Alice didn't want to take any chances, just in case someone was waiting inside for her.

She listened for several minutes but she saw and heard no movement. Carefully, she opened the door and stepped inside. She made sure to close the door behind her before moving further into the house.

Memories flashed in front of her eyes as she looked around the room. She saw Greyson sitting on the floor next to the couch she was laying on. She smiled, remembering how he had pulled her off the couch and onto his lap.

She blinked and she saw him reading a book to Asher while holding Avery. Alice shook her head. She needed to focus. She headed for the stairs and climbed them quickly. She paused on the threshold of their room. The bed was still not made and Greyson's shirt was on the floor.

Alice slowly walked over to it and picked it up. She hugged it to her chest as she took in a deep breath. His scent was still on it. It was faint, but it was still there. Alice looked around and spotted a satchel in the corner. She picked it up and put Greyson's shirt in it.

Rowan would tease her for taking Greyson's dirty shirt. What Rowan did not understand was the gaping hole Alice felt with Greyson's absence. His scent made her feel grounded and calmed her. She didn't realize how much she had needed that, or how much she would miss and need him.

Alice began pulling out clothing of hers and stuffing them in the bag. Once she had several changes of clothes, Alice moved back downstairs. She made her way outside and to the barn. She stopped when she saw that the stalls were empty. Where had the horses gone? Alice looked around. The barn looked to have been empty for a long time. Maybe the Finn's came and got them. With nothing else to get, Alice closed the barn and house again and set out towards the store.

Alice stopped as the Finn's store came into view. A memory of the last time Greyson brought her here came back to her. It was nearing the end of their visit and Asher was having a rough time. He wanted to go home with them. His cries had been hard for Alice to hear. She wanted him to go home with them, too. She missed having the kids there.

She had been fighting back tears as they headed for the horses. Before she could climb on top of Prince, Greyson had pulled her to him and held her close until her tears dried. Greyson had pressed a kiss to her forehead before helping her up into the saddle.

Alice shook her head. She crossed the street and entered the store. Mr. Finn looked up from his place behind the counter and froze. He looked at her as if he wasn't sure if she was actually standing there or not. He finally shook off the shock and hurried around the counter to her. He pulled her into a tight hug.

"Dear Alice." His voice broke. "We have been so worried about you." He finally stepped back and held her at arm's length as he studied her. "How are you holding up?"

"I am hanging in there." Alice took in a breath and slowly let it out. "How is everyone?" Alice asked, looking around.

"Let me close up the shop and we can go upstairs. The kids will be so happy to see you." Mr. Finn walked to the door and locked it before leading the way up the stairs to the Finn's living quarters. "Look who came to the store today." He called loudly.

Alice heard little feet running down the small hall followed by Mrs. Finn telling Asher to slow down. When Asher saw her, he stopped for a moment before launching himself at her. Alice caught him to her and hugged him tight. Tears started running down her cheeks as the boy's small arms wrapped around her neck. "How is my boy doing?" She whispered into his ear.

"I've missed you." Asher's excitement at seeing her had him bouncing on his feet. "Where is Greyson?" he asked, looking behind her as if Greyson would climb the stairs any second.

"Alice!" Mrs. Finn came into the room. Alice stood from her crouched position to accept the hug of the older woman. "How are you, dear?"

"I'm okay." Alice answered with a forced smile. "Where are Avery and Alisha?"

"Alisha is reading to Avery. Asher, why don't you go get your sisters." Mrs. Finn suggested. Asher reluctantly left Alice's side and moved back down the hallway. As soon as he was out of earshot, Mrs. Finn turned back to Alice. "What are you doing back here? I thought you were in danger."

"I am." Alice said quietly. "I am on my way to Valencia. I figured I could stop in and see some of my favorite people while I purchase supplies."

"Why are you heading to Valencia? It's not the friendliest of countries to visit." Mr. Finn asked.

"My uncle and brother are there. I need to meet up with them." Alice tried to skirt around the truth. She didn't want them to know too much. Greyson seemed to trust them, but he often left out specific details, so she followed his example.

A moment later, Alisha, carrying Avery, stepped into the living room with Dante at their side. Her face lit up as she hurried to Alice. Alice hugged Alisha close for a minute before Avery was handed over to her. "She started to try to walk." Alisha said with a smile.

"Oh Avery, baby. You are getting so big." Alice pressed a kiss to the baby's cheek. Alice smiled at Alisha. "I've missed you. What have you been up to?"

"Reading and helping with Avery and Asher. Did Greyson stay behind?" Alisha asked with a furrowed brow.

Alice closed her eyes. She knew the kids were not trying to cause her pain, but it didn't hurt any less being reminded that Greyson wasn't with her. Had Mr. and Mrs. Finn not told the kids that Greyson was most likely dead?

"Umm. He is gone right now." Alice felt so guilty. She hated lying, but she also did not want to tell the kids that Greyson had been killed. She didn't even know if he really was dead or if he was a prisoner somewhere.

Alice spent the rest of the day with the kids and the Finns. Mrs. Finn was grateful to have Alice there to help with the kids so she could get some of their laundry done while Mr. Finn went back to the store. Dante stayed at her side the whole day. He whined periodically, and each time, Alice expected to hear Greyson's growl, but didn't. Just another reminder of his absence.

Alice played with the kids and read to them. She had missed them so much over the past several months. She sang to them at bedtime until they fell asleep. Mr. Finn helped Alice get the supplies she needed and loaded them into the saddle bags.

He did have her and Greyson's horses, which was a huge relief. She took Prince, but left Greyson's horse Midnight. Alice figured she and Greyson could pick him up when they returned. Alice set out soon after the kids were asleep. It was going to be a difficult journey from here on out since she was going into unfamiliar territory.

Chapter 3

The sound of a heavy lock grinding against metal roused Greyson from his restless sleep. He inwardly groaned as he sat up. The stone floor was not very comfortable. He had been moved several times over the past nine months, but this cell was worse than the others.

The ceiling was no more than five feet tall, making it impossible for his six-foot frame to stand up straight. The floor, walls, and ceiling were made of stone. There was a small window at the very top of the cell. It was about six inches tall and eighteen inches wide, just big enough to mark the passage of time. There was a leaking pipe somewhere that caused the floor to be permanently damp. The air was thick with the smell of mildew and blood.

The door opened wide and his usual two guards stood there with grim expressions on their faces. Greyson let out a heavy sigh. He struggled to his feet, still in pain from the whipping several days ago. He gave the men a nod as he stepped toward them, ready for whatever they decided to do to him that day.

He had vowed that he would not make a sound no matter what they did to him, and so far, he had kept his promise to himself. He was taught that the key to withstanding torture was to take his mind somewhere else. He was six when he was forced to master the skill. The last several months, he retreated to one of his memories of Alice.

The guard on the left was burly with a thick beard. He acted tough, but Greyson saw the respect in his eyes grow with each month that Greyson had been there. He had overheard the guards talking and found out the man's name was Phil.

The guard on Greyson's right was short but built like an ox. Phil had called him John. In contrast to Phil's dark brown hair, John had long blonde hair that was pulled back into a bun at the base of his head. Both weren't terrible men, but they had a job to do. Greyson could understand that. He had spent years doing things he was not proud of because it had been his job.

They grabbed Greyson's arms, as to their normal routine. Greyson still hadn't really figured out if it was to help support him or to keep him from trying to run. They led him through the winding corridors of the prison. They passed the door to the torture room, so it looked like it was another day of the whip.

Greyson took a deep breath as he began to prepare himself for the pain. But to his surprise, he was pulled past the whipping post and through another set of doors. Greyson was confused, this was not the normal routine that he had gotten used to. Normally, Phil and John showed up at his cell and escorted him to one of two places: either the whipping post or the torture room. It had been that way for nearly eight months.

After another ten minutes of walking, Phil opened a door and shoved Greyson in before following him inside. "The Alpha wishes to see you today. Time to clean you up and get you presentable." Phil's deep voice explained.

Before Greyson could fully process the words, a cold bucket of water was dumped on him. John pulled the rags off of him that were serving as pants as another bucket of cold water was dumped over his head. "Here is the soap. Start scrubbing." John commanded.

Greyson accepted the bar of soap and did as he was asked. The soap burned his still healing wounds on his chest and arms. When Phil started scrubbing his back, Greyson let out a soft hiss of pain. These two weren't his enemy so he didn't bother to hide his discomfort from them. Phil and John paused and looked at one another.

A flash of pity crossed their features before they replaced it with their emotionless masks. After he was clean, John cut Greyson's hair so it was only a few inches long, while Phil shaved the beard that was growing thick and long on his face. It felt good to have his beard off, at least something good was coming from this. John tossed him a pair of clean pants and Greyson quickly slid them on.

Once done, his trusty guards placed thick metal cuffs on his wrists. Greyson knew that these cuffs were laced with something that prevented him from shifting, same as the rooms in the prison. He had tried several times after he had first gotten there to escape, but without his wolf senses it was hard to know where guards were without seeing them.

Not to mention that he wasn't physically up to fighting his way out. They made sure that he was constantly beaten and tortured to keep him from being able to do much. Greyson had become resigned to his fate. With no hope of escape, he would take his knowledge of Alice to the grave.

Now that he was clean and had pants on, Phill grabbed his arm and dragged Greyson out of the room and up a flight of stairs. They entered an enormous chamber. Greyson had not realized they were in a castle, but now that he was standing in the huge space, he recognized it as a throne room.

There were at least a hundred people standing along the sides leaving a clear path to the front of the room where a raised platform was situated. A large man with black hair sat on a chair in the center of the platform. To his right sat a woman with dark reddish-brown hair.

Phil nudged Greyson forward and the three of them walked to stand in front of the man and woman. Greyson smiled as John bent down and hooked a chain that was bolted to the floor, to the cuffs on his wrists. Phil and John stepped back leaving Greyson standing alone.

The man on the platform sat silently as he observed Greyson. Greyson stood tall despite his injuries. He felt fresh blood dripping down his back, no doubt the wounds had reopened from Phil scrubbing them.

Greyson kept a neutral expression on his face as he waited. His eyes flicked to the woman sitting next to the man. Something about her seemed...familiar. He studied her more closely. Her dark reddish-brown hair flowed down around her shoulders, and she sat tall. There was an elegance about her that seemed to draw him in. He looked at her eyes and their gazes locked. She had the same amber colored eyes that Matthew and he had. He continued to watch her until a throat cleared.

"Is there a reason you keep looking at my wife, boy?" The man growled out and Greyson turned his attention back to the man, but didn't answer. "Let me introduce myself, I am Alpha Maddox, and this is my wife, Queen Isabel. I hear from Lady Sasha that you are a Shifter, is that true?" Greyson kept silent. "How old are you?" Alpha Maddox started tapping his fingers on the arm of his chair. "Where is the girl who has visions? " Alpha Maddox yelled as he slammed his fist on the chair. "Can he even speak?" Alpha Maddox turned and glared at John and Phil.

Greyson glanced back at Queen Isabel who was watching him with wide eyes that glimmered with unshed tears. Greyson gave her a quick bow. "Queen Isabel, it's nice to finally meet you." His voice was raw from not using it for so long and it came out scratchy and low.

"Get him some water." Queen Isabel commanded and in seconds Phil handed Greyson a cup. He drank the whole thing quickly before setting the cup down on the floor at his feet. He grimaced as he stood back up as the pain in his back intensified. "What is your name?"

Greyson debated how he should answer. He was pretty sure that Queen Isabel was the same woman from Alice's vision about Matthew being taken to the orphanage. If Alpha Maddox was the same Alpha she was afraid of back then, he didn't want to get her in trouble now. "Greyson Hunt." He finally said. There was no reason to believe that Alpha Maddox would know his name.

He watched as recognition, surprise, disbelief, wonder and then indifference flashed through the queen's eyes. He knew it. She was his mother. He swallowed hard as he pulled his eyes from Queen Isabel back to Alpha Maddox.

If Queen Isabel was his mother, Alpha Maddox was probably his father. Greyson narrowed his eyes and glared at the man. The Alpha was breathing hard with his fists clenched. His face was a deep shade of red.

"You have been silent for nine months, and now you speak to my wife!" He roared. Greyson knew the Alpha was close to shifting as veins bulged on his neck as he glared down at Greyson with steel grey eyes. Greyson needed to be careful since he could not shift himself. "Take him back to his cell!" In seconds, Phil had unlocked the chains and was dragging Greyson back toward the door at the opposite end of the throne room.

John followed close behind as they trekked back to Greyson's cell. Phil opened the cell door and Greyson walked in before turning around and holding out his arms, presenting his shackled wrists. John unlocked his cuffs and Greyson rubbed his raw skin.

He gave the guards an appreciative smile and walked back to his place by the wall. Phil hesitated before closing the door. Greyson let out a heavy sigh. Queen Isabel and Alpha Maddox were his parents, he did not see that coming.

As the day stretched on, his thoughts turned back to Alice, like they always did. He missed her. He hoped that she had contacted her uncle and not just stayed in the underground shelter.

He knew that they had not kidnapped her yet because they were still trying to get her location from him. He smiled at the thought of her threatening him and making him promise to make it back from the library. His smile faded as his thoughts turned to her searching for her fated mate.

Had she found him yet? A growl escaped from him at the thought. Closing his eyes, Greyson thought about fated mates and the connection they shared. If only he and Alice were, he would not have to give her up.

He began to replay the six months they were together. The longer they had been together, the more he was drawn to her. He could chalk that up to his growing attraction and love for her. Then there was his hypersensitivity to her emotions. He had not really lived with a woman before. Wasn't it normal to eventually sense her emotions, especially with his wolf senses?

He cursed under his breath. He needed to do something to clear his mind. Thoughts of Alice usually calmed him, but when he thought of her finding her mate, it ticked him off. Alice was *his* wife. And he wasn't planning on giving her up to anyone. He let out another curse. He really couldn't do anything being trapped in this prison.

Greyson moved to his hands and feet before he began doing push-ups. He had been alternating between doing push-ups and squats for hours causing sweat to burn the wounds in his back and chest. He ignored the pain and started a new set of push-ups. Greyson's cell door opened, and he could feel eyes on him.

He glanced over as he lowered himself into another push-up. His guards stood in the doorway watching him. When they didn't say anything or move into the cell, Greyson did five more push-ups before standing as much as he could with the low ceiling. He walked over to them, and they wordlessly grabbed his arms and led him from his cell.

They walked past the torture room and out into the courtyard that had the whipping posts. Phil and John slowed their steps as they walked towards Greyson's usual post. Greyson did not fight them. After the first month, he found that it went by faster if he just let them get it over with.

He had gotten quicker at mentally escaping the tortures that they forced on him. The real pain came after he was dumped back in his cell and left alone. He would come out of his mental block and had to endure the residual pain from the injuries.

As Phil and John finished chaining his arms above his head, Greyson looked over at them. He gave them a small nod and he saw their jaws tighten. He knew they hated to see this but were forced to. They never participated in actually hurting him, and often times apologized quietly as they returned him to his cell. Their job was to transport him from his cell to whatever torture was on the schedule for the day.

A movement behind Phil's shoulder caught Greyson's attention. A young soldier stood near a pillar. His wide eyes were trained on Greyson. Eyes Greyson knew well. Matthew. What was Matt doing here?

A man behind Greyson called out thirty stripes, but Greyson barely heard him. Greyson didn't want to draw attention to his brother but couldn't seem to look away. The whip came down hard on Greyson's back. He squeezed his eyes closed and took a deep breath. He gripped onto the chains with his hands with all his strength. *Stay Silent. Do not give them anything.* He reminded himself.

He opened his eyes and met Matthew's again. A hard expression was on his face, and his eyes showed anger, pain, and grief. The whip came down again. The thin leather straps sliced through Greyson's skin easily. Clenching his jaw, he closed his eyes. Alice. He needed his Alice.

He thought of his first training session with her back at the house. Another hit from the whip near his shoulder. She was so determined and wanted to know everything. She was a good fighter; her father taught her well, but she didn't put as much power as she could into each punch.

Greyson fixed her posture and then stood behind her. He had grabbed her fists in his and showed her the movement she should be making by guiding her fists. He had then stepped back and watched her complete the move several times against the punching bag. She wasn't rotating her hips. He stepped back up behind her, placing his hands gently on her hips. As she threw her next punch, Greyson rotated her hips while telling her that her real power comes from her whole body, not just her arm.

They had moved to the sparring arena after he watched her throw a few more punches. Up until this point, Greyson had always ended up winning with Alice barely getting any hits on him. It had frustrated her to no end. A few minutes into their match, Alice had delivered a punch straight to his face. It had split open his lip and he couldn't have been more proud of her.

Alice had been so surprised that she froze in her attack. After a moment, Alice's stunned expression had turned into an apologetic one. He pulled her to him and pressed his lips to hers. That was the last time he had kissed her until they were underground in the bunker. He had realized he was completely in love with her. He shouldn't have kept his distance. He should have treasured his time with her.

Hands began trying to loosen his grip on the chains. Greyson's back was on fire as he looked around him. John and Phil were trying to pull his right hand off the chain while Matt and another guard were working on his left. Taking a deep breath, Greyson released the chains.

As soon as the chains slackened on his wrists, he stumbled to his side. He fell against Matt, who still had a clenched jaw. As Phil and John hoisted him off Matt, Matt slipped something into Greyson's hand. He tightened both hands into tight fists so no one would know he had something in his hand.

It took everything in Greyson not to turn back around and look at his brother one last time. He still wasn't sure if he truly did see Matt. Maybe all the torture was finally breaking his mind and he was starting to see things. Phil and John were half dragging, half carrying Greyson down the long hallway. Once they were close to Greyson's cell, they slowed their steps.

"The Queen isn't going to like this." John whispered.

"When has she ever liked hearing about this?" Phil shot back.

"We should call for the healer. They did far more than the thirty stripes. I don't think there is a single untouched piece of skin on the kid's back." John said angrily.

"Once he is in the cell, you can send the new kid down to the infirmary to get the healer." Phil said quietly as the sound of a metal door creaking open reached Greyson's ears. "Come on kid, let's get you laying down."

Greyson was laid on his stomach gently. He kept his hands clenched. By the occasional breeze touching his face and back, Greyson did not need to open his eyes to know that the cell door was still open. It wasn't long until he heard footsteps approaching him. He slowly opened his eyes, trying to move as little as possible. He knew the more he moved, the more painful his back would be.

"You did well, kid. I thought it would take you longer to find the infirmary." John said tensely.

"Thank you, sir." Matthew's voice was a healing balm of its own. But panic kicked in quickly. Matt could not stay here. If they found out who he was, they would kill him. "Is this kind of thing normal?"

"For this poor man, yes." Phil said quietly.

Greyson's whole body tensed as the familiar warm rags full of healing herbs and oils were set on his back. Not only did they sting and burn his raw flesh, but they also tended to give him a headache.

"Queen Isabel assigned you here so there are a few things you need to know. This prisoner is your only priority. He does not speak or make any noise. The first time I have ever heard him speak in eight months, was a few hours ago when he was speaking with the Queen. Your job is to take him to and from his various sessions that the Alpha has assigned and protecting him from the other guards and prisoners."

"I need help rolling him. It looks like there are several lacerations along his sides." The healer spoke softly.

Greyson clenched his jaw. If she was going to heal his wounds, she might as well get the ones on his chest, too. He pushed himself onto his hands and his knees. He was breathing hard against the pain as he straightened up. The Healer's eyes were wide with surprise, while John, Phil and Matt moved quickly to his side. He was still on his knees when they reached him.

"If you're going to do it, just do it." Greyson said through clenched teeth. Matthew's mouth twitched slightly before settling back into indifference. The Healer quickly applied the nasty smelling rags to his wounds before using a long white strip of cloth that she wound around his entire torso, from his armpits to his waist. The Healer gathered her things quickly and left with John escorting her out. Greyson was trying his hardest not to throw up from the severity of the pain he was experiencing.

"Help me lay him back down on his stomach." Phil said to Matt. Greyson felt hands helping him lay back down.

"Phil." An angry man called from the door.

"Make sure he's not in any of the water." Phil said quietly as he got to his feet. "What can I do for you, sir?" He sounded like he stepped outside of the cell.

"Why was the Healer here?" The man said.

"The Queen has charged me with making sure this prisoner doesn't die before the information she needs is acquired." Phil said calmly.

"Grey?" Matt's quiet voice barely reached Greyson's ears.

"In the flesh, little brother." Greyson kept his voice low as he squeezed his eyes closed as pain shot through his body.

"What have they done to you?" Matt whispered.

"You shouldn't be here." A spasm of pain shot across Greyson's back again. "Alice?"

"She's alive, if that is what you are asking." Matt moved to Greyson's legs and pulled him a little more into the drier area of the cell. He moved back towards Greyson's head as he glanced back at the door and the angry voices that were coming through it. "She is a ghost of herself since she's been back. She heard everything that happened at the hunting lodge, including the gunshot. She is torn between thinking you are alive somewhere and thinking you died."

Greyson tried to get up, but Matt put a hand on him to stop his attempt. "Get out of here, Matt." Greyson felt his consciousness slipping. He met his brother's eyes, knowing it would not be much longer for the medicinal concoction in the bandages to knock him out. "Tell her I am dead. Keep her safe and help her find her mate." The blessed darkness claimed him, taking him away from all the pain and all of his swirling thoughts.

Chapter 4

Alice woke again drenched in sweat. She was spending the night in a cave she found in Valencia. Greyson was being whipped again. This time he was whipped until there was nothing but raw and bleeding skin left on his back.

Tears poured from her eyes as she hugged her knees to her chest. She almost wished Greyson were dead if her dreams were actual visions of him. These new nightmares are worse than the ones she had as a little girl. At least when he was little, he had a fighting chance. Now he was strapped down or chained.

She had been in Valencia for just over a week and she had no idea where to go. She had found her way into a small pack on her second day in the country. While there, Alice sold Prince so she could have money for supplies. It was hard to watch him go. Prince had been her wedding gift from Greyson, but she had to say goodbye in order to have the funds to find Greyson. Maybe after she had Grey back, she would think about getting another horse.

Alice also learned more about how Valencia was run, while at the market. She was told that much of the country was divided into packs. Some packs were very welcoming to travelers while others were not.

Alice was warned away from the Howling Meadows Pack multiple times while she was restocking her supplies. The only problem was that the Howling Meadows Pack was the same pack name that Matt had mentioned in the rumors, and where Uncle Isaac mentioned he was going.

Alice wiped her cheeks as she debated on what to do. If she went to the Howling Meadows Pack, she would be walking into the very pack whose Alpha was hunting her. But if she didn't, what were the chances Greyson would be in one of the other packs?

Alice started gathering her things and putting them back in her bags. Yesterday, she learned that the Howling Meadows Pack would open their main gate today in order to allow trade from other packs. She would walk in with all the other traders and find out all the information she could. She would leave during the next trade day. How hard would it be to blend in with all the other pack members? She didn't have a problem or stood out when she visited the other packs.

Stepping out into the warm morning sunlight, Alice began making her way down the steep hill that hid her little cave. She was twelve miles from the Howling Meadows Pack. She was tempted to shift to her wolf to travel faster, but she did not want to let anyone know she was a Shifter, let alone the white wolf.

Alice hiked her bags higher up on her shoulder as she began walking down the road. It did not take long for her to find more travelers. Not wanting to be seen travelling alone, Alice stayed close to a group of women, making it look like she was part of their group.

Once she was inside the pack, she could find her uncle or even Matt. It wasn't like they could send her away at this point. She would be trapped within the dangerous pack, so they would have to keep her close. Alice would be able to get information more quickly from their investigations.

The day rapidly grew hot. Valencia was much more dry and warmer than Arlania. Back home the nights were starting to turn cold, and snow was not far off. The temperature grew warmer and warmer as she descended the mountain pass that separated the two countries. Alice realized during this week that she didn't care too much for the heat, preferring the cooler weather and snow.

Miles passed and Alice had worked up a nice sweat. She glanced down at her clothes that she had purchased several days ago. They were covered in dust from all the foot traffic and carts travelling in front of her on the dirt road. She let out a sigh.

It looked like she was going to have to do laundry in the next day or two. At this point, the only semi-clean clothes she had was Greyson's shirt. And even that could probably use a wash. It had been the shirt Greyson had used during training the day before they went to the bunker. However, it was the only thing she refused to wash. It still had his scent on it and there was no way she was giving that up.

The number of people around her seemed to be growing. Soon she was shoulder to shoulder in a massive crowd of people that was barely moving. Standing on her tip toes, Alice tried to get a better look at what was holding everyone up, but she couldn't see above the mass of heads in front of her.

She wiped her brow and focused on her surroundings. The group of women she was travelling behind were still directly in front of her, so she stayed close to them. Other than them, there were carts loaded down with all sorts of goods to sell. There were items from wooden furniture to different foods to animals.

It took another three hours before she was standing in front of a large gate. Guards were roaming around as they checked people for weapons and looking over the goods to be sold. Once they cleared a group, the guards allowed the merchants to pass through the open gate.

Alice stayed as close as she could to the women who carried bundles of fabric. Her heart was pounding as three guards approached her group. One of the guardsmen spoke with a woman upfront. He looked over all of them with a bored expression on his face. He nodded and they were all ushered through the gate.

Alice let out a sigh of relief. She had made it into the Howling Meadows Pack without causing a scene. She moved with the women as they walked through the crowded streets, just in case the guards were still watching her. As they approached the town center, Alice was enthralled with all the colors and smells. If only Grey was there with her. She would have loved to slowly wander around the stalls to see everything that the traders had to offer.

She smiled as she saw a group of children running and laughing. There were carts selling beautiful jewelry and clothing. A man called out in a loud voice drawing attention to his array of freshly baked goods. A woman sat behind a table that held wooden figurines that looked like toys. Alice moved closer as she looked over all the different figures. There was a large black wolf with yellow eyes that drew her attention.

"How much for this one?" Alice asked. Asher would love it.

A man stepped up to the woman's side and looked Alice up and down with disapproval. "Twenty." The man sneered.

Alice gave him a smile. Their currency was the same in Valencia as it was in Arlania. She drew out the exact amount of money and passed it over to the surprised man.

She knew the price was ridiculously high, but she did not want to draw attention to herself by haggling. She had plenty of money, so it wasn't a big deal to just give this conman what he asked for. He hesitantly took the money and Alice grabbed the Greyson look-a-like carving. She slipped it into her bag before looking around.

She had lost the group of women. Alice fought her rising panic. She would be fine. She would walk around like she was meant to be there, and no one would ever know the difference. Alice moved confidently away from the wood carvings and farther down the road. She kept an eye out for the women or her uncle or Matt. She found a few more things that she purchased. She found a small dress in a vibrant blue that would be so cute on Avery and a book she thought Alisha would enjoy reading.

Alice continued to wander around confidently. She spotted another vender selling buns. She moved over to the cart and gave the man a friendly smile. "One please."

"Here you are, that will be two." The baker smiled at her.

"I'll get it for you, My Lady." A man spoke from beside her and Alice turned to find a handsome man with dark brown eyes. He was giving her a charming smile, but Alice felt annoyed by him.

"Thank you for your generosity, but I will purchase my own food, thank you." Alice said firmly as she handed the baker the money. The baker gave her an amused smile as she turned away from the annoying man and began walking.

"My name is Cain." The stranger said as he followed Alice, and she rolled her eyes. When she ignored him, he continued. "What's yours?"

Alice stopped walking and turned towards him with a glare. "I am sorry. Did I give you the impression that I wished to further our association? If I did, I'm sorry. That was not my intention. Good day, sir." Alice tried to walk away, but he grabbed her arm.

She looked down at his hand and slowly raised her eyes to meet his. His eyes had gone hard, and she began to feel nervous. "What is your name?" he asked stiffly.

Alice pulled her arm from his grasp. "Do not touch me. This is your only warning." She continued to glare at him until he scratched the back of his neck.

"There you are!" A woman called. Alice turned to see one of the women she had been following earlier. The woman slipped her arm through Alice's and began pulling her through the crowd. Once they were a good distance from the man, the woman leaned in close to Alice. "That is Cain Micheals. He is the son of the Howling Meadows Beta. He always gets what he wants. Rumor is he will be the next Alpha of the pack, since Alpha Maddox does not have any sons of his own."

"Well, he can't have me." Alice said glaring over her shoulder at the man that was still watching her. He had his head cocked to the side with a smirk on his face. He looked like he was listening. Since he was a Shifter, he probably was. Alice turned back around and smiled at the girl that rescued her. "I am already married."

"Really?" The girl's smile widened. "You must tell me about him. Is he handsome?" The girl blushed at her own question.

Alice laughed. "My husband is very handsome. His hair is so thick and soft I want to run my hands through it all the time. When he smiles, he has dimples that are irresistible." They moved behind the display that the women had set up and Alice caught sight of a scowling Cain through the crowd. He had moved closer, probably to stay within earshot.

"How long have you been married?" The girl asked.

"Just over a year. He is the love of my life." Alice gave a small shrug as she felt her cheeks warm. She had only admitted to two people that she was in love with Grey: Matt and her uncle. Telling this stranger made her feel almost giddy. She was starting to tell the world about her feelings, now she just needed to find the infuriating man, so she could tell him.

"I can't wait to fall in love." The girl said wistfully.

"Do not let any man con you into thinking he loves you. Find the one that would do anything for you. Even if it is something he hates." Alice laughed. "My man and I found an injured dog once. I love dogs, he hates them, and they are not fans of him either. Anyway, I asked if I could help the poor thing and he grudgingly agreed. After the dog was healed, he wanted to get rid of it. I knew how he felt about the dog, and I wasn't going to beg him to keep the poor thing. I was saying my good-byes to the pup when he came and sat down next to me." Alice's smile widened. "He had a pained expression on his face when he turned to me. He told me I could keep the dog. I fell even more in love with him at that moment." Okay, so maybe that was when she had first started to fall for him and not after he stole her heart, but no one needed to know that.

"That is the cutest thing I have ever heard." The girl sighed.

"Do not settle. Find the right one." Alice bumped the girl's shoulder. She looked back over the crowd but did not see Cain anywhere. Thank goodness. Alice turned back to the girl. "Thank you for the save. That man was getting a bit much."

"I don't think I have ever seen anyone tell him 'No' before." The girl lowered her voice. "My name is Tara. You are not from around here, are you?"

Alice shook her head. "Is it that obvious?"

"Only because you don't know who Cain is. Everyone in Valancia knows who Cain Michaels is. He is the Beta's son of the second most powerful pack in the country."

"What is a Beta?" Alice asked. She knew what an Alpha was, but only because her great grandmother claimed Greyson as one.

"They are the second in command. They are bigger than a normal wolf Shifter, but smaller than an Alpha Shifter. They are also stronger and faster than normal wolf Shifters. If Cain is made Alpha, he would be the first Beta turned Alpha. He will be weaker than all the other Alphas. Because of that, he is brutal and merciless. Be careful. He has set his sights on you, and he will not give up easily. I hope your husband is willing to fight for you."

"My husband would set the whole world on fire to protect me." Alice glanced back over the crowd again. Cain was still nowhere to be seen, but she felt eyes on her, and it made her uneasy.

The rest of the day Alice helped Tara at the booth. They occasionally saw Cain among the hundreds of faces in the square. Alice was careful not to give her name or any specific details as she talked with Tara. She did not want to chance Cain hearing anything that he could use against her or Greyson.

Evening was approaching and the two people Alice had wanted to see the most had not shown up. Her plan had hinged on finding Isaac or Matt and being able to stay with them, but it looked like she was going to have to find a place to stay for the night. She would have to look for them tomorrow.

"Do you have a place to stay?" Tara asked as they began closing their booth.

"I haven't figured that part out, yet." Alice admitted in a soft voice.

"No matter. You can stay with me at my aunt's house. She lives here in the Howling Meadows Pack." Tara smiled at her before hooking her arm through Alice's as they began walking through the dwindling crowd.

Tara and Alice ended up walking in the direction of a castle style building that Tara had mentioned was the Alpha's house. Tara's aunt owned one of the nicer inns within the pack. They were ushered upstairs to a room that had two single beds. Tara's aunt sent up dinner for them and the girls settled in for the night.

Alice changed into Greyson's shirt and a pair of her workout pants. She crawled into the bed and wrapped her arms around herself. Greyson's scent filled her senses, and she began to relax.

"Can I ask you something?" Tara asked into the darkened room.

"Sure." Alice said half asleep.

"Who are you and why are you here?" Tara's voice was thick with curiosity.

"I am…it's complicated." Alice raised up on her elbow and looked across the small space to Tara.

"Howling Meadows is a dangerous pack to be wandering around in. If you do not have to be here, you should probably leave as soon as you can." Tara said softly.

"My husband was attacked, and I think he is here in Howling Meadows. I need to know if he is here or not." Alice whispered. It felt good to confide in someone who was not so close to the situation.

"If he was attacked and then disappeared, he very well could be here. Alpha Maddox is known for making people disappear if they do not do what he wants. But you have to know that there isn't anything you can do. If Alpha Maddox has your man, then he is most likely dead or close to it." Tara sat up in her bed and watched Alice with an anxious expression. "I don't mean to sound insensitive, but you should escape this place while you can."

"I hear what you are saying, Tara. But I have to know if he is alive. I cannot leave until I know." Alice said firmly.

Tara let out a long breath. "I can understand that. Especially after the way you talked about him earlier today. But be careful, okay?" Tara laid back down and silence fell between them.

Alice lifted the collar of Greyson's shirt to her nose and took a deep breath. A tear fell from her eye as she settled back on the mattress. If nothing else, she needed to know what happened to Greyson, even if he was dead.

Alice and Tara woke early and got dressed for the day. Alice planned on going back to the market with Tara to keep an eye out for Isaac and Matthew. They were her only hope of staying after tomorrow.

Tara was leaving with the rest of the other women that were selling the fabrics, so Alice would be on her own. They were descending the stairs when a familiar voice reached her ears.

"He is in a bad way. The healer was called at least. Phil said that he should be mostly healed by tomorrow, but sir, what I saw was nothing new. From what I was able to gather, it happens every couple of days." Matt said in a tense whisper. He was speaking with someone at the bottom of the stairs.

Alice told Tara to go ahead before heading back up the stairs. If Matt was here, then he should have a room. She took a deep breath, allowing her wolf senses to open up. She caught the familiar scents of both Matt and Isaac. She moved down the hall where the smells were a bit stronger and came to a door.

Alice glanced over her shoulder to make sure she was alone in the hallway before quickly picking the lock with a pin from her hair. She slipped into the room and closed the door. She heard footsteps approaching and her heartrate accelerated. She ran across the room and climbed into the small wardrobe near the window, just as the door opened.

"Is there any way we can get him out before his next session?" Isaac's voice was low, but Alice was still able to easily hear him.

"He is heavily guarded and on the lowest floor of the dungeon. Right now, they have medicated him to help with the healing process. Maybe if he was more himself, but not in his current state." Matt sounded defeated.

"What do you mean, himself?" Isaac asked sounding concerned.

"Alice is a shell of her feisty self; Grey is not even that. He has lost a lot of weight. He is pale and submissive in a way. I was able to talk with him for a few minutes after..." Matt cleared his throat. "I have never heard him like that."

"Matt, we both know that Greyson would never give up." Isaac started to say, but he was cut off by Matt slamming his fist on the small table near the door.

"He has not given up; he is resigned to his fate. He told me to tell Alice that he was dead. He knows he is not getting out of there alive and wants her to move on." Matthew was furious. Alice heard him take a deep breath to calm himself. "He literally told me to get out of there and tell Alice he was dead. He asked me to take care of her and help her find her mate."

Alice covered her mouth to try to keep herself quiet. Greyson was alive. He was alive and wanting her to believe he was dead. Tears coursed down her cheeks as her heart screamed out for him.

"It's like he had no more fight left in him. If he were attacked, I do not think he would even fight at this point. He will not break when it comes to anything involving Alice, but he isn't the same Greyson we knew."

There was a long silence following Matt's words. Alice fought the sobs that threatened to give away her hiding place. Was Greyson really willing to give up on fighting for his life? Alice could not see him ever getting to that point. Her Greyson was strong and unmoving. He would get through this. He had to. She needed him to.

"Tomorrow Alpha Maddox is speaking with the representatives from other packs. I was told he would hear me then. We will get him out of there and back home. I am sure he will be back to his normal self once he is no longer in that place. Until then, we should appear to be enjoying the festivities. When do you go back on shift?" Isaac asked.

"I go back in a few hours. I need to get some sleep before I head back. I will be off when the conference is being held." Matt said in a calmer voice. Back to business. Alice had no idea how he and Greyson were able to be so upset about something but be able to talk about it as if it were nothing but the weather.

"Very well. I will be back in a few hours. If I do not see you before you leave; good luck." Isaac said just before a door clicked closed.

It was quiet for a minute before Matt let out a frustrated growl as something hard slammed against her hiding place. She let out a startled squeak. Before she could calm her racing heart, the door to her hiding place was thrown open and she screamed. Matthew stood there with a shocked look on his face. For a few minutes, they just stared at each other.

"Long time no see." Alice finally broke the tense silence as she slowly started to move out of the wardrobe.

Her movements snapped Matt from his shocked state. "What are you doing here? How?" He shook his head as he watched her walk to the end of the bed. Alice sat down slowly.

"I will tell you everything, but first, did you really see him?" Alice watched Matt closely.

He let out a tense breath as he ran his hand through his hair. "I should have known you wouldn't stay home." He muttered as he began pacing. "Grey is going to kill me when he finds out you are here."

"Did you really see him, Matt?" Alice was desperate for all the details.

"Yeah." He sighed. "Alice, he is not... They have done a number on him."

"Tell me." Alice felt tears burning her eyes again. She knew she was not going to like what she heard, but she needed to know. "Please, Matt. Tell me."

"Alice, I don't even know everything. I only saw the one whipping. It went on for an hour and we had to carry him back to his cell where a healer was required to treat his wounds. According to Phil and John, this isn't the first time. The torture room, I heard, can be much worse." Matt's voice broke.

"When did it happen?" Alice asked softly as tears started to blur her vision.

"Two days ago."

"I saw it." Alice managed to get out before she started crying. Matt moved quickly to her side and pulled her into a hug. She clung to him as she realized that all of her nightmares of Greyson were actually visions of his time here. "My nightmares. They were visions." She sobbed.

"Shh. It's going to be okay. We are going to get him back, Alice." Matt tried to soothe her, but it did not work. The images of the dreams came back to her causing her to cry harder.

Once she was able to get a hold of her emotions, Alice leaned back and looked up at Matt. "Will you see him again when you go back on duty?"

"Isaac and The Pheonix were able to get me assigned directly under the two guards in charge of Grey. I should be able to see him at some point on my shift. Why?" Matt furrowed his brow as he looked down at her.

"I need you to deliver a message." Alice said as she wiped her cheeks.

After leaving her message with Matthew, Alice went back up to her room. Matt was not happy that she didn't stay with him, but when she promised she would stay in her room until his shift ended, he finally let her go. Once in her room, she locked the door before pulling Greyson's shirt over her clothes. She climbed back into bed and cried herself to sleep.

Chapter 5

The metal bolt to Greyson's cell door ground back and the door creaked open. He laid still. He had not moved from when they laid him there after the whipping the other day. Maybe if they thought he was still in a lot of pain or unconscious they would leave him alone for another day. He held his breath as he waited to see if they would enter his cell or close the door.

"Check to make sure he is still breathing, kid." Phil said with no emotion in his voice.

Greyson racked his brain trying to remember who the new guard was. He had vague memories of a new face helping him get back to his cell. He remembered having a dream of Matt coming to him, but he knew that was impossible. Oh, how he wished to see his brother's face one more time.

Greyson felt hands touch his neck as the person searched for his pulse. "Is he alive?" There was a pause. "We need to remove his bandages then." John added from the doorway.

Whoever was kneeling next to him began cutting at the bandages that surrounded his torso. Greyson was afraid to move, not wanting the guard to cut him. He felt the tight pressure of the bandage slowly release as the man cut more and more of the wrappings away.

Once they were completely gone, Greyson took a deep breath and let it out slowly. His back was no longer burning. Whatever the healer put into her poultices accelerated the healing process tremendously. Which was a blessing and a curse. Since he was mostly healed, he would be taken back to the whipping post or the torture room.

"How's he looking?" Phil had moved closer. A big hand shook his shoulder. "Come on, get up." Phil's voice was low.

Greyson knew he could not pretend to be asleep. He shook his head as he pushed himself up into a sitting position. When he finally looked up, he came face to face with Matthew. Greyson froze, unable to believe what his eyes were telling him. He blinked several times to clear the hallucination, but his brother remained in front of him.

"It's really me." Matt said quietly as Phil patted Matt on the shoulder and moved toward the door.

"What? How?" Greyson mumbled in disbelief.

"There is no time for that right now. I have a message." Matt said glancing over his shoulder before returning his attention to Greyson. "Do you still have the thing I gave you?" Matt grabbed Greyson's hand and took the vial from him.

"Message from whom?" Greyson furrowed his brows in confusion. How was Matthew here in the dungeon dressed as a guard? What was going on? Matt twisted a small vial and a needle extended from one end. Greyson didn't even flinch when Matt stabbed him in the shoulder. They had used the drugs often while growing up. They gave the person a temporary energy boost and helped with healing.

"Your wife." Matt said, his whole body was full of tension. Greyson could tell that Matt wasn't happy with Alice.

"Alice? She's here? How could you let her come here?" Greyson said angrily. He kept his voice down, but he was ready to throttle his brother for bringing Alice into such a dangerous place.

"I did not bring her; she ran away from home and came on her own. I found her hiding in the wardrobe in my room. She told me to tell you that if you roll over and give up, she is going to march up to the Alpha's house and trade her life for yours." Matt's jaw tightened.

"She can't be serious." Greyson got to his feet, bumping his head on the low ceiling. "Why would she do something so stupid?"

"She is completely serious, Grey. And thanks to you training her and her determination, I have no doubt that she would succeed. I cannot even begin to anticipate her next move, so don't even try telling me to outsmart her." Matt growled out. "If I were you, I would figure out a way to get out of this because she didn't like it when I told her you were dead."

"How is the prisoner, kid?" John asked again as if he hadn't asked the question a few minutes ago.

"Still not too good, sir." Matt said, glaring at Greyson. But added in a quieter voice. "It is good to see you up and moving, Grey. Now figure out a way to show your wife that you are willing to fight."

Matt walked from the room and the door closed firmly behind him. Greyson was reeling from seeing Matt and the fact that Alice was going to give herself over to Alpha Maddox in order to free him.

He hunched his shoulders while keeping his head low and began pacing the small space. How was he going to show her he still had fight left in him? He let out a frustrated growl as he slammed his fist into the stone wall. He needed to unscramble his thoughts. He needed to clear his mind so he could think rationally. He dropped to the ground and began doing push-ups.

Greyson spent several hours working out until his muscles felt like jelly. Several times throughout the day, the cell door opened, but no one spoke to him and he ignored their presence. When the door closed, he would find a good amount of food on a tray. Greyson gratefully ate every bite. He needed to regain as much of his strength as he could. He was a long way from what he had been before his capture, but he had to start somewhere. After an hour or so of rest, he got back to doing exercises again.

As he pushed his body again and again to its breaking point, he thought of what he could do to keep Alice safe. He was sure that Matt would do everything in his power to keep her from giving herself to the Alpha, but she was smart, and it sounded like she learned a lot from him. He smiled at the thought, but at the same time, he wished he hadn't trained her.

Greyson placed both hands on the wall and leaned his forehead against its cold surface. There was no way he could escape. He thought of every time he was removed from his cell. When he walked the halls to the whipping post or to the torture room; there were too many guards. Too many corridors to get lost in.

Not to mention the fact that he could not shift. He growled as he punched the wall again. What he wouldn't give for a punching bag at that moment. Or Alice. Her scent of vanilla and her warmth. The sound of the cell door opening jolted him from his thoughts.

John stepped into the small space with Phil right behind him. He held a tray of food and a large mug of some dark colored liquid. "Eat up, kid." He said as he placed the tray carefully on the floor. "Drink everything and get some rest." Both men walked from the cell and sealed Greyson back inside.

Greyson moved to the tray and carried it to the dry corner where he spent his time. He quickly ate his meal but hesitated at the odd drink that was provided for him. He sniffed it, but it didn't have an odd smell. He took a small sip and coughed. It tasted disgusting.

Greyson did not think it was poison. Considering Phil and John were the ones that brought it to him, he was inclined to believe that the drink was some sort of medicinal drink to help him recover. Taking a deep breath and a leap of faith, Greyson chugged the entire contents of the mug. An involuntary shutter ran down his spine.

He was tired after spending most of the day being physically active. It had been a long time since he had done such a thing. Greyson leaned back against the wall and closed his eyes. His back was still a little tender, but not nearly as bad as it could have been. It did not take long for him to fall asleep.

Dreams of Alice coming face to face with Alpha Maddox made his sleep less than restful. He had given up on falling back to sleep just before the sun rose in the sky. He went back to doing push-ups, feeling stronger than he had in months.

Matt's injection combined with whatever was in that drink definitely helped his recovery. He had been at it for nearly an hour when his cell door opened. He looked over, hoping to see Matt, but he was disappointed. Phil and John stood in the entrance with their characteristic masks of indifference.

"It's a bit early for you boys to be here, isn't it?" Greyson asked as he lowered himself into another pushup.

"Uh. Your presence is requested, again, by the Alpha." Phil responded.

Greyson scoffed as he got to his feet. It wasn't like he could deny the request, even if he wanted to. The exercise had not helped settle his mind, instead it fueled his frustrations. Pressure began to build within him.

Knowing Alice was close made him tense and ready to fight anyone who would hurt her. He hadn't felt this familiar pressure in a while. His wolf was pushing to the surface, but unable to shift. He needed to calm down.

He closed his eyes, and an image of Alice's smiling face came to mind. Greyson took a deep breath and felt slightly calmer. Opening his eyes again, he moved to the door and out into the hall without waiting for Phil or John.

"Let's get this over with." Greyson grumbled.

He saw the shocked look on John and Phil's faces as they walked beside him. They didn't say anything as they walked through the halls. The large doors to the throne room opened as they approached, and Greyson's steps didn't falter as he continued up to the front of the room. When he got to the same spot as he had before, he waited. John tried to put the cuffs on him.

"Try it and I'll end you, John." Greyson growled. The man stopped and looked nervously at the Alpha.

"It is fine. It's not like he can do anything in here." The Alpha watched Greyson with a curious look on his face. "You seem more talkative."

"Look sir, I don't know who you think you are, but I am done playing this game with you and your men." Greyson felt his wolf pushing to the surface again. It felt good to feel it. It was crazy to think he use to hate it.

"Sir?" Alpha Maddox laughed menacingly. "I am your Alpha."

"You're not my Alpha." Greyson spat on the floor.

"You dare challenge me?" Greyson could hear the anger rising within the man. "You will kneel to me, boy. Now!" Greyson watched as Alpha Maddox's eyes glowed as he tried to push his command on Greyson.

Greyson could feel the powerful aura filling the room as all those in the room bowed to the Alpha in submission. He, however, stood tall and did not break eye contact with his father. Greyson smirked at the frustrated Alpha.

Alpha Maddox got to his feet as he glared down at Greyson standing tall, meeting his glare with one of his own. A loud growl echoed through the deafening silence of the hall. Alpha Maddox looked ready to shift as a vein in his forehead pulsed.

"Calm down, Maddox." Queen Isabel touched the Alpha's arm in an attempt to calm him. Greyson made eye contact with the Queen. Her gaze darted quickly to Greyson's left side before returning to his face. "I think all that time in the prison messed with the boy's mind." Again, she darted her eyes off to Greyson's left.

Was she trying to tell him something? If he looked now, he would draw everyone's attention to it, so he waited. Tapping into his wolf's sense of smell, Greyson took a slow deep breath through his nose. There were several scents that were unfamiliar to him, but then one caught his attention: Isaac. But how was he there? First Matthew, then Alice, now Isaac?

He gave a small nod to the Queen as she spoke again. "Maybe we need to send him to the infirmary to see if they can do anything to help."

"I want to know how he withstood my command. He has been here for over six months. He is automatically a member of the pack now." Alpha Maddox roared. Greyson folded his arms over his chest, unwilling to answer the man. "Your previous pack's link would have broken after six months of being here. The only other way is if you are not a wolf Shifter, or you are also an Alpha." Alpha Maddox marched down the steps towards Greyson as he studied him carefully. "You aren't any Alpha I know." Alpha Maddox mused. "But from all reports, you are a wolf Shifter."

Greyson watched Alpha Maddox's every move. He could feel the aura around the Alpha continue to push on him, trying to get him to submit. He heard a whimper from someone behind him. Alpha Maddox circled around Greyson as he continued to study him. As he walked behind Greyson, the Queen gave him a tiny shake of her head. Greyson bit the inside of his cheek to keep quiet.

"Have we met before?" Alpha Maddox asked.

"The other day, but I have never seen you before then." Greyson answered honestly.

"Hmm." Alpha Maddox continued to watch Greyson. "Well, unfortunately I do not have time for you right now. Chain him up to the slave's post." He called out to John and Phil. "After I speak with my next appointment, we'll continue to chat." John and Phil stepped forward and clamped the cuffs on Greyson's wrists quickly before dragging him off to the side.

There were large metal rings lined up on the wall to the right of the room. As they pulled the chain through the ring, Phil gave Greyson a barely audible apology before yanking his arms high over his head. At the abrupt movement, the skin on Greyson's back pulled apart, his wounds reopening. Something warm began to slowly roll down his back. There was no slack on his arms unless he rose on his toes. Phil and John stood on either side of him as they waited for their next order.

"Bring him forward." Alpha Maddox called.

Several people were standing in the way and Greyson was unable to see who was walking to the front. He could see Queen Isabel and she looked nervous. Her eyes kept glancing over at him before returning to someone in the crowd. "Maddox, shouldn't we have our foreign visitor go first?"

"Nonsense, Lars is a good friend of mine. Now, what can I do for you, my friend?"

"My Alpha, may I first say how glad I am to see you in such good health." Alpha Maddox gave Lars a nod. Greyson rolled his eyes at the other man's obvious attempt to flatter the Alpha. "I have come here to ask for more slaves. I am running a bit low, and I need to replenish my stocks before profits start to dip."

"I see. And how many are you needing, Lars?" The Alpha looked amused.

"A dozen or so. They need to be strong so that they can last more than a few minutes." Alpha Maddox sat back in his chair with a thoughtful look.

"I can probably get you ten men. I can have them ready for you in the morning." Queen Isabel paled as her gaze locked with Greyson's.

"The prisoner that was here a moment ago, he looked strong and would make a fine showing. It would not take long for him to make us a very handsome profit, Alpha." Lars's voice sounded excited at the prospect.

The hall was quiet for a long moment and Greyson watched as Queen Isabel blinked back tears. Alpha Maddox finally nodded his head. "Very well, he is yours. He has not provided me with any information in the nine months that he has been a prisoner."

What was happening? Had he just been sold into slavery? This could not be happening. Greyson started pulling at the chains, trying to break himself free.

"Sedate him." Alpha Maddox yelled.

Greyson struggled harder causing the chains to cut into his skin. John and Phil tried to stop him, but he kicked John causing him to stumble back. Placing his feet on the wall, Greyson grabbed the chains and pulled.

To his relief, the ring started pulling out of the wall. Just before it could give way, Greyson felt a sharp stabbing pain in his neck. He turned and saw Phil standing there with an empty syringe in his hand.

"Sorry, kid." He whispered as Greyson felt his body growing weak. His feet slipped off the wall and he looked around. His eyes landed on the worried face of Isaac Young just as his vision went black.

Chapter 6

He had been so close. How could he have been so close only for Greyson to be yanked out of his grasp? Isaac stormed into his room at the inn before slamming the door. He jumped when he saw Alice sitting in the chair by the fireplace.

"What are you doing here? How did you even get in here?" He yelled. His frustration over the day's events combining with the shock of seeing Alice caused his voice to come out sharper than he intended.

"Good to see you too, Uncle." Alice stood and moved to stand in front of him. "Greyson taught me several new skills, like how to get in and out of locked rooms. How did your meeting with the Alpha go?" There was a guarded hope shining in her eyes.

"He was there, Alice. Greyson was there and alive." Alice gasped as Isaac ran a hand through his hair. She had not expected Greyson to be there at the meeting.

"H-How was he?" she asked as tears gathered in her eyes.

"Not good. It looked like he had been whipped recently and he had bruises all over his chest and face. There are cuts and scars all over him, more so than before." Isaac shook his head as the tears spilled out onto Alice's cheeks.

"Were you able to talk with him?" Alice held her breath. She knew he was physically damaged, but she needed to know if he was okay mentally.

"He spoke with the Alpha. He was not at all how Matthew portrayed him. Matt said Grey was not very talkative and had pulled into himself. But Greyson stood his ground and did not let the Alpha intimidate him. He was able to hold his own against Alpha Maddox's Alpha command while everyone else bowed and whimpered, which made Alpha Maddox angry." Isaac's lips curled up slightly at the corners in a small smile.

Alice let out a laugh through her tears. Matt must have delivered her message. Greyson was fighting. "Where is he now?"

"He was chained to the wall, but before I could even petition for his release, he was sold to a slave trader. He nearly pulled the chain out of the wall. Men ran towards him in order to stop him from escaping. They sedated him and he was dragged from the room. I asked to see him, but they refused. I tried to speak with the slave trader and Alpha Maddox about purchasing him, but they both refused to hear me out. I am so sorry, Alice." Isaac shook his head as he rubbed the back of his neck.

Alice moved away from her uncle and sat back on the chair she had just vacated. She closed her eyes and thought of Greyson. They had been so close. Her nightmares had been accurate with the scars and fresh wounds she had seen on him and from what Matthew and Uncle Isaac had said he looked like now.

Concentrating, she tried to feel him, but there was nothing. He was most likely still sedated, making it impossible for her to feel him close by. Her hand went to her wolf pendant, and she traced the outline of it. She narrowed her eyes. She could not give up. No matter where they took him, she would find him.

"You look tired, Uncle Isaac. You should rest for a while. We can come up with a plan later." Alice said tiredly. "I need to send a message to Matthew and let him know that the meeting was cut short."

"Matthew knows you're here?" Isaac asked in shock.

"Of course, he does. He is too smart for his own good. He found me the other day and I got a huge lecture about leaving home on my own." Alice rolled her eyes at the memory. Matthew had turned out to be just as protective as Rowan. "Now rest for an hour and then we can have dinner."

Isaac ran a hand down his face before finally agreeing. He looked like he hadn't slept in the last several days. Before he fell asleep, he made Alice promise she would not leave the room.

Alice had spent a good hour thinking over the new information Isaac gave her. She wished she could have been there with her uncle so she could have at least seen him in person. Her heart ached to see him again. The feelings of frustration and restlessness caused Alice to move to the window and she looked out at the street below.

The market was coming to a close and many of the booths were being dismantled. Some of the merchants had already collected what was left of their goods and packed them away. She watched as several headed for the large gates that would be closing in a matter of hours.

As soon as the sun dipped behind the horizon, the gates would be closed for the night. Tomorrow they would be open until midday and then they would close again. This time they would remain locked until the next market festival. Only those with travel papers signed by the Alpha or Queen would be allowed to pass through the gates.

Matthew said he would be back by dinner. She wasn't sure what he was doing, but she needed to let him know that Greyson had been sold. They needed to figure out when he would be moved from the castle. Maybe this was a good thing. It would be easier to plan an escape when Greyson was being transported, than when he was inside the castle dungeon.

Alice's restlessness continued, so she did what she usually did to release the pent-up energy; she began working out. She alternated between pushups and sit-ups as she tried to center her mind. She had too many thoughts about all the possible what-ifs that could happen in their rescue attempt.

Should they try to get him when he was being transported, or wait until he was taken to the slave trader's base? What if they didn't get to him in time and he was sold again? What if they were unable to follow him and they ended up back at square one; not knowing where he was?

The door opened and Matt slipped inside. He looked tired and defeated. He closed the door behind him but paused when he saw her drenched in sweat and mid-pushup.

"I'm guessing Issac told you about Greyson?" Matt said quietly. Alice nodded as she rotated into a sitting position. "The sedative was not staying in his system very long and he did a lot of damage to several of the guards. They knocked him out and drugged him with the slave trader's special blend. I thought I heard someone say that if Grey were a Shifter, it would make it impossible for him to shift." Matt sat down on the floor and leaned against the bed. "It was good to see him fighting back instead of taking the abuse, though."

"When do they take him?" Alice asked, not sure she wanted to know any more details about what they did to Greyson.

"Lars is taking the slaves in the morning. Greyson should be among them."

"Can we help Greyson escape during transport?" Alice asked hopefully.

"Unfortunately, no." Matt scrubbed his hand over his face. "Not only does Greyson not have any of his Shifter abilities, but Lars, the slave trader, has a long-standing agreement with Alpha Maddox. The caravan will be heavily guarded until it reaches the slave trader's men. The only thing we can hope for is the ability to track where they take Greyson and get him out later." Alice felt her heart constrict.

They were so close to him, but he was still out of their reach. She wondered if she were to ask the Alpha if she could see Greyson, if he would allow it. Alice shook her head. There was no way she could do that. If she asked, Alpha Maddox would most likely know she was the one they were looking for and that would be too big of a risk. So, as much as she wanted to see Greyson, she was going to have to be patient.

Matthew woke Isaac and they sent for dinner. Isaac also asked for information on any houses within the pack that were available to rent. The innkeeper promised to have a list of people that could help them look for temporary lodging ready for them by morning. Isaac thought it would be best if Alice concealed her presence from everyone the best she could. That meant she was to be locked away in the room and had to stay away from the window.

Even with the quarters being very confined, Alice would take it any day in order to get as much information on Greyson as she could. And so far, both Isaac and Matt had given her more than she could have found out on her own.

She knew he was alive and relatively well considering the abuse he had been under for nearly a year. He was sold to a man that was known as the biggest slave trader in Valencia and would be moved from a stronghold of a dungeon in the morning. Alice wished she knew where this Lars guy would be taking Grey. If they did, they could meet the slave caravan there and get Greyson back quickly.

"Alice, you have that look on your face." Matt commented as he took a bite of his potatoes.

"What look?" She asked not looking up.

"The look that says you are thinking about something that usually leads to you getting yourself into trouble." Isaac pointed his fork at her.

"What if I pose as a healer or guard or something. Maybe I could get close enough to Greyson to either heal him or find out where they are taking him." Alice looked up at her uncle and brother-in-law.

"Alice, I know you want to see him. I know it is killing you to be this close and not able to be there with him, but it is too dangerous. If Alpha Maddox discovers you are the one he is looking for, then he won't hesitate to kill Greyson or anyone else to get to you. If not for your own safety, think of Greyson's. We need to keep you away from the Alpha at all costs." Matt gave her an apologetic look. "Plus, Greyson got your message, and he kept up his end of the deal, you need to keep yours."

"What message?" Isaac asked, putting his fork down.

"Alice asked me to give Greyson a message. Pretty much if he did not start fighting to stay alive, Alice was going to turn herself over to Alpha Maddox in exchange for Greyson's release." Matt crossed his arms over his chest and gave Alice a pointed stare. He was clearly not happy with her willingness to trade her life for Greyson's.

"Alice." Isaac pinched the bridge of his nose.

"Don't Alice me, Uncle Isaac. My message got Greyson willing to fight again. Maybe now he can help us to get himself out of there."

"But he would never want you to give yourself up for him." Isaac pointed out.

Alice stood from the table and threw her arms out to the side. "Exactly." She huffed. "He would do anything to keep me from doing that, so he had no choice. He will fight tooth and nail to make sure I stay away from Alpha Maddox and that is what I am counting on."

"You wanted him to feel desperate to keep you safe." Matthew's smile lit up his face. It had been too long since Alice had seen him truly smile. "You gave him a choice that was not really a choice at all. You manipulated him."

"I wouldn't really call it manipulating. I just know his weakness is duty. And at the moment, his duty is to protect me." Alice shrugged.

"You're wrong, Alice. Greyson's weakness isn't duty." Matthew said as he winked at her, and Alice felt her cheeks warm.

She hoped that was the case, that she was his weakness, but she didn't want to get her hopes up. She knew they were only together because he was assigned to protect her. Even though Alice had fallen in love with him, Greyson's feelings towards her could only be that of a protecter and his assignment. Sure, he was crazy protective of her due to the mate bond, but he could still reject it and her.

Alice was quiet for the rest of the night. She listened as Isaac and Matt discussed the layout of the town and castle. Matt wished they had a tracker that they could put on the caravan when it passed through the town. He said Sasha claimed her daughter had the ability to bind objects to each other. Once the bond was set, you could put a piece of the object on a map, and it would be attracted to the location of the other object. That is how they tracked the boys.

Since they didn't have the trackers, Matt was going to try to follow the caravan and send a message once he knew where they were going. Uncle Isaac kept reassuring her that they would get Greyson back, but she could tell they were not fully confident they would be able too, at least not anytime soon.

Alice stood from the table and walked over to the small couch where she had dropped her bags earlier that day. She pulled out Greyson's shirt and put it on before lying down on the couch with her back facing her uncle and Matt. She needed rest if she was going to be up and ready by morning.

It was quiet for several minutes and Alice began to relax with Greyson's scent around her. "Is that Greyson's shirt?" Isaac asked quietly.

Alice was about to answer, but Matt responded first. "That's my guess. At least she has found something to help comfort her at night."

"Has she really been that bad?" Isaac asked, and Alice could feel their eyes on her.

"She has nightmares of Greyson being tortured. Given what I have seen, they probably were visions. She started training so hard that she was falling asleep during meals. Rowan took it upon himself to make sure she ate, because she had no appetite. This was the first time in months that I have seen her eat without someone reminding her to take a bite." Matt let out a long sigh. "She and Grey need each other. The sooner we can get Greyson back, the better it will be for both of them."

"I was debating on whether one of us should take her back home while the other one trails Greyson, but I think it might be better for Alice if we keep her close. She might be the key to getting Greyson to fight to escape." Isaac said as he moved across the room.

A chair scooted across the wood floor. "Even if you did send Alice home, she would just come back. It will be safer keeping her close. The Beta's son, Cain, is looking into a young woman who rebuffed him at the market. He lost track of her a day or so ago. I was sent to question the ladies she was seen with the first day of the market. A young woman named Tara said the young woman left early to return to the Twin River Pack. Apparently, her family sent word that she was needed back home."

"I don't understand what this has to do with either Alice or Greyson." Isaac said, but Alice's heart rate picked up. Cain was still looking for her and Tara had covered for her. Alice was going to have to be extremely careful whenever she went out.

"By the description I was given, the girl Cain is looking for is Alice. He is determined to find her. We need to keep her close. If we send her away and she returns here, Cain will get her." Matt clarified.

Isaac let out a heavy sigh. "Let's just get some rest. We need to be in position by the time the slave traders set out." Alice heard them moving around the room for a few minutes before the candles were blown out.

Alice lay there in the dark as her mind replayed what her uncle and Matt had said. Why was Cain still looking for her? He was a cocky arrogant man who knew she was married. Why couldn't he leave her alone? Matt and Isaac would never allow her to leave the inn with Cain searching for her. Hopefully, Tara telling him that she skipped town would get him to stop his search.

Alice woke up early. It had been a while since she had felt so rested. As she stretched and yawned, she realized something felt different. She felt so much calmer this morning than she had in nearly a year.

Alice looked around the room, but both Isaac and Matt were gone. She stood and moved to the table where there was a breakfast tray. Next to the tray was a note. It was short but gave Alice all the information she needed. Isaac and Matt left already to follow the caravan.

Alice's stomach growled. She sat down at the table and ate her eggs and bacon. Once she was done, she pulled Greyson's shirt off and folded it before putting it back into her bag. She always felt a loss when she took it off.

Alice let out a growl of frustration as she wiped a tear from her cheek. She was so tired of crying. At least she knew that Greyson was alive. Now it was only a matter of time before they were able to break him out of his imprisonment. Alice moved to the window, careful to stay out of sight, and looked out over the crowded streets.

It amazed her how many people were up and moving around at this hour of the day. But then again, it was the last day the merchants from other packs were allowed to freely leave. From her vantage point, Alice could almost see the gates that were a mile away from the town center. In the opposite direction, she could see water in the distance.

Tara had mentioned that the Howling Meadows Pack sat on the coastline with a dock within the pack lands. Alice sighed and leaned against the wall. She watched the crowd making their way towards the gate. The mass of people started moving off to the sides of the street and Alice shifted to see what was causing everyone to make way.

A large cage on wheels pulled by four horses moved slowly through the crowded streets. As it passed by her window, she gasped. The cage was full of men! At least fifteen men were crammed into it. Her stomach twisted seeing the hopelessness in the eyes of several of them. She looked at each of the men and a pair of amber eyes caused her heart to skip a beat. She placed her hand on the window as butterflies took flight in her stomach.

Greyson's hair was much shorter than how he usually wore it, and his face was covered in bruises. But his eyes were the same. She kept her eyes locked on his face as she tried to open a mind-link with him. "Greyson!" she shouted in her head.

"Alice?" His voice was full of disbelief as his eyes widened.

"Oh, Grey." Alice felt tears rolling down her cheeks.

"Alice, how are you in my head?" He sounded confused. His eyes seemed to scan the crowd around him before they settled on her. "Maybe they did break my mind? I'm seeing and hearing things that can't possibly be there."

"You are insufferable, you know that?" Alice growled at him.

"Princess? Is that really you?" The carriage continued its slow pace through the crowds. She could see Greyson sit up straighter. "You should not be here. You cannot be here."

Alice was so happy to see him but was also getting so frustrated with him. Her emotions competed with one another, she wanted to kiss him, but at the same time she wanted to punch his handsome face.

"Don't you dare start trying to tell me what to do." Alice felt more tears start falling and she tried to hold in her sobs.

"I'm sorry, Princess. I just...I wouldn't be able to live with myself if anything happened to you. Please baby, go back home where it is safe." Greyson pleaded.

"Baby?" Alice sniffled. Her heart picked up speed and she closed her eyes as she tried to picture Greyson now that he was out of her view. The crowd had returned to the streets as the wagon passed.

"You look good, Ali." Greyson said.

"You look terrible." Alice shook her head as she fought her grin. "Maybe next time you shouldn't antagonize someone with a gun."

"I am so sorry, Ali. I didn't know what else to do." Greyson pleaded. "I couldn't let them find you. I had seen what they do to women and there was no way I was going to even chance them putting a finger on you."

"Grey." Alice sighed. Just hearing his voice was soothing.

"Shoot." He cut her off. She could feel his anxiety through the bond.

"What's going on, Greyson? Talk to me." Panic filled her and she grabbed the windowsill to keep her hands from shaking.

"We stopped at a dock. Looks like I will be boarding a boat." Alice felt her heart constrict. "Alice, is there a range on our ability to mind-link?"

"It seems to be. I have not been able to feel you from the time you were shot, to when I just reached out to you." Alice wanted to run to him but knew she wouldn't be able to free him without getting herself caught.

"Do you still have the Stone?" He asked and she confirmed she did. "Have you found your mate? Are you able to destroy it yet?" He sounded unsure of himself as he asked.

Alice had never known Greyson to lack confidence, but he was radiating it. "Are you serious?" Alice felt like punching something. How could he not have figured it out by now?

"We have not seen or talked in nine months. How are you mad at me already?" Alice could almost see Greyson's frustrated scowl.

"When I see you again, sir, you are going to get what I promised you all those months ago." Alice promised. She could hear him chuckle in her head. Alice began feeling their connection weakening. "Greyson? What's going on?"

"They are sedating all the slaves, Princess." He sounded close to falling asleep. "Man, I have missed you, Alice."

"No, Greyson, please. Stay with me. Do not leave me again." She was desperate to keep their connection. She needed him.

"I promise we will see each other again, Princess." Alice dropped to her knees as his voice faded to little more than a whisper.

"Come back to me, Grey. Please." Alice could not hold in her sobs anymore as she felt her connection to him fully disappear, again.

Chapter 7

Greyson woke up with a pounding headache. His wrists and ankles were chained to the wooden floor. By the rocking motion, Greyson guessed he was in the belly of a boat. He studied his surroundings and was shocked to see that an additional twenty or so men were added to the fifteen men he boarded with.

Those that were awake had bleak and hopeless expressions on their faces. How long had he been out? He closed his eyes and tried to remember the events that led him here. Maybe he could figure out where they were going, so he could plan an escape.

The image of Alice standing in an upstairs window with tears streaming down her face popped into his mind. The relief and excitement from seeing her had given way to panic and worry that she was so close to the man that wanted to capture her.

Hearing her voice inside his head had been a complete shock, but he loved every minute of it. Maybe they were still close enough for him to hear her and he could talk with her again.

"Alice?" He held his breath. "Please, Princess. I need to hear your voice, Love." To his disappointment there was no response. He tried to feel if she was close or if she was angry with him, but there was nothing. He was too far away from her again.

Taking a deep breath, Greyson opened his eyes and met the stare of a man. "Who's Alice?" The man's gruff voice broke the depressing silence. Greyson furrowed his brow at the man. How did he know about Alice? "You've been calling out for her periodically for hours." The man added while watching Greyson curiously.

"My mother." Greyson answered coolly.

The man laughed heartily. "If this Alice woman is your mother, than I am the Alpha King. Do not worry boy, we all have loved ones we were taken away from. I, myself, haven't seen my Gwen in nearly three years." He gave a sad smile and the merriment that sparked in his eyes moments ago dimmed.

"I only asked who Alice was because I have found it helps keep their memories fresh when one speaks about them."

Silence fell between them while Greyson studied his fellow prisoner. Greyson could see the man's pain and longing for his Gwen in the man's whole demeanor. Greyson leaned his head back against the side of the boat and took a breath. Maybe it would be good to talk about her a little. He would be careful about the information he shared, but he could at least share a little.

"She's, my wife." Greyson said softly as he swallowed hard. Gads, he missed her.

"How long were you two married?" The man's gruff voice held compassion.

"We were married for almost six months when I was taken. I've been a prisoner of Alpha Maddox for eight or nine months." Greyson responded.

"Wow. Sorry kid, that's heartbreaking. Gwen and I have been married for nearly twenty years. I have two daughters that were fourteen and sixteen when I was arrested." The man closed his eyes and shook his head.

"My name is Greyson." Greyson gave the older man a small smile. For some reason, Greyson felt a kinship with this man. Almost like some sort of connection that bonded them. "Why were you arrested?"

"The name's Drake. I was arrested because someone overheard me questioning Alpha Maddox's ability to lead the pack." Drake shrugged his shoulders.

"Why were you questioning your Alpha?" Greyson was curious to learn more about Drake and how he became unhappy with his Alpha. From everything he learned as a prisoner, Alphas were held in great respect. Pack members were loyal to their Alpha to a fault.

"Alpha Maddox has always been drunk with gaining power. He even married Queen Isabel to gain more power."

"Queen Isabel? How would marrying her be a power move?" Greyson was eager to learn more about his own family history.

"Where have you been, Greyson? Everyone knows about Queen Isabel." Drake looked shocked at Greyson's ignorance.

"I grew up in Arlania. I know nothing about Valencia's history or its politics." Greyson gave him a quick shrug.

"Ah. I see." Drake mused before continuing. "Queen Isabel is the daughter of the First Moon Pack's Alpha. It is said that the Alpha family from the First Moon Pack are descendants of the Alpha King. Queen Isabel was kind and compassionate and everyone loved her. She was sought after for her strong bloodlines. Alpha Maddox ended up twisting her father's arm in a way he could not refuse. Soon after, Isabel was married to Alpha Maddox." A look of disgust flashed across his face.

"To Alpha Maddox's great disappointment, Queen Isabel gave birth to three daughters. Her fourth and fifth children were sons, but they both died in childbirth. Queen Isabel was devastated by the losses, but Alpha Maddox only became angrier and more desperate. A human visited Howling Meadows and she constantly talked about a stone of some sort that could grant the beholder a stronger Alpha presence. Maddox asked about its location and the visiting human claimed that only a woman with the ability to see visions could locate it. She knew the girl's location but could not get to her."

Greyson felt the blood drain from his face. If this happened three years ago, that would explain Barnett's increased desperation to get to Alice. "Since Alpha Maddox did not have sons that he could manipulate and train to take over other packs, he turned all his attention to finding the girl. It became an obsession for the last two decades." So not Alice, but Kyrie? "Someone overheard me say that the Alpha needed to be challenged so that we could find a more suitable leader to follow. Two decades is a long time to be looking for an object that doesn't exist. I was picked up the next day while on guard duty and thrown in a cell for treason."

"I am so sorry, Drake. That's awful." Greyson felt sorry for the man. Alpha Maddox was definitely not a good or sane leader. "I thought Alphas were supposed to provide, protect, and care for their packs, not be dictators."

Drake laughed again. "You would think. Several Alpha's are kind and good, but unfortunately, most are more like Alpha Maddox. Where do you think all these men came from? All were prisoners of different packs before being turned over to Lars."

"Who is this Lars person anyway?" Greyson asked. The more information he could learn about his captors the better.

"Lars is a rat. He acquires men to fight in the arenas at Trevor's Cove. He makes his money off the bets placed on the fights. Beast vs beast, man vs beast, man vs man. It doesn't matter. To keep things interesting, Lars even injects a toxin he calls the Equalizer into the slaves that makes it impossible for Shifters to shift, either into their animal form or back to their human form, depending on when it is given. If he can make money off it, he will do it." Drake shook his head as anger flashed through his eyes. "I'm pretty sure Alpha Maddox also makes money off of the fights."

Perfect. Greyson closed his eyes as he thought about what Drake had told him. His mother was supposedly nice, but his father was a complete monster. No wonder she hid Matthew and him at the orphanage. What would he be like if he had grown up with a father like Alpha Maddox? He understood her desperation to hide them away and he was glad she gave them up.

Once Greyson got out of his current situation, he was going to challenge Alpha Maddox and free all the people that his father had oppressed. He would save his mother. And he would stop his father from hunting Alice. Maybe he could get Drake's help to do it? His blood began to boil with his anger towards his father.

"Greyson, are you okay? Your hands are shaking." Drake asked in concern. Greyson opened his eyes and stared at Drake. "Holy crap! Your eyes are glowing!" Drake gasped. Greyson could hear several of the other prisoners starting to move around and he could feel their eyes on him.

"I think I'm going to shift." Greyson growled out through clenched teeth as he tried to fight his wolf. If only Alice were there to calm him. His breathing increased and he knew he was losing the battle. He needed to control himself, there were too many people around and he did not want to hurt anyone.

He turned his attention back to Drake as the man scooted closer to him with concern in his eyes. "Sorry, kid." He said as he swung his chained fist into Greyson's face. The impact slammed Greyson's head against the side of the boat with enough force to knock him out.

Several gasps were heard from the men that were close and Drake scooted back to his spot. Running footsteps overhead signaled that the guards had heard the commotion. Drake leaned back against the post he was chained to and got comfortable just as three guards descended the stairs.

"What is going on down here?" One of them yelled. No one spoke and when nothing seemed out of place, the guards retreated up the stairs, slamming the hatch door back in place.

"Why'd you do that to the kid, Drake?" Luther asked in disbelief.

"Did you notice anything strange about young Greyson?" Drake asked as a small smile spread across his face.

"Other than him almost shifting and being from Arlania, no." Luther answered, confused. Luther scooted as close as he could to Drake so they could talk without anyone else hearing them.

"He has the same eyes as our Queen and his eyes started to glow. He even started to shift." Drake said quietly.

"So?" Luther was still lost.

"You were there with me both times when we took Queen Isabel to Miss Mary's Orphanage." Drake's eyes sparked with renewed hope, but he kept his voice low enough no one else could overhear him. "I believe we have found one of the lost princes. His eyes glowing is a sign he is an Alpha, and judging by his ability to shift, even with the toxin in his system, he is a strong one." Drake smiled widely at Luther. "We need to protect the prince, Luther. We swore an oath to our Queen."

Luther studied Greyson more closely. Drake was right. If this was one of the princes, they needed to do everything in their power to keep him alive. Since they were being taken to Trevor's Cove, it was going to be difficult. He hoped the kid knew at least a little about fighting.

Drake and Luther had accompanied Queen Isabel to the Howling Meadows Pack when she married Alpha Maddox. Their loyalties had always remained with Queen Isabel. They had sworn an oath that if their paths ever crossed with the lost princes, they would assist the boys in bringing down the tyranny of Alpha Maddox. And he was more than ready to see that day happen. All they had to do was survive this death camp, train Greyson to be able to challenge Maddox, and take him back to the Howling Meadows Pack so he could.

"I hope you are right, Drake. And I hope the kid can survive the cove long enough for us to escape." Luther whispered as he sat back and studied the boy.

Chapter 8

A week had passed since Alice had seen Greyson. Her uncle refused to allow her to leave the home they were renting. She ended up spending her days reading her books that she brought, and training. In the evenings, Matthew would work with her on throwing her daggers.

After returning to Barnett's compound, Greyson had apparently taught Matthew the skill. Matthew claimed to be nowhere near Greyson's skill level even after three years of practice. Alice was curious how good Greyson actually was, considering Matthew never missed the bullseye.

It was midday and Alice was going stir crazy. The sun was shining and the temperature outside was mild. Isaac had left for the docks to try to find more information about the boat Greyson was taken on, while Matthew meandered through the street asking discrete questions.

She could not take it anymore. Alice tucked a dagger into her boot and stepped outside. She took a deep breath of the fresh air and headed toward the marketplace. Alice smiled as a group of kids ran through the street laughing and playing.

Alice moved from stall to stall examining the wares. There were vendors selling everything from clothing to food, jewelry to weapons. As she passed a group of women, she noticed that they did not have any wedding rings on and were accompanied by a man.

Alice studied the crowds closer. The only women that were not accompanied by men were those that wore wedding rings.

Alice covered her left hand with her right. Greyson had not given her a ring since they were in hiding and she had never thought about it. She had the feeling she needed to get a ring before anyone noticed her alone and without one.

Keeping her left hand covered, she meandered over to a jewelry cart. The merchant looked excited as she approached. She gave him a smile before looking at the rings. There were several plain bands along with rings with small stones on them.

"Can I help you, Miss?" the merchant asked.

"Mrs. and yes. The ring my husband bought me a couple of years ago has become too small for me. He asked that I see if I can find one that would fit me."

"I see. Where is he now? Shouldn't he be here with you?" The merchant narrowed his eyes.

Alice felt a hand touch her lower back and she stiffened. "Did you find something you like?" Matthew asked.

Alice was so relieved to see him. "I think so." She smiled and looked up at him. Matthew wore a stern look on his face and she quickly turned back to the rings. "That one. The one with the deep blue stone." Alice pointed to a ring in the center of the third row.

The merchant picked it up and handed it over to Matthew. Matthew passed the ring over to Alice. She examined it closely. It was a simple silver band with six small diamonds surrounding a single dark blue sapphire. She slipped it on her finger, surprised that it fit her perfectly. She held her hand out for examination.

"What do you think?" Alice asked as she continued to study it.

"It looks beautiful. How much?" Matthew turned to the merchant. They settled on a price and then Matthew grabbed Alice's elbow and dragged her away from the stall toward a less populated area of the market. "Why are you not at the house?"

"We needed groceries, and I needed fresh air. Then I noticed that unmarried women were all accompanied by men. I did not want to draw attention, so I tried to get a ring." Alice explained in a quiet voice.

"I'm supposed to be meeting with someone in a minute, so I can't take you back. Promise me you will go back on your own. I should be home in about two hours." Matthew begged.

"Matthew, I'm not going to just sit around the house with nothing to do. I am not an idiot who can't defend herself. I will hang around the market and you can come find me when you are done with whatever it is you are doing." Alice said as she crossed her arms over her chest.

"How did Greyson deal with you?" Matthew muttered before letting out a heavy sigh. "Fine. But stay in heavily populated areas."

"Greyson didn't ever learn, it seemed like we were always fighting over something." Alice smirked.

"Meet at the wolf fountain in two hours." Matthew said before stepping away from her and heading down the street.

Alice watched Matthew until he disappeared into the crowd of people. Smiling to herself, Alice was pleased that she was not being forced to go back to the house. She continued down the street in the opposite direction Matthew went, taking her time to examine every stall until she reached a merchant selling books.

"Can I help you?" A blonde-haired woman asked as she stood from a stool.

"Um...yes actually. We have recently moved to the area, and I was hoping to learn a little more about the history. Do you have any books that could help us?" Alice asked with a big smile.

"I do." The woman reached below the shelves, pulled out a thick book, and handed it to her. "What brought you to the Howling Meadows Pack?" The woman asked as Alice paid for her new book.

"My uncle, brother, and my husband and I all came here for research. My husband must have done something wrong because he was arrested." Alice looked down. She didn't know why she added that last part.

"I'm so sorry to hear that." The woman's voice quieted to a whisper. "My husband was also arrested a few years ago. Have you been to any of the Matron Gatherings?"

"No, I haven't. I don't even know what that is." Alice looked at the woman, confused.

"The Matron Gathering only comes around twice a year. It is a gathering put on by Queen Isabel for the women who have been affected by their husbands being arrested or killed. I was just about to head there now. Would you like to come?" the merchant asked with a kind smile.

Alice hesitated for only a moment. "I would love to, thank you."

"Great. Let me close up really quickly and we can be on our way." The woman began to move the books off the display table and into a lockable chest. Alice assisted her and within five minutes, the two women were making their way toward the Alpha's castle. "By the way, I'm Gwen."

"Ali...son. My name is Alison." Alice said quickly. The people hunting her knew her name, so Alice decided to use an alternative name while in Valencia.

"Well Alison, I am glad you decided to come. Queen Isabel is very generous and kind. You will love her." Gwen said.

"What exactly is the Matron Gathering?" Alice asked curiously.

"Queen Isabel lost two sons during childbirth nearly two decades ago. In remembrance of the lost princes, she hosts this event twice a year, one for each prince. She hands out clothing, food, learning supplies, and other things to help the families that have been affected by their husbands being taken from them. It is held in the Queen's Garden where the Alpha does not go, so that the families can feel comfortable." Gwen's voice was so quiet Alice could hardly hear her. "The Gathering is always held the day before one of the princes' birthdays."

"Which prince are we remembering today?" Alice asked. She was intrigued with Queen Isabel and the charity and service she gives to her pack. From what she had gathered, Alpha Maddox was a very cruel man.

"The younger one. He would be eighteen if he had lived." Gwen said as she led Alice off the main path towards a large building.

The walls were made of stone for about ten feet before it turned to glass. The glass rose another five feet before curving over the top, creating a domed ceiling.

They walked along the stone wall and Alice took in the spectacular structure. When they rounded the corner of the building, two guards stood on either side of a metal door. They watched as Gwen and Alice approached.

"Good afternoon, Phil. John. How are you both today?" Gwen greeted them.

"Just fine, Gwen. It's nice to no longer be stationed within the prison." Phil answered as he frowned.

"What happened?" Gwen sounded worried.

"You know the young prisoner I told you about? Well, I will not have to see him tortured anymore." Seeing Gwen's confused face, Phil continued. "He was shipped off to Trevor's Cove."

"That poor boy! Why would they send him there? He has been here less than a year." Gwen put a hand over her heart in total shock. Alice watched the interaction in confusion.

"At least he will have a chance to protect himself at Trevor's Cove. I'm glad I don't have to watch him go through all the stuff he has been through the last eight months." John said.

"This is the one that never made a sound, right?" Gwen asked. Alice felt her heart drop to her stomach. Were they talking about Greyson?

"Yes. Until he was brought before the Alpha and Queen. The Alpha was angry that the prisoner talked with the Queen after being silent for so long." Phil answered. Suddenly Phil stiffened. He glanced around before settling his gaze back on Gwen and Alice. "Who is your friend, Gwen? You know that the Queen is very strict with who is allowed to the Gathering."

Gwen became slightly nervous with Phil's change in demeanor. "This is Alison. Her husband is in the prison. This is her first gathering since she is new to the area."

"Very well." John turned and unlocked the metal door and pulled it open. "Enter one at a time. There is a barrier at this door and one at the next." Alice peeked through the door and saw another metal door about ten feet in. "The door prevents anyone from hearing what is going on inside the Queen's Garden. Once you are both in the antechamber, one of us will accompany you to unlock the next door. Gwen, lead the way please."

Gwen gave the guards a nod before stepping through the first door and walking toward the other one. Just before she reached the door, she looked back at Alice and gave her an encouraging smile as she waited. Alice glanced at Phil who gestured her inside.

Taking a deep breath, Alice stepped over the threshold and gasped. All sound disappeared except for her own breathing. She moved toward Gwen when she felt a large presence behind her. Glancing over her shoulder, she saw Phil following her, and John closing the door behind them. She didn't even hear the door click closed.

Phil squeezed past her as he quickly unlocked the second door and Gwen stepped through. Gwen waited patiently for Alice to walk through the doorway, but Alice hesitated when Phil gestured her forward.

"Is something wrong?" Phil's deep voice echoed strangely around her.

"What was the prisoner's name?" Alice asked. She was desperate to know if the prisoner he was talking about was Greyson. If it were, she would know where to look for him next, Trevor's Cove.

"Like I said, he never spoke or made a sound." Phil narrowed his eyes at her.

Tears gathered in her eyes. "Please." Alice begged. "I need to know his name." Phil crossed his arms over his chest as he continued to glare at her. "Was his name Greyson?" Alice could not stop the tears that escaped and ran down her cheeks. Phil's hands dropped to his sides as his eyes widened in surprise. "Please, I need to know." Alice whispered.

She could see Gwen's concerned face as she watched her from the other side of the door. Alice didn't care. If the prisoner was Greyson, she just learned that even his own prison guards hated the way he had been treated and that he was sent somewhere that was worse than staying at the prison.

Phil regained his emotionless composure before answering her. "Why would you need to know if the prisoner's name was Greyson or not? There are hundreds of prisoners, why are you concerned about this one?"

"Because." Alice swallowed hard as she squeezed her eyes closed for a moment before locking her eyes with Phil's. "Greyson is my husband."

Phil's face paled as he watched Alice. Her chin was quivering as she tried to regain control over her emotions. He opened his mouth as if to say something, but shut it again. He ducked his head as he remained silent. His continued silence was in a way, confirmation that the prisoner was Greyson, but she needed to hear the prisoner's name from Phil.

Gwen came back through the door and wrapped her arms around Alice. Phil looked back up at Alice, unshed tears in his own eyes. "Yes." He quietly whispered. Alice nodded her understanding, her stomach still twisted painfully.

"What is going on?" Gwen asked, clearly upset. "Why is Alison so upset, Phil?"

"She is the Silent Prisoner's wife." Phil's voice was so quiet that even in the complete silence of the antechamber, Alice barely heard him. Gwen gasped beside her.

"Please, do not say anything about me being his wife. I don't want any trouble with the Alpha. Please." Alice looked between Phil and Gwen with pleading eyes.

"He earned my respect, but I was unable to do anything to help him. I will do whatever I can to keep his wife safe as a way of paying him back for his kindness to me, even when I was the one taking him to his punishments." Phil straightened his shoulders and gave her a determined look. "I never agreed with the Alpha's treatment of the prisoner and wouldn't mind getting back at him any way I can."

"You do not have to worry about me, Alison. I hate Alpha Maddox. My loyalty is only to Queen Isabel." Gwen said firmly.

Alice nearly collapsed in relief. "Thank you." She wiped the remaining tears off her face and took a calming breath. "I'm sorry for holding you back from your work, Phil."

He gave her a kind smile. Gwen grabbed her hand and led her out the door. As Alice passed the threshold, her ears were assaulted by all sorts of sounds. It was a little disorienting coming from the antechamber with absolutely no sound, to hearing birds singing, people talking and kids laughing.

The garden was beautiful. There were hundreds of flowers in flower beds that lined the many paths that webbed out from the center. There were trees that provided shade on grassy patches, and some had swings hanging down from the thick branches. Birds flew through the air, filling the garden with their unique songs.

Gwen continued to pull Alice behind her as she greeted several women while they walked toward the center. A tall woman wearing a beautiful dark blue dress was standing with her back to them as they approached. She had long reddish-brown hair. Streaks of grey were barely visible through the long thick braid that hung down her back.

Gwen slowed her steps as they approached the woman and stopped a couple of feet away. Gwen watched the woman as she waited for her to finish her current conversation. Alice's mind was replaying the conversation she overheard between Gwen and the guards. Greyson was on his way to Trevor's Cove. When the woman was done with her conversation, Gwen stepped up to her with a smile.

"Queen Isabel, it is good to see you." Gwen gave a curtsey and Alice quickly did the same. "May I introduce Alison. Her husband was invited by Alpha Maddox to the lower levels of the castle."

Alice kept her head lowered as she waited to be addressed. She had never met anyone of high ranking, let alone a queen, and did not want to offend her. Not to mention that her eyes were probably red from crying.

"I see." Queen Isabel said sadly. "I am truly sorry for the Alpha's aggressive behavior. I do not believe I have seen you before, are you new to our pack?" Queen Isabel asked in a kind voice.

"We are just visiting. My uncle and brother accompanied me here while we try to find a way to free my husband." Alice looked up into the queen's face. Alice gasped as she put a shaking hand over her mouth. Greyson's amber eyes were staring back at her from the queen's face. "I...I'm sorry." Alice took a few steps back as Queen Isabel's lips pressed into a thin line and her brow furrowed with concern. "I think I need to sit." Alice's mind was racing as she tried to find an explanation for the Queen and Greyson having the same eyes.

"My dear, you are pale." Gwen grabbed Alice's arm and led her to a secluded corner of the garden. Queen Isabel had followed them carrying a glass of water, which she offered to Alice. Alice gratefully took it and downed the whole cup in a few seconds. "What is the matter, Alison?"

Alice could only shake her head, unable to pull her eyes from the queen's. "I will sit with her, Gwen. Why don't you go get what you need for you and your girls." Queen Isabel said calmly as she took the seat next to Alice. Gwen hesitantly nodded before she headed back to the tables in the center of the garden. "You look like you have seen a ghost. Are you sure you are alright?" Queen Isabel was studying Alice carefully.

Alice could not help but say something. She needed to know how Greyson, Matthew, and Queen Isabel have the same eye color. "You have his same eyes." Alice finally said.

Queen Isabel's worried expression turned to one of anxiety. "I'm sorry, who's?"

"My husband and brother-in-law both have amber colored eyes, like yours. I have never met anyone with their eye color before." Alice whispered while continuing to look at the queen's eyes.

Queen Isabel put a hand to her mouth as her eyes filled with tears and her chin trembled. It took several moments for Queen Isabel to compose herself. "What are their names?" Her voice was barely louder than a whisper.

"I am married to Greyson, and Matthew is his brother." Alice watched as a single tear fell from her eye. She quickly wiped it away as a sad smile pulled up the corners of her mouth.

"I am so sorry to tell you, but your Greyson was sold to Lars, the slave trader. I tried to get Alpha Maddox to reconsider, but his mind was made up." There was a bleakness in Queen Isabel's eyes that told of regret and helplessness. Queen Isabel grabbed Alice's hand in a gesture of comfort.

"I know." Alice gave the queen's hand a gentle squeeze. "My Lady, how is it possible that the three of you share the same eye color? Is it a more common shade here in Valencia?" Alice asked.

Queen Isabel looked around for several minutes. They were completely alone, with the closest person being Gwen, nearly one hundred feet away. "It has been long forgotten that amber colored eyes are a sign of having the Alpha King's bloodline. Queen Mara alone had amber eyes and only her descendants have the gene."

"So, you really are a royal?" Alice asked in surprise. "But, if only those with the royal bloodline have amber eyes, then Greyson and Matthew..." Her voice trailed off as she stared wide-eyed at Queen Isabel.

"Then they are of royal blood as well." Queen Isabel nodded.

"But how? They both came from an orphanage." Alice released the queen's hand as she began to run her finger over the wolf pendant. Her vision. The one where the woman was giving up her child. Did Queen Isabel give up her sons?

"Where did you get that?" Queen Isabel grabbed Alice's wrist as she studied the pendant with surprise and fear.

Alice looked at the Queen in alarm. Her complete demeanor changed from sad, but hopeful, to almost angry and accusatory. "Greyson gave it to me." Alice pulled her arm out of the queen's grasp.

"Do you realize what this is?" The queen whispered urgently. Alice shook her head in confusion. "I need to go be with the other ladies, but will you please meet me here tomorrow for breakfast? Bring your uncle and brother if you would like. Please. And be here at eight." Queen Isabel stood up quickly and gave Alice one last look before walking back to the center of the garden.

Alice was so confused by Queen Isabel's behavior. She went from concerned over Alice's shock, to somewhat quiet while talking about the royal bloodline, to nearly panicked when she saw Alice's bracelet. A headache started forming and Alice wished she were back at their rented house. Standing up, Alice walked over to Gwen and gave her a small smile.

"Thank you for bringing me. I was not planning on being a total wreck today and I am so sorry for any trouble I have caused you. I think I am going to go home and rest for a bit." Alice said as Gwen gave her a hug.

"It gets a little easier over time. My Drake was arrested three years ago and for the first year the littlest things would set me off. I understand exactly how you feel. If you need anything, my home is just south of the market square, the fifth house on the left. It has a blue door." Gwen said as she walked with Alice back to the metal door. She pulled a rope and waited.

A minute later, the door swung open, and John stepped aside allowing room for Alice to enter the antechamber. Gwen gave her another quick hug just before Alice stepped over the threshold. Once inside, she started heading for the other door.

She was about halfway there when a large hand grabbed her arm. Her training kicked in and she spun around and threw her left fist into her attacker's face. John stumbled back a step. Taking advantage of his surprise, Alice kicked his feet out from under him. After he landed hard on his back, Alice placed a knee on his chest as she pulled out one of her daggers and held it to his throat.

"Wow! Hold on!" John lifted his hands to show her that he meant no harm. "I'm sorry if I scared you. I promise I am not going to hurt you. I just want to ask you something."

Alice blinked several times and took a deep breath. She had reacted so quickly that she didn't even have time to think. Embarrassed, Alice got back to her feet and sheathed her dagger. "I'm sorry. I didn't even think." She mumbled as she kept an eye on John.

Keeping his eyes on her, John slowly got to his feet. "Who taught you to fight like that?" His voice was filled with amazement.

"Which part?" Alice laughed softly. "My father has been teaching me to fight since I was young. My brother-in-law taught me to use daggers. But my husband helped refine my fighting skills and taught me how to make every punch count." Alice smiled as John's mouth fell open.

"The Silent Prisoner taught you to throw punches like that?" John used the back of his hand to wipe his face. Blood was coming from a cut on his cheek and a split lip. "Maybe he does have a decent chance at surviving Trevor's Cove."

"What is Trevor's Cove?" Alice asked.

"Trevor's Cove is where Lars takes the men he collects to fight in the arena. People come from all around Valencia to watch the fights and place bets. Slaves either die in the ring or, if they're lucky, become so good that they can earn their freedom after ten years." John explained. "I didn't stop you in order to talk about Trevor's Cove though. I needed to ask you something." Alice watched as John's amazed expression turned serious as he told her about Trevor's Cove. John's whole posture radiated with uncertainty. "Are you the girl they kept asking him about? Phil thinks that you are?"

Alice kept her facial expressions neutral. "What makes you think that?" Alice could hear her anxiety in her own voice and knew John probably could too.

"I can't think of any other person for a young man to be so determined to keep safe, than the woman he loves. And since you are his wife, we are assuming he loves you." John answered.

"And why would I trust a man that was one of the guards that took my husband back and forth between his prison cell and different forms of tortures?"

Alice narrowed her eyes. She needed to figure out if she could trust this man or if she needed to get as far away from here as possible. At least she knew Greyson was going to Trevor's Cove.

"I'm not proud of what I had to do for the last eight months. As the Queen's guards, the Queen asked Phil and me to watch out for the prisoner and report back to her on everything the Alpha did to him. The Alpha agreed to permit us to be the kid's guards, but we were unable to intervene, per the Alpha's command. We have sworn our allegiance to our Queen, but unfortunately, we still have to follow the Alpha's commands." John explained. "I don't expect you to trust me. I just wanted to issue a warning. If you are the girl the Alpha is after, get out of pack lands as fast as possible and do not come back. Alpha Maddox is a very dangerous man."

"You don't sound like you hold any love for your Alpha." Alice commented while studying John's face as he moved to unlock the door to the outside.

"I don't." John said firmly as he glanced over at her. He wiped the blood off his face again.

He opened the door, but Alice made no move to leave. "If another Alpha came to the Howling Meadows Pack to challenge Alpha Maddox, who would you follow?" Alice was curious, if Greyson were to return, would he have support from some of the pack members?

"That would depend on the other Alpha. There are worse ones out there than Maddox." John shrugged as he continued to hold the door open.

"What if it were Greyson? Would you swear your allegiance to him or Alpha Maddox?" Alice asked before she stepped over the threshold and walked several steps away.

She heard the door click behind her and she turned around. Both Phil and John were watching her closely. "The first." John said firmly while holding her gaze. "There is no question."

Phil turned to look at John with a confused look, but when he saw John's bloody and slightly swollen face, his eyes went wide. "What happened to you?"

John nodded in Alice's direction and Phil let out a surprised laugh. Alice smiled as well. "He surprised me. It was just a reaction. And I really am sorry, John." John gave her a smile and a nod of his head. She gave them both a wave before heading back to the house.

She opened the door and stepped inside. She paused when she saw both Uncle Isaac and Matthew glaring at her. The tension in the room was palpable as Alice closed the door behind her. She could see the worry and frustration in her uncle's eyes and anger in Matthew's.

"Where were you?" Matthew growled out. "We were supposed to meet up an hour ago at the fountain, Alice."

Isaac placed a hand on Matthew's shoulder to try to calm him as he looked at Alice expectantly. "While here in Valencia, I am Alison. And I was invited to meet Queen Isabel at a private gathering for women." Alice answered.

"That was dangerous, Alison. We have no idea where Queen Isabel's loyalties lie. What if she tells Alpha Maddox about you?" Isaac asked sternly. He was clearly frustrated as he ran his hand through his hair.

"She won't tell the Alpha about me, and you can find out for yourselves what kind of person she is in the morning. She has invited all three of us to have breakfast with her at eight and I'm planning on going." Alice said as she headed toward her room. "Oh, and I know where they took Greyson." She called over her shoulder.

"How?" Matthew was flabbergasted.

"We can talk about it more tomorrow. I'm exhausted and I am going to bed." It was still somewhat early to be going to bed, but Alice didn't want to talk about anything she learned today outside of the Queen's Garden. She was worried that someone might overhear and report back to Alpha Maddox or Cain. And she did not want to do anything that would jeopardize getting to Trevor's Cove as quickly as possible.

Chapter 9

Greyson woke to the creaking of the boat. No sun shone down through the grates in the ceiling making the interior very dark. Greyson used his wolf's sense to see better in the darkness. As he scanned the space, he noticed Drake watching him. Greyson glared at the man.

"You punched me." Greyson said trying to keep his voice low enough to not draw attention.

"You were about to shift, what would you have had me do?" Drake shrugged as he smirked at Greyson. "Besides, if we have any hope of getting you out of here, we need to keep the guards thinking that the Equalizer affects you normally."

"Why are you so concerned about me? You don't even know me." Greyson moved to get into a more comfortable position.

Drake confused him. Sure, they both had been taken from their families and were enroute to a fighting ring, but Drake seemed to have singled Greyson out as an ally. The question Greyson had was, why him and not one of the other prisoners?

"That is where you are wrong, my young friend. We knew you as a baby and I even held you for a few minutes while your mother gathered several things for you." Drake smiled and Greyson saw a spark of mischief in the older man's eyes.

Greyson was wary of the man. Growing up under the thumb of Bradley Barnett had taught Greyson to question everything and not trust anyone. He had learned to trust some, but that trust was not won easily.

"Forgive me for being a bit skeptical of your claims, sir. My childhood was unique and your claims of knowing me as a baby are farfetched. And who are 'we'?"

"Luther and I delivered you and your mother to Miss Mary's in order to hide you." A slight movement to Drake's left drew Greyson's attention and he saw another man watching him intently. Greyson could feel his heart rate increase as he watched the two men sitting in front of him. They knew he was at Miss Mary's. That was a part of his history that very few people knew. Not even Bradley knew where Greyson came from.

"Judging by your silence, I am sure you don't fully believe us." The second man whispered. "My name is Luther. Maybe it would help if we told you how we are connected to your mother and why she felt like giving you to Miss Mary was her only option." Luther cleared his throat when Greyson remained silent. "Your mother is the daughter of the Alpha of the First Moon Pack. She was forced to marry Alpha Maddox. Drake and I were your mother's personal guards before her marriage and our Alpha insisted on us accompanying Isabel to her new home in the Howling Meadows Pack. Alpha Maddox desperately wanted a son so that he could teach his heir the proper way to rule a pack and to expand the pack borders."

"That is a nice way of saying Alpha Maddox wanted to take over other packs, using his son." Drake cut in.

"Anyway, Isabel gave birth to three daughters within the first five years of their marriage. Maddox became more and more aggressive and desperate for a son. When Isabel gave birth to you, she panicked knowing what fate would befall you if your father knew she had finally given birth to a son. Within an hour of your birth, Drake and I were assisting Queen Isabel into the orphanage where she met with Miss Mary. She told the Alpha that a son was born, but died during childbirth. The grief she felt over having to give you up was enough to convince her husband that the child actually died. Four years later, another son was born, and we again took the Queen and infant to Miss Mary's." Luther continued to explain, and Greyson could feel the truth in the man's words.

"Queen Isabel swore Luther and me to secrecy and issued an Alpha command strong enough that even Alpha Maddox's command wouldn't be able to break it. We pledged to our Queen that if we ever found one of the lost princes, we would assist him in challenging Alpha Maddox and restoring peace to the pack and freeing the people from his tyranny." Drake picked up the story. Greyson's mind was reeling from all the information Drake and Luther told him.

"What makes you think I am one of the lost princes?" Greyson asked. He wanted to double check to make sure he was the person they thought he was. He could get on board with the idea of his mother giving him up to protect him from Alpha Maddox, but a lost prince? He was having a hard time believing that part.

"Queen Isabel comes from the royal bloodline that originated from Queen Mara and Alpha King Tyson. Their line alone has the amber colored eyes that you have. If the eye color didn't give it away, you seem to have a greater strength than most wolf Shifters." Luther replied.

"Who said I was a wolf Shifter?" Greyson questioned as he raised one of his eyebrows.

"Touche." Drake laughed lightly. "Whatever Shifter you are, the Equalizer should have made it impossible for you to shift, yet I had to knock you out in order to keep you from doing just that. Only a powerful Shifter would be able to resist its effects."

"Now that we have gotten our history out of the way, let us talk about our future. How well can you fight, Greyson?" Luther asked seriously.

"Uh…Well…Um…" Greyson didn't know how to answer. He could easily hold his own, but he did not want the slave traders to know that. Or his fellow prisoners. He didn't trust them fully, yet.

"That's okay, kid. Luther and I can help teach you some things while we are at Trevor's' Cove. Once we escape, we can get you ready to challenge Alpha Maddox." Drake leaned back against the post he was chained to and closed his eyes. "For now, try to rest. And remember to act as if the Equalizer toxin affects you just as it does us."

Greyson nodded his head. He settled back against the hull and thought about his mother's history. She must have been desperate to keep her sons from her husband. To surrender your children within an hour of giving birth to them would take a great amount of strength. He still struggled with having to leave Alisha, Asher, and Avery, and they were not even his own flesh and blood.

Greyson's thoughts turned to the three kids that he had grown so fond of. Avery had to be at least a year old by now. Was she walking yet? She had been so tiny when he last saw her. Had Mr. Finn started teaching Asher how to ride yet? The boy would be a natural on horseback. And then there was Alisha. She was shy, but smart. She would have loved the library at the Witches' Castle. He missed them all. As soon as he escaped, he would take out Alpha Maddox, and find Alice. Then they were going to go see the kids.

The rocking of the ship started to lull Greyson to sleep. He reached out with his mind trying to feel Alice. He needed to know she was still okay. He was almost desperate to talk with her again after they had mind-linked before he boarded the boat.

Suddenly, he felt a wave of panic and fear wash over him. The feeling quickly changed to disbelief and anxiousness. Something was going on with Alice and it ate at him to not be able to do anything about it. He knew he should close the link to her, but he could not bring himself to break the connection. He tried to push his own uncertainties aside and send comforting thoughts and feelings her way. He hoped it would help.

Days passed and Greyson lost track of how long they had been in the boat. The guards would periodically come down and administer more rounds of the Equalizer in order to keep the prisoners sedated. Luckily for him, the drug only seemed to knock him out for a few hours. He had learned that for Drake and Luther, the drug knocked them out for hours and once they woke up, they were groggy for days.

While pretending to be asleep, Greyson used his wolf hearing and learned that the drugs they were injected with was a combination of the Equalizer and a powerful sedative. He also learned that the journey was almost over.

Greyson's muscles screamed at not being able to stretch or be used for so long. At night when most of the prisoners and guards were asleep, he took to doing pushups to keep himself active. The seas were calm, and Greyson was doing push-ups as he thought about Alice. Was she safe? He really hoped that Matt and Isaac had gotten her away from Alpha Maddox.

"How do you have the stamina to do that for so long?" Luther asked.

Greyson smiled as he rotated to a sitting position. "My cell didn't provide much room to stand. I have had eight months of practice at this single workout. Before that, I was quite active as well." He wiped the sweat off his brow with the back of his hand. "I don't do well sitting in one place for very long."

"You might want to cool your enthusiasm, Greyson. You do not want the guards to notice how much energy you have." Luther warned.

Greyson rested his head back on the side of the boat. Luther was right. He was sweaty and breathing hard. If any of the guards came down to check on the prisoners, they could easily notice that he had been up to something. He took a deep breath and slowly let it out. "You are right. I'll try to refrain for the remainder of our boat trip."

Luther gave him a nod before closing his eyes. "It is obvious that you do a lot of physical work, but have you ever fought?"

"What do you mean?" Greyson asked. He knew what Luther meant but still did not want anyone to know the extent of his fighting skills. He had decided several days ago that he would pretend to not know how to even throw a proper punch. Luther opened his eyes and gave Greyson a look that he interpreted as Luther thinking him an idiot. "I have a brother that I fought with a few times growing up." It was true. To a degree. All the boys were taught to think of each other as brothers. He had also sparred more than a few times with Matt.

"That's a start, I guess." Luther grumbled.

Silence once again filled the space around them. Greyson could hear the vague sounds of conversations taking place on the deck above but didn't bother trying to overhear what was being said. He closed his eyes and allowed his mind to replay every moment he spent with Alice. She was the only thing keeping him sane.

Chapter 10

Alice bolted upright in bed. Another scream tore through the night air and Alice scrambled out of her bed. She ran out of her bedroom and down the hall. She followed the screams to Matthew's room. Isaac was already there just standing back and watching as Matthew tossed and turned on the floor while continuing to scream out in pain.

"What's going on? Why aren't you helping him?" Alice yelled at her uncle as she tried to run to Matthew, but Isaac grabbed her arm and held her back.

"He is shifting, Alice. Hopefully, it will end soon. He has been tossing and turning and groaning in pain for the last four hours. Like Greyson, he has a high pain tolerance, so he must be close now." Isaac said calmly while he pulled Alice into a hug.

Alice's fear from waking up to screams changed to worry for Matthew. She remembered what it felt like when she had shifted and wished she could help lessen Matthew's pain in some way.

A feeling of comfort spread from within her, and she closed her eyes. An image of Greyson popped up in her mind. She wished he were there to hold her and see his brother's shift. If this feeling of comfort was coming from him, then at least he was safe at the moment and he wasn't blocking her from him.

She stood by her uncle for twenty more minutes before Matthew finally shifted. His wolf was almost the size of Greyson's. His body was such a dark grey it appeared like salt and pepper. All four of his legs and both ears were a solid black.

Alice walked over to him and patted his head. She scratched behind his ears and his tail wagged. Alice laughed. "You are so cute! I love your ears, Matt." He let out a playful growl before looking over at Isaac. Isaac walked over to the large wolf.

"You ready to shift back to human?" Isaac asked with a smile.

Isaac and Alice moved back to give Matt a bit more space. Isaac told Matt how to shift back and Matthew shifted quickly before pulling Alice into a hug. "That was crazy!" He laughed. "No wonder Greyson was so tired the night of your shift, Alice. I cannot imagine going through that again without shifting. What did I look like?" Matthew was rambling as he always did when he was excited. While researching, Matt brought up the thought that Greyson was feeling Alice's pain through the mate bond while she shifted.

"Your wolf is amazing. You are dark grey with black legs and black ears." Alice grinned at him. "But I am going back to bed. Congratulations on shifting, Matt." She gave him another hug. "Remember we leave for the Queen's Garden in…" She looked at the clock. "…two hours."

Alice awoke to Matthew shaking her shoulder. He informed her that she had just twenty minutes until they were supposed to arrive at the Queen's Garden. She jumped from bed and quickly dressed.

By the time she made it to the living room, Isaac and Matthew were waiting for her. They didn't say much as they left the small house and headed in the direction of the castle. Just as they were passing the wolf fountain, a man stepped out of a nearby shop.

"Finally, I have found my mystery woman." Cain smiled widely at Alice. She felt both Isaac and Matt step closer to her as she continued to walk without acknowledging Cain. "I have been looking everywhere for you but couldn't seem to find you."

"You would think that a man as smart as the rumors claim you are, would get the hint." Alice mumbled.

Cain stepped in front of Alice causing her to stop, and Matt moved even closer to her. "Is this your husband?" The glint in Cain's eyes when he sized Matthew up made Alice immediately uneasy.

"My brother. Now get out of my way, sir." Alice kept her chin up. She would not back down. She feared if she did, he would only see it as her giving in to him.

Cain reached for her right hand, but she quickly tucked it behind her back. He narrowed his eyes when he saw the ring on her left hand. "A new ring? You are not trying to fabricate a husband, are you?"

"My sister is married. A fact she apparently has told you before." Matt narrowed his eyes at Cain. "If you will excuse us, we have an appointment this morning that we are already running late for." Matt put an arm around Alice's shoulders and guided her around Cain.

Alice refused to look back even though she could feel Cain's eyes on her as they walked away. When they finally turned down the path to the garden, Alice shivered. "Are you okay?" Isaac asked quietly.

"You should have told him I was your husband." Matt grumbled.

"Did you see the look in his eyes when he asked? I would not put it past him to try to kill you in order to make me a widow." Alice shook her head. "That man just cannot accept the fact that I turned him down. Tara said as much, too." They rounded the corner of the garden and Alice smiled when she saw Phil and John standing guard by the door. "Good morning, gentlemen." Alice greeted them.

John gave her a big smile as they both gave her a quick bow. "Good morning to you, My Lady." John said. "Who are your companions?"

"This is my Uncle Isaac and my brother, Matt." Alice made the introductions, and noticed the look that Phil and John gave Matthew. She would ask them when they were within the antechamber. "The queen is expecting us."

Phil gave a quick nod as he unlocked and opened the door. "One at a time please. Alison, lead the way."

Alice stepped through the doorway and shook her head. The complete absence of noise once again taking her off guard. She moved to the other door and turned to watch as Matt, Isaac and Phil followed her in. Matt yawned and stuck his finger in his ear as if trying to clear it. "This is weird." He commented.

"So, how do you know each other?" Alice asked with a raised brow.

Phil laughed. "Beautiful, a fighter and smart. No wonder the Silent Prisoner protected you so fiercely." Alice just continued to stare at him. "Queen Isabel assigned Matthew under John and me for a few days when we were your man's guards."

That explained how Matthew was able to get her message to Greyson. Matt seemed more at ease after seeing Phil and John guarding the entrance.

She nodded in acceptance of the answer and Phil unlocked the inner door. Alice walked into the garden and waited for Matt and Isaac to join her. They followed her along the path towards the center where Alice had first met Queen Isabel. Alice stopped once she saw Queen Isabel standing near a large bush with flowers. She appeared to be smelling the blossoms.

Matt nudged her shoulder, and she began walking again. The moment Queen Isabel heard them approaching, she turned around to greet them. Alice watched as the woman placed a shaky hand over her abdomen.

When they were within a few feet of her, Alice dipped into a curtsey. She felt Isaac and Matt bow beside her. "Good morning, Queen Isabel." Alice said quietly.

"Good morning, dear. I am so glad you accepted my invitation and that your brother and uncle were able to make it as well." Queen Isabel gestured towards a table and the group took their seats.

Alice watched as Queen Isabel fought to remain in control of her emotions as she continued to stare at Matthew. Alice cleared her throat after a few moments of silence. "I don't mean to be rude, but I think we both know that Matthew is more than just my brother." Alice crossed her arms and narrowed her eyes at Queen Isabel.

"Alison!" Isaac choked out in horrified shock.

"No. It's alright." Queen Isabel gave Isaac a reassuring smile before turning her attention back to Alice. "You are correct. And I am sure you have many more questions you wish answered." Alice nodded. "I will do my best to answer them all, but first, will you allow me to tell you a story?"

Alice glanced over at Matthew and Isaac's confused expressions before giving a small nod. "That sounds fair."

"Why don't you three eat while I begin." Alice took a small bite of eggs as Queen Isabel took a deep breath. "I was nearly nineteen when my father called me into his office. An Alpha from a nearby pack had approached him and asked for my hand in marriage. This Alpha was known for being hard and unforgiving. At first my father rejected him, but the Alpha would not accept that answer. My father was loving and kind, however, he is a man and made mistakes early on when he took over as Alpha. My father informed me that the Alpha was trying to blackmail him. He gave me the choice whether to accept the man's proposal or to weather the storm that would come if I refused."

Alice had put her fork down as she was swept up in the story. "I chose to protect my father and marry the Alpha. In the beginning, Alpha Maddox was not as bad as I had feared, but he still was hard and emotionless. When I became pregnant not long after our wedding, he became very protective of me and doted on my every need. When a daughter was born, Maddox became angry. His anger only became more unpredictable after two more daughters were born. He wanted a son so badly. Someone that he could teach to take over the pack for him. I was secretly glad that each of our babies were girls because I knew Maddox would destroy any good in a boy. He would have raised them to be worse than he was. I had even heard him talking with his advisor about attacking other packs to become stronger."

Alice glanced over at Matthew who had grown still. "When I became pregnant again, I was terrified for the child. If I had another girl, I was afraid of what Maddox would do to me or the child. When I went into labor a month early and a son was born…" Queen Isabel squeezed her eyes closed and took a deep breath. "Luckily, Maddox was gone visiting a neighboring pack. I could not allow Maddox to hurt my baby. I was desperate to save my son from his father. I took my most trusted guards that came with me from my home pack and went to a friend's orphanage. I knew Mary would be able to give my son the love that I would not be allowed to give him. I named him Grey, said good-bye and returned home before I could change my mind."

Alice wiped a tear from her own cheek as she watched the remorse and sadness on Queen Isabel's face. Matthew's jaw tightened as he glared at his plate. "I told Maddox that the child came too early and died moments after being born. Four years later, Maddox was in a conference when my second son was born. I again made the journey to see Mary. I named him Lawrence Matthew after my father. I nearly took the child back with me. It killed me to have to lose another child, but his father had become even more aggressive. I knew that if I did not hide my baby, Maddox would either kill him in his quest for power or my sweet baby would be conditioned into a monster. Just like Maddox." Queen Isabel began to sob. "I could not let that happen. I had to protect them, even if that meant giving them up."

Alice slid off her chair and moved to Queen Isabel's side. She wrapped her arms around the older woman and hugged her tight. Queen Isabel returned the hug as she continued to cry. Matthew remained silent, watching the queen. After several minutes, Queen Isabel sat back and wiped her cheeks. She gave Alice a watery smile. She glanced over at Matthew but did not meet his eyes.

"Thank you." Matthew quietly said. Queen Isabel's head snapped up and stared at him in surprise. "Thank you for trying to protect Grey and me from Alpha Maddox." Matthew slowly got to his feet and moved over to Queen Isabel's side. He grabbed her hand and helped her to her feet. As soon as she stood, Matthew pulled her into a tight hug. "You did the right thing, mother." He whispered.

Queen Isabel started crying again as she clung to Matthew. Matt buried his face into his mother's neck and Alice watched as he squeezed his eyes shut. "I never thought I would hear those words from my sons." Queen Isabel sniffled. Matthew retrieved a napkin from the table and handed it to her. She gave him a smile before retaking her seat. "I am so glad you have grown into such a good man."

Matt cleared his throat and shifted uncomfortably in his chair. "That is mostly Grey's influence. I'm not sure how he remained how he is, but lucky for me, he taught me well." When Queen Isabel gave him a questioning look. Matt explained about the false adoptions and the training camps where he and Greyson were raised. Queen Isabel's face paled as she listened, but she did not interrupt.

"I am so sorry. I should have..."

"No." Matt interrupted his mother. "I told you before that you did the right thing. If you had not sent us away, there wouldn't have been a chance that we would have come out okay." Queen Isabel hesitantly nodded as she wiped her cheeks. "And Grey is the best of men. Even having gone through everything he has. His training was so much more...intense than mine was. They sent him up north to the Assassin's Guild when he was five, I think. He was there for several years. But somehow, he is selfless and kind. He is everything I wish to be when I grow up."

Alice smiled softly at that. Greyson really was selfless and kind. She watched as Queen Isabel patted Matt's hand before looking back to Alice. "And you are Grey's wife." Alice nodded. "I am sorry we were unable to get him out of the dungeon before he was sold to Lars."

"I am sorry too." Alice sighed as she sat back in her chair. She began tapping her finger on the table as her brows furrowed. Now that Queen Isabel had confirmed she was Greyson's and Matthew's mother, Alice had several more questions. Why did the sight of her wolf pendant upset her? How did she know so much about their plan to get Greyson out of the dungeon?

"I know you still have questions, but I am afraid I must be going. Alpha Maddox requires that I sit with him as he meets with Beta Cain." Queen Isabel stood. They stood with her. She shook Isaac's hand and hugged Matthew before turning to Alice. "I must ask that you all leave the pack today. Maddox is not happy that he has not been able to locate someone." She reached for a stack of papers that sat in the center of the table. "Here are your travelling papers. Grey is being taken to Trevor's Cove. If you are able to reach him before he is killed, you will have the easiest chance of freeing him there." She handed the papers to Isaac. "My dear Alison, I am so glad Grey has a sweet girl like you. Please, stay safe and best of luck." Alice was pulled into a tight embrace before Queen Isabel kissed her forehead.

"Thank you, Queen Isabel. But..." Alice began.

"We can speak again once you return with Grey." They all nodded before turning towards the exit. "Please do not speak of any of this until you are far away from here. Maddox has spies everywhere." And with that, Queen Isabel turned and headed for a door opposite the one they had entered.

Alice once again led the way. No one spoke until they reached their little house. Isaac told them all to pack as quickly as possible. Within an hour, Alice found herself walking between Isaac and Matthew as they approached the pack gates. Isaac had given them each their travel papers before they left the house. He nudged her forward now, allowing her to go first.

Alice stepped up to the guard and gave him a smile. She handed him her papers and waited. He began looking over the documents as another guard stepped up to assist Matthew and Isaac. Both made it through the gate as her guard continued to look at her papers. Anxiety began to knot her stomach as she glanced over the guard's shoulder to where her uncle and Matt waited for her. They both wore matching frowns.

"Is something wrong, sir?" Alice finally asked.

The guard looked up at her with an apologetic expression. "I'm sorry Miss, but I cannot allow you through."

"It is Mrs. and why not? Is there something wrong with my paperwork?" Alice masked her nervousness with frustration.

"Your paperwork is fine but..." The guard looked away from her and cleared his throat.

"But what?" Alice glared at the man. "If my paperwork is in order, I will be leaving."

"We are under orders to not allow you to leave the pack. I am sorry." The man looked back at her, and she could see he really wished he could let her leave.

"What's going on?" Isaac spoke as he tried to come back to her, but he was stopped by a different guard.

"I'm sorry sir, but you only have papers to leave, not enter." The new guard said.

"I have papers to leave but you are refusing to let me." Alice shot back at the guard. The guard assisting her winced.

"We have our orders. You must stay, but they are free to go."

"If I had known you were not going to allow my sister to leave, I wouldn't have left either. Is she a prisoner?" Matt stepped close to the guard. Alice could feel a powerful aura coming from Matt as he glared down at the man. Both guards visibly swallowed and bowed their heads. Matt's eyes began to flicker like Greyson's did when fighting his wolf.

"She is not a prisoner, sir. I promise. We just cannot let her pass." The guard nearest her said in a rush as his eyes were fixed on the ground. "I truly am sorry."

Alice placed a hand on her stomach as she took several deep breaths. She looked between all the men and the several more guards approaching. "It's alright, Matt. I will go back to our friend and see what all this is about. You and Uncle need to continue to our destination. I will meet you there." Alice gave them a pleading look. Isaac gave her a small nod before grabbing Matt's arm.

Alice didn't wait to watch them leave, instead she turned and headed directly for the Queen's Garden. She knew she would find sanctuary there. She kept her head down and her pace quick. When she saw Phil and John standing at their post, Alice nearly broke into a run. Both men glanced at each other before giving her a puzzled look. By the time she reached them tears were sliding down her cheeks. Phil did not ask any questions but quickly opened the door for her and followed her inside.

"What has happened?" He asked as soon as the door closed behind them.

"I don't know." Alice wiped her cheeks. "Queen Isabel gave us papers to leave. They let my uncle and Matthew through but told me they were under orders not to allow me to leave even though my paperwork was correct. They refused to allow Matt and Uncle Isacc back in. I don't know what to do." Phil pulled Alice into a quick hug.

"Stay in the garden. You will be safe in there." Alice nodded as she stepped back. "It sounds like either Alpha Maddox issued the order or Cain did." Phil rubbed his jaw.

"I would put money on Cain. He has taken an interest in me even though I have told him to leave me alone." Alice tucked her hair behind her ear and looked down at the ground.

"Definitely stay here then. I will let the Queen know about the situation. She will know what to do." Phil patted her shoulder.

"Thank you, Phil." Alice stepped aside so that Phil could unlock the inner door. He gave her a reassuring smile as she walked back into the garden.

Alice spent the next half hour wondering the paths that wove around the vibrant flowers. She spotted a bench in the shade of a large tree and walked towards it. She settled herself on the bench and opened her bag. Alice pulled out Greyson's shirt and the wooden wolf figure she had purchased for Asher.

She raised the shirt to her nose and took a deep breath. Cinnamon. She put the shirt back in the bag so it would not get dirtier than it already was, before turning her attention to the figure. It looked so much like Grey's wolf. Alice closed her eyes, picturing Grey as he smiled and winked at her from across the room while he read Asher a book.

Chapter 11

Alice heard the rustle of skirts, and she opened her eyes. Queen Isabel rushed towards her with a concerned expression. As soon as she reached Alice, she took a seat on the bench and grabbed her hand. "Tell me everything." Queen Isabel gave Alice's hand a gentle squeeze.

Alice took a deep breath before starting. She told the queen about entering the pack with the group of women and then Cain's attentions. She told her of Matt's assignment to ask about Cain's mystery woman to try to find her. Alice mentioned when Cain saw them on their way to breakfast and then what happened at the gate.

"I didn't know what else to do." Alice said. "Matt was so angry, and more guards were starting to show up. I did not want him to end up arrested, too. Trying to rescue Grey is enough without having to try to get Matthew out as well. So, I told them to go on without me."

"You did good. Matthew would definitely have been arrested if he had tried to enter pack lands again." Queen Isabel gave Alice's hand another squeeze. "Your uncle is smart. He will keep Matthew out of trouble. Once they get Greyson, they will be back for you. Now, we need to make sure Cain cannot get to you."

"How are we going to do that? He will know soon enough that I am here without my protectors. He will double his efforts to get me."

"Hmm." Queen Isabel let go of Alice's hand as she stood and began to pace slowly. "You are not without protectors, Alison. Phil and John would willingly take you in, but I think I have a better idea, if you agree." Alice gave her a nod to continue. "If you were to be my companion, you would be in an adjoining room to mine and you would be wherever I am. You would be protected at all times."

Alice mulled over her options. She could always ask to stay in the garden, but hiding for who knows how long, alone, didn't seem like much fun. But if she did agree to be the Queen's companion, she would need to act submissive to the Alpha and Queen. She would also be close to Alpha Maddox.

Alice looked up at Queen Isabel. Although, as a companion, Alice would also get to know her mother-in-law. The idea made her smile. "I think I would like to be your companion." The smile that lit Queen Isabel's face warmed Alice's heart and set her nerves at ease. "Though I must be honest with you." Queen Isabel raised an eyebrow in question. "My name is not Alison, it's Alice. But please continue calling me Alison. Considering our newfound relationship, I felt like you should know my real name."

"I think Alice fits you better, but I agree. You shall remain Alison while here." Queen Isabel smiled at Alice. "And when we are alone, please call me Isabel. Now, I need to go speak with the Alpha about having a companion. If he is agreeable, I will be back, and we can start getting you an acceptable wardrobe for the position. If not, we will make you a comfortable place to stay within the garden." Alice nodded and watched Isabel quickly walk away.

Not having anything better to do, Alice put the figurine back into her bag and moved to the ground. She propped her feet up on the bench and began to do pushups. Doing them with her feet elevated was much tougher than when on flat ground. Alice relished the challenge. By the time she got to her second set of thirty, she noticed Isabel approaching.

"So, this is what you do to fill the time?" Isabel smiled. Alice moved her feet to the ground and stood. "I should have known you did something like this, considering Phil and John mentioned Grey doing something similar in his cell."

Alice could not help the small smile that lifted the corners of her lips. "If he needs to think or work through something or even just do something, Grey will work out. He favors a punching bag most of the time."

"Would you like me to get you one for your new room?" Isabel asked. Alice paused in grabbing her bag before looking over at Isabel. "The Alpha agreed that I need a companion so that he does not have to spend so much time with me. Come with me, and I will show you your room."

Isabel linked her arm through Alice's as they walked through the garden towards the door that Isabel always used. To Alice's surprise, the castle was relatively empty. They only saw three people as they wound through the halls and up multiple sets of stairs. They finally reached a set of double doors, and Isabel stopped. She pulled a chain from around her neck and used the key that hung on it to unlock the door.

When Alice entered, her breath caught. The room was huge. There was a deep purple blanket on the bed with matching curtains. White wood furniture lined the walls. There were several large windows that let in tons of natural light and several couches were situated near a stone fireplace.

"Your room is through here." Isabel gestured to a door next to a tall bookcase. Alice followed as Isabel walked through the door. "It was the nursery for my babies. The only door is through my room, so you will not have to worry about unwanted visitors."

The room was about half the size of Isabel's, but just as beautiful. Alice would be very comfortable in here, especially knowing that no one would be able to enter without coming through the Queen's chamber. "May I ask you something personal?" Alice asked as she turned back to Isabel.

"Of course, dear. Just like the garden, both my room and this room have a protective barrier." Isabel sat on a small sofa near one of the two large windows in Alice's room.

"How are there protective barriers? I mean, what caused the…enchantment? Magic?" Alice furrowed her brows as she tried to phrase her question correctly.

Isabel laughed. "You are the girl with the visions that Maddox is looking for, correct?" Alice hesitantly nodded. "I think you might be able to understand more than anyone. I have a gift similar to your visions. My gift is to create protective barriers to prevent sound from passing through them, as well as unwanted guests. Maddox is unaware of my gift. I only placed the barrier on my private rooms after he stopped coming to them."

"You are a Guardian?" Alice asked in disbelief.

"That is a term I have not heard in a very, very long time. My father told me about the great massacre of the Guardians and the war within Arlania that soon followed." Isabel gestured for Alice to take a seat. Once she did, Isabel continued. "A great treasure was lost during that time."

Alice didn't know if she should mention the Stone to the Queen, so she chose to say something about her grandmother. "My great grandmother survived the massacre. She told me a little about her life before the betrayal. Do you know Sasha?"

Isabel's expression hardened. "That woman is manipulative and evil. She came to the pack shortly after Maddox and I were married. I always thought that she should have been Maddox's wife. The two are cut from the same cloth. It took a few years, but I later found out that, before I was in the picture, Maddox and Sasha had a son together. Maddox refused to accept the child until he knew if the boy was a Shifter."

"What?" Alice gasped.

"When she returned with her son, she married another of our pack members. That was when she started talking about a powerful stone that could control wolf Shifters. Maddox became obsessed." Isabel's face looked as if she smelled something disgusting.

"Do you know what the son's name is?" Alice hated to ask, but at the same time needed to know.

"Bradley, I believe. Do you know him?"

Alice felt all the blood drain from her face. Bradley Barnett was Greyson's and Matt's half-brother? He tortured Greyson growing up and shot him. It seemed more and more that the Stone has more to do with Greyson's family than it did hers.

But the prophecy did say that a blood descendant would be able to use it. Which could only be Isabel, Grey, and Matt. So why would Maddox and Sasha want it if they could not use it? Did they know they couldn't?

"Alice?" Isabel's anxious voice pulled her from her thoughts, and she blinked several times. "Are you alright?"

"Yes, I just was thinking." Alice shook her head to continue to clear her mind.

"What has Bradley done that has upset you so?" Isabel continued to watch Alice closely. Alice relayed all she knew about Bradley, which wasn't much. But it was enough to give Isabel a clear picture. "A horrible man, just like his father and mother." She let out a huff before taking several deep breaths. "I think we have had quite an eventful day. Why don't we rest for a while before we must dress for dinner."

Alice agreed and moved to the bed on the far wall. Isabel left the door between their rooms open so that if Alice needed anything she could call out to her. Alice smiled at the motherly action.

Alice pulled out Greyson's shirt and slipped it on over her clothes before climbing under the blankets. The bed was the most comfortable bed she had ever slept in. Closing her eyes, images of Greyson appeared. Between the mattress's softness and the memories of Greyson, sleep came quickly.

*   *   *

It was late and the moon shone brightly. There were several people standing in the shadows of the trees with their breath making little clouds in the chilly air. Several of the shadowy figures moved to huddle together before speaking in hushed tones. Alice moved closer to hear what was being said, but before she could reach them, the men moved off in different directions. They moved quickly but quietly as they hunched to stay within the shadows.

The figures slowed as they reached a darkened building. A building Alice recognized. Alice began moving forward with her heart pounding hard in her chest. She was almost to the back stairs when the sound of breaking glass was followed by a flickering light in the window. Smoke began to billow out of the opening. Alice screamed.

Movement in an upstairs window drew her attention. Alice saw the terrified faces of Asher and Alisha before a large man grabbed them and pulled them out of sight. Fear like she had never felt before consumed her. She had to save her kids.

The flames from the ground floor began to spread quickly and Alice was unable to do anything. Time slowed as her fear for the kids' safety grew. The moment she saw the kids burst through the back door; Alice fell to her knees in relief. Her relief, however, was short lived.

Two men dragged the kids down the stairs. Asher was crying as he fought against the man holding him, and Alisha was holding Avery tight while Avery screamed. One of the men slapped Asher, causing him to fall down the last few steps. The boy cried out in pain and the man lifted him off the ground by his shirt.

"Please. Our grandparents are in there. Save them, please." Alisha begged.

"No, I don't think we will. We only need you three." One of the men laughed. "Plus, fire can't hurt what isn't alive."

Alisha hugged Avery closer as the little girl continued to scream. Alice looked back at the Finn's two-story home to see the whole thing engulfed in flames. Tears coursed down her face as she turned away from the inferno and quickly followed after the men and kids. By the time she reached them, the kids were loaded into a cart similar to the one Greyson was in when he was taken to the boat.

Alisha sat in the farthest corner of the cart with Asher pressed to her side and Avery clinging to her neck. One of the men threw in a few blankets before slamming the door closed. All three kids were crying as the wagon began to move. Alice tried to follow but something grabbed her and shook her hard.

* * *

Alice's eyes flew open as she gasped for air. She frantically looked around to find herself in her room at the castle. Queen Isabel sat on the edge of the bed with a worried look in her eyes. Her lips were pulled into a thin line as she observed Alice. Alice became more aware of her current surroundings and the fact that she was drenched in sweat.

"Thank goodness." Isabel breathed out in relief. "What happened? Are you all right?"

"I-I." Alice started to say, but stopped. She ran a shaking hand down her face as she sat up. "I think I had another vision."

"Do all your visions have you screaming and crying in your sleep?" Isabel asked, still concerned. Alice did not pull away when Isabel reached for her hand. The contact felt grounding, comforting.

"No. Not all of them." Alice proceeded to tell Isabel about the time she and Greyson watched over the kids while their grandparents travelled. She told her of the bond she had with the kids. Tears began to fall again as Alice told Isabel about what she had seen in her vision and the fear she still had for the kids' safety.

"Oh dear, I am so sorry." Isabel wrapped her arms around Alice.

"What am I to do? How am I going to find them? Who took them and why?" Alice clung to Isabel. Her whole body was trembling. She needed to find them. She needed to protect them.

"Shh." Isabel soothed as she rubbed slow circles on Alice's back. "I will help you find them." Alice nodded against the older woman's shoulder. "I promise. We will find them."

"Alice!" Greyson's desperate voice echoed faintly in her head, and she gasped. "Alice!" It came again. Alice froze as she closed her eyes and tried to concentrate on Greyson.

"I'm here." She said back, but after several minutes of nothing, Alice figured it was just her stressed mind conjuring up his soothing voice. Just hearing him, even if it was just in her head, brought a measure of comfort that she desperately needed and she fell back asleep.

Chapter 12

Greyson jolted awake. He was filled with terror and hopelessness. He started breathing hard as he looked around him. He was still in the hull of the boat surrounded by his fellow slaves. Both Luther and Drake were watching him with matching looks of concern on their faces. Greyson raised his hand to rub his forehead and was surprised to see it shaking.

"You, okay?" Drake asked quietly as he scooted to get closer to Greyson.

Ignoring Drake, Greyson squeezed his eyes shut as he tried to reason out what was happening. Like a sudden kick to the chest, he knew. Alice. Something was wrong with Alice. The feeling of hopelessness and worry intensified as his own feelings mixed with hers. He felt something touch his foot, but he shook his head to let Luther and Drake know to leave him alone.

He emptied his mind and tried to push the overwhelming feelings aside as he took several deep breaths. He brought up an image of Alice in his mind and concentrated on her and her alone. "Alice!" He yelled in his head, desperate to reach out to her in any way he could. He had not been able to feel her for days. She must really be upset for her emotions to reach him now. "Alice!" He tried again. Nothing. But the overwhelming emotions began to fade.

"Greyson?" Luther asked hesitantly.

"I'm fine. It's my wife. Something is wrong." Greyson looked over at the two men.

"How do you know?" Drake asked curiously.

"I..." Greyson began but shouting on the deck above cut him off.

All heads turned up to the dark ceiling and Greyson tuned into his wolf hearing to hear what was going on. After several minutes the shouting calmed, and all fell silent again.

"Well, that was new." Luther commented.

"Someone spotted land. We will be at Trevor's Cove just after daybreak." Greyson said. Several of the other prisoners heard and passed the information on. Unease settled upon the prisoners as their minds turned to thoughts of what the next day would bring.

No one spoke and Greyson's thoughts once again returned to Alice. He wished he could be there with her to hold and comfort her. He wished he could take away whatever had frightened her. He let out a heavy sigh and settled back against the side of the boat. He would make it back to her, no matter what it took.

Sleep eluded him for the rest of the night. His mind was too worked up with what could be wrong with Alice and ways for him to escape from Trevor's Cove. From all the accounts he had heard from his fellow prisoners and listening to the guards above deck, Greyson concluded it wouldn't be nearly as difficult to get out compared to Alpha Maddox's dungeon.

From what he understood, Trevor's Cove was mostly underground. The arena and training grounds being the only two locations open to the sky but still below ground level. The slaves were all housed underground.

Greyson hoped once they got to Trevor's Cove, the guards would be just as lazy as the ones on the boat. If he was confident that no one would get hurt, he would have already tried to overpower the guards on board. But he needed to be patient. He needed to see which of the other prisoners he could trust, and who would betray him if he attempted anything.

The hours ticked by slowly and by the time the call to drop anchor came, Greyson was eager to be off the boat. Reminding himself that he needed to act groggy and weak. They had been on the boat for nearly two weeks and the guards only brought down food once a day. Not one prisoner seemed reluctant to leave the vessel even though they seemed apprehensive about what their futures would bring.

The unloading of the prisoners was a painfully slow affair. Greyson kept his eyes closed and pretended to be asleep as he listened to the prisoners on the other side of the boat go first.

By the time the guards reached Greyson, Drake, and Luther, it was late afternoon. The guard called out to Greyson, but he didn't move. The guard tried again, but Greyson only groaned. Finally losing patience, the guard kicked Greyson's leg and Greyson jolted upright. He made a show of looking around as if he were disoriented.

"Get up!" A guard yelled at him. Greyson stumbled to his feet and fell against Drake who raised his brow in question.

Greyson was grabbed by two guards and shoved up the stairs onto the deck behind Luther and Drake. He was the last slave, so the two guards continued to assist Greyson as he stumbled his way down the gangplank and onto the dock.

He was shoved roughly into a caged wagon, and he fell against the side. Once they were moving, no more guards were directly beside them, and Greyson glanced over at Luther and Drake. They sat across from him, watching him closely.

Luther opened his mouth as if to ask something, but Greyson gave a small shake of his head before giving them a wink. Drake coughed and Greyson fought his own smile that threatened to surface.

They hadn't traveled far when the wagon came to a stop. Greyson looked around and listened carefully. There was a group of twelve slaves lined up in two rows. In front of them stood Lars and another man. Lars was speaking to the slaves and Greyson tuned into his wolf.

"You all are lucky to be here. You will be given the best food and sleeping arrangements. You will be given a number you will need to remember. These numbers will be your assigned fighting class. But for today, you will all be given time to bathe, eat and rest. Tomorrow, bright and early, you will be put through a series of tests in order to gage your skills and put you into the right groups. Now, follow your handlers and we will see you tomorrow." Lars motioned for his men to escort the prisoners to a door.

Once they all disappeared, guards began unloading Greyson's wagon. He once again stumbled out and a guard roughly dragged Greyson to his spot in front of Lars. Luther and Drake were on either side of him. They stood tall as they faced Lars, but Greyson hunched his shoulders and kept his head bowed. He listened to the same speech he heard Lars give the previous group while taking note of the number of guards and the details of the terrain. The speech ended and Greyson's group was directed to the door.

He blinked several times once inside the dimly lit hall. His eyes adjusted quickly as he was dragged through a series of locked doors. Greyson took note of their path through the tunnels, the number of doors and guards, and the weapons the guards possessed.

They turned down a hallway and passed through one more door. This area was different. The lighting was brighter, the passageways were cleaner, and wider. Doors lined each side of the hall. Near the end of it, before it turned in a different direction, the guard leading the way opened one of the doors and gestured for Greyson to enter.

"Three to a room for now. After your trial, you will be taken to a different room, and you will probably have different roommates." Drake and Luther were shoved in after Greyson and the door slammed closed.

No one moved for a long time, and Greyson tried to tune into his wolf to hear if anyone was on the other side of the door, but couldn't sense anything. "I cannot use my wolf's senses. Just like in Alpha Maddox's dungeon." Greyson took stock of his surroundings.

Three beds lined a wall with a toilet in a corner. He moved to one of the beds and sat down. The bed was surprisingly soft. Greyson laid down and let out a sigh.

It had been so long since he had slept on a bed. The last time was when he held Alice. He didn't count when he was so angry that he shifted and laid next to Alice because he didn't actually sleep. He rubbed a hand over his face before letting out a frustrated growl. That woman and all her talk about finding her mate.

"You okay, kid?" Luther asked from the bed next to him.

"Just thinking." Greyson growled out.

"For a man that seems skilled at keeping his cool, you seem to be losing control. Is there anything we can do to help?" Drake asked from his other side.

"It's Ali." Greyson had taken to calling her Ali whenever he spoke aloud about her. "It's complicated." He finally said.

"She is your wife. Nothing about having a woman in your life is ever simple." Drake said.

"For us, it's even more complicated than most couples. We had an arranged marriage of sorts." Greyson let out a long breath. That was the simplest way he could explain it without saying he was her protection detail.

"And you fell in love with her. We can see it all over your face. So, what's the sudden sour mood for?" Luther commented with a smile.

"She wants to find her fated mate." Greyson admitted. "Just before I was shot and captured, she expressed the need to find him even if it meant going to random clubs and kissing men until she found him." His frustrations during that conversation resurfaced. He felt his wolf trying to push through. At least he wasn't able to shift at the moment.

Greyson got to his feet and began pacing the small space. He flexed and clenched his fist multiple times as he tried to calm himself. He stopped when he heard Luther's chuckle. Greyson turned to face him with a scowl.

"I'm sorry, kid. I don't mean to laugh, but it is a bit funny." Luther's smile spread ear to ear. Greyson had the intense urge to punch the smirk off the man's face.

"Be nice, Luther." Drake scolded his friend. "No need to add salt to the wound. We want him motivated to fight his way out of here, not us."

"I fail to see what is so amusing about this." Greyson said through clenched teeth as he tried to reign in his anger.

"Being raised in Valencia and in the First Moon Pack, we are taught about fated mates. It is part of our culture, but it doesn't seem like common knowledge in Arlania." Drake sat back on the bed and leaned his back against the wall.

"It's not. Ali's great grandmother gave her a book about them. I had not heard anything about them until shortly after we were married." Greyson continued to stand as he crossed his arms over his chest. He was still agitated.

"The thing with fated mates is their fierce need to protect one another and their ability to feel one another." Drake started to explain.

"We haven't seen you with your Ali and I don't think we need to." Luther laughed. "By your extreme reaction to her suggesting finding her fated mate..." He chuckled again.

"I'm in love with her. Of course, I hate the idea of her wanting to find another man." Greyson defended himself.

"Even with this place laced with whatever it is they put in it to stop us from shifting, your eyes are glowing, and your veins are bulging. You are very near shifting, still." Drake pointed out. "You love her. You are jealous. A normal husband would be angry. A mate's reaction would be close to blind rage. It would affect every part of you, including your wolf."

"You, my young friend, are acting like a mate." Luther added. Greyson shook his head. His anger slowly faded as he thought about what Drake and Luther were saying. A part of him wanted to believe them, but there was still a part of him that refused to believe he could be so lucky. "What happened last night on the boat when you woke up having a panic attack? You said your Ali was in trouble. How did you know?"

Greyson closed his eyes and took a deep breath. He moved back to the bed and sat down heavily. "I don't know. I could feel she was scared and worried about something."

"Is that the only time you have been able to feel her emotions?" Drake asked.

"No. It came on gradually, but a month or so after meeting her, I could almost read her emotions. I thought I was just picking up on her change in demeanor or voice." Greyson ran his hand through his hair. Were they fated mates?

"That could have been, but I would lean on the side that you are indeed, her fated mate." Drake said softly.

Greyson let out a curse and laid back on the bed. Luther laughed as he settled back on his own bed. Silence fell between them. Greyson figured they were probably giving him time to process what they had discussed. Closing his eyes, Greyson thought back on all his time with Alice with a new perspective. He did not know how much time passed before he sat up again. He looked over at Luther who seemed to be asleep, before looking over at Drake.

Drake was laying down but staring at the ceiling. "Do mates have a strong scent about them that calms the other? And does one tend to get irritable when unable to be near their mate for a while?" he asked softly.

Drake slowly turned his head until he faced Greyson. "My Gwen smells like fresh baked cookies. She said I smell like sandalwood. Her presence calms me even when I am close to losing complete control. I don't sleep well without her near." Drake gave Greyson a sad smile.

Greyson studied the man for a minute, feeling sorry for him. He had been away from his wife and daughters for three years. How had he managed it? He was going crazy, and it had only been a year. Greyson took a deep breath and slowly let it out.

"I think you and Luther are right." Greyson groaned. "We need to get out of here. I need to get to her, and you need to return to Gwen."

"We will see how tomorrow goes before we try to make any plans. We need to figure out who we can trust and who will turn on us. The more allies we have, the better." Greyson nodded in agreement.

Greyson settled back on his bed and put an arm over his face to block out the light. He had been so blind. Looking back, he could see the signs so clearly. Even when they had first met as teenagers, Greyson had felt an overwhelming sense of protectiveness towards Alice. The only other person he had felt even the slightest bit protective of was Matthew.

He hadn't understood what he had been feeling at the time for Alice. All he knew was he could not let any harm come to the pushy girl. He felt out of control whenever he thought about the Barnetts or anyone else doing harm to her. It scared him and he ran.

Years later when she had stepped into the room after Sir Lance attacked him, all the strong emotions slammed into him. He needed to be close to her. He needed to protect her. The pull he felt towards her was undeniable now. Luke had been right on at least one thing, Greyson and Alice always seemed to move closer to one another when they were in the same room. Even if they had not known it then.

The door to their cell opened and Greyson got to his feet. A man stood in the doorway. "Your turn for the showers. Come along."

Greyson, Drake, and Luther exchanged a look before following the man out into the hallway. As they followed the guard, Greyson continued to mentally draw a map of the facility. It wasn't long before the guard opened a door and gestured them inside.

Luther let out a low whistle. The room was brightly lit with a light grey tiled floor and white walls. A couple of large bowls with small spouts curving over them sat in front of a large mirror along one side of the room. On the adjacent side were five large stalls with spouts high on the wall. Shelving made up the rest of that side of the room. On the opposite side were cabinets made of dark wood.

"There are five showers against that wall. Fresh towels on the shelves over there. Clean clothes are in the cabinets on that side. Get yourselves cleaned up and select a single set of clothes. You will be getting your uniforms when you are placed tomorrow. You gentlemen have one hour and do not worry, there is plenty of hot water. I will be just outside if you need anything." The guard stepped from the room and closed the door.

"Well. I was not expecting this." Drake commented.

Greyson began pulling off his smelly and dirty clothes as he moved toward the showers. He had never seen anything like it before. It only took him a few seconds to realize he needed to turn the knobs. When he did, water sprayed from the faucet above his head. He stepped into the spray and closed his eyes. Resting his hands on the back wall, Greyson hung his head and allowed the water to rush over him. His back still stung, but at the same time, the water felt so good.

After a few more minutes, Greyson noticed a bar of soap on the floor. He picked it up and scrubbed his whole body several times before he turned off the water and reached for a towel.

Greyson moved to the sinks as he wrapped the towel around his waist. He looked at himself in the mirror for the first time in over a year.

He had several more scars on his chest and abdomen, courtesy of his father. He ran his hand over the several weeks' worth of facial hair. It didn't look terrible, but he wasn't a fan of it. He used to shave daily. A small smile tugged at his lips. Alice had said she liked it when he allowed a few days' worth of scruff to grow, and then they had kissed.

"What's that look for?" Luther moved to his side. He had a towel around his waist while he used a second one to dry his hair.

"I was just thinking." Greyson shrugged as he got ready to shave.

"With a look like that, I'm guessing it has something to do with your Ali?" Drake stepped up to Greyson's other side with a knowing smile.

Greyson gave a noncommittal grunt. He finished shaving and moved to the cabinets that stored the clothes. His eyes widened at the numerous sizes available. He quickly found clothes that fit him and pulled on his pants.

As he was about to put on his shirt, the guard walked back in. He stopped suddenly when he saw Greyson's back. Greyson ignored him as he continued to get dressed. It was taking a while for his last whipping to fully heal. Every time he did a push up or when his back brushed against the side of the boat, his wounds had reopened.

Ten minutes later, the guard locked them back in their room. The three men were surprised to see trays heaped with food on each of their beds. They remained silent as they ate their meals. Greyson was nearly finished with his food when the door opened again.

The guard from earlier stepped into their room. He moved his weight nervously from one foot to the other before straightening his shoulders and focusing on Greyson. "I noticed that your back is still healing from what I am assuming was a whip." Greyson remained silent as he watched the man. The guard cleared his throat and took a step closer to Greyson as he extended his arm. In his hand was a medium sized jar. "This helps reduce scarring significantly. Apply two to three times a day. With the extent of your injuries, if it scars, you will most likely lose some range of motion. You cannot afford the risk of that happening here."

Greyson hesitantly accepted the jar from the man while continuing to observe him. "Thank you." He said quietly. The guard nodded once before quickly leaving. "Interesting." Greyson said thoughtfully after the door clicked closed.

"He seems like a nice enough fellow." Luther commented. "Especially for a prison guard."

"Some people are forced to do things they hate in order to survive." Greyson continued to stare at the closed door.

He had been one of those people. So had Matthew. Something about the guard told Greyson he could trust him, but he was not going to be rash. He needed to make sure before he put his life in the man's hands.

"I have had to do things that go against who I am in order to survive. We should keep an eye on him. We might be able to use him to get out of this place. And if we do, he is coming with us."

Drake and Luther nodded thoughtfully. Drake helped apply the ointment to Greyson's back before they all settled in for the night. Greyson's mind drifted back to the guard. He had a feeling that they had just found their first ally and when they finally escaped, the guard would be with them.

*   *   *

Greyson stood in the second row of men. There were four rows with ten men in each one. Drake and Luther stood on either side of him as they waited for their instructions. Greyson was taking the time to take stock of his surroundings and his fellow slaves.

They were in a large arena that sat twenty or so feet below ground level but was open to the sky. He counted thirty guards from where he stood. The ones on the ground level were looking down on them while the others were in the pit with the prisoners. Training equipment filled one half of the arena. On the other half were four sparring arenas.

"Good morning, men." Lars's voice pulled Greyson's attention back forward. The slave trader once again stood next to the same man he had the day before. "Today you will be put through a series of tests. Based on your skill level, you will be assigned a number. Remember this number. You will be split into four groups. Marc and I will be moving among you as you go through your stations to gage your skill levels. Put all you have into these tests." Four men made their way to the front of the group. None of them smiled and Greyson was reminded of Bash, his trainer up North.

Each one of the four men took a row of prisoners to different areas of the arena. Greyson's group was led to the punching bags in the corner. He and Luther were assigned the same bag. Greyson was momentarily excited to be in front of a punching bag again. Then he remembered he couldn't let loose like he craved to do.

It took every bit of self-control not to assume his normal fighting stance. It had been so engrained in him over the last twenty years, but he fought the habit. Instead, he fully faced the punching bag, keeping his feet square with his shoulders. He intentionally stood too close to the bag and then he swung his fist. It felt so wrong, but he gritted his teeth and swung again.

After several pathetic punches, Greyson growled in mock frustration and took two steps back. This put him too far from the bag and he had to lean forward in order to make contact. He hated every second of this. He just wanted to enjoy a good workout instead of pretending he was four again.

Five minutes passed before Luther moved to his side. "Okay, stop. You are painful to watch."

Greyson bit the inside of his cheek to keep from smiling. It couldn't have been any more painful to watch than it was to execute such ridiculous punches. Luther proceeded to instruct Greyson on how to place his feet and hold his fists near his face.

He took a good ten minutes to help Greyson "learn" the basics before moving back to his side of the punching bag. Greyson was relieved Luther took the time so that he could actually throw proper punches. He intentionally kept his swings slow and measured. He still wanted to appear inexperienced.

The rest of the morning was a new form of torture for Greyson. He had to constantly remind himself that he did not know what he was doing. He allowed himself to be pummeled in the sparring ring by one of the guards. Drake and Luther took turns trying to teach Greyson defensive moves, proper fighting stances, how to throw a proper punch, basic footwork, and dodges. Nothing they had shown him was incorrect, but he itched to let loose and push himself like he used to.

They were back in their lines. Lars and Marc were once again standing in front of the groups. The slaves were all dirty and exhausted from a morning of training. "You all did well this morning. Marc will walk the lines and give you your number. You will be bunking with those of your same number group." Marc began moving along the lines of slaves.

To Greyson's surprise he, Luther, and Drake were placed within group four. Once Marc returned to the front, Lars continued. "You each will be given a tattoo. This tattoo will be your identity while you are here. It will also allow the spectators to easily identify their fighters. As soon as you are done getting cleaned up and have eaten a good lunch, you will get your new identity." Lars turned and left the arena.

The prisoners were led back to their cells. They were once again taken room by room to the showers before being led down a different hallway. Drake was escorted into the first room and Luther into the second. Greyson entered the third room and froze just inside the door.

A wood table sat in the center of the room. Next to it was a tall desk with various instruments lined up on it. A man stood near the table with a forced smile on his face. The set up reminded him of the torture room in Alpha Maddox's dungeon. Well, all except the man. In the torture room, the man usually wore an eager smile like he could not wait to inflict pain. This man looked almost apologetic.

"Why don't you have a seat and take off your shirt. Let's see what we have to work with." Greyson hesitated before slowly doing as the man said. When he saw Greyson's back, he went still.

"With these wounds still being raw, we will need to place the tattoo on your chest or shoulder." The man moved to stand in front of Greyson. "Lay down on your back and stay still. There will be some pain involved but I will do my best to minimize any discomfort you might experience." Greyson laid down and nodded.

The man started busying himself with the instruments on the table. "Can I ask what it is you plan on doing?" Greyson asked.

"Lars has assigned you a wolf." The man said without looking at Greyson.

"Can I make a request for location and the type of wolf?" Greyson watched the man for his reaction.

The man stopped what he was doing and turned to look at Greyson. "I don't think I have ever had a slave ask such a thing." He was quiet for several moments before continuing. "But I do not see why not. You are getting a wolf regardless."

Hours later, Greyson entered his new cell. He smiled when he saw both Luther and Drake eating at a small table in the corner. This room was a little bigger than their last one. The beds lined one wall and there was a table in a corner with a small room that was off to the right side. Both men had their shirts off as they ate dinner. Greyson moved to the table and took a seat.

"So how did your sessions go?" Greyson asked as he dished up a plate of food.

"I was given a snake." Luther scoffed as he turned to show his back to Greyson. The image of a coiled snake was on Luther's right shoulder blade. It was very well done and looked life-like.

"I think it fits you very well." Greyson sent Luther a smirk as he took a bite of potatoes. "What about you, Drake?"

"A dragon." Drake shrugged. Greyson leaned back to get a look at the older man's back. It was the full body of a dragon on his right shoulder. The tattoo looked really good, just like Luther's. "What is yours? Isn't your shirt irritating it?"

Greyson pulled up his sleeve to expose his right shoulder. There was the head of a wolf. The wolf's face was divided. One half was black with a yellow eye and the other was a white wolf with a blue eye. He chose it to represent him and Alice.

The man had been impressed with the design and was excited to do it. Adding the slight color for the eyes was the man's idea and Greyson hadn't minded. It turned out quite well and Greyson was pleased with it.

"That is impressive." Luther moved to get a closer look. "The guy that did your tattoo is very good. All the tattoos I have seen done have all been pretty simple. But this one is very detailed. The point where the two wolves blend together makes it look like one."

"Why two wolves?" Drake asked.

"Because I asked him to." Greyson answered as he took another bite.

"You were allowed to pick yours?" Luther asked incredulously.

"Kind of." Greyson sat back a little to get more comfortable. "The man told me I was getting a wolf. I asked if I could have some input on how it looked, and he didn't have a problem with what I wanted."

"I should have asked my guy." Luther complained. "I don't think I have seen any slave with their brand on their shoulder like yours, either."

Greyson laughed. "Apparently, my back isn't healed enough to allow a tattoo. I was given the option between my chest or shoulder."

Silence fell among them as they continued to eat. Greyson finally pushed his empty plate away and sat back. What he wouldn't give to be able to go back to the training grounds and make use of the punching bag. He itched to get back in shape.

Unfortunately, he needed to exercise patience. He needed to sell the idea that he could not fight if he wanted to escape as quickly as possible. And he needed to get out of Trevor's Cove so that he could make his way back to Alice.

Chapter 13

Alice heard the door creak open behind her. She resisted the urge to turn around to see who entered as she threw her fist into the punching bag. She took a deep breath and recognized Isabel's now familiar scent.

Through the past several weeks, Alice had learned from Phil that each person had an individual scent. Phil and John had been helping Alice learn more about her wolf. Greyson had taught her how to use her wolf senses while in human form which both men had not known was possible.

"Do you plan on practicing all day or would you like to join me and Gwen in the garden for lunch?" Isabel asked.

Alice could hear the smile in the Queen's voice. Isabel had openly admitted how much she admired Alice for her fighting skills and enjoyed watching as she trained. They had agreed that they needed to keep her skills a secret for the time being.

Alice turned around with a large smile on her face. She had grown close to both Isabel and Gwen over her forced stay in the Howling Meadow's Pack. The two older women were very close friends and Isabel had taken the role of mother while Gwen had taken the role of favorite aunt to Alice.

"I would love to join you. I just need to get cleaned up and I will be ready to go."

As Alice moved toward the already filled bathing tub, Queen Isabel turned to leave her room. Over her shoulder, Isabel called. "You have an hour, my dear." And then she closed the door softly.

Alice stripped off her sweat drenched workout clothes and stepped into the tub. She sucked in a quick breath as she sat in the freezing water. She must have trained longer than she thought for the water to be as cold as it was.

Alice didn't waste any time getting herself clean and escaping the cold water with her teeth chattering. Due to her position as the Queen's companion, Alice was expected to wear dresses. She scrunched her nose as she pulled on her sage green dress. Alice refused to wear the slippers that went with the dress and pulled on her boots. Her dresses hid them anyway.

Crossing her room to the door, Alice gave a quick knock before opening it and stepping into Queen Isabel's room. They left their rooms and walked through the halls in companiable silence.

They entered the garden and Alice took a deep breath of the fragrant air. The flowers were blooming and memories of a walk through her mother's small garden flashed through her mind. Greyson walked next to her and then held her close. Their near kiss and Greyson cursing her mother for interrupting them. A small smile touched her lips at the memory.

Gwen was waiting at the tables located in the center of the garden. Alice waved when Gwen smiled and began heading in their direction. She noticed Gwen's overly large smile and raised a questioning brow. She watched as Isabel and Gwen hugged in greeting before they continued making their way to the table. The older women caught up on what had been going on in the town for several minutes; Gwen's smile never fading.

Once there was a lull in the conversation, Alice piped up unable to control her curiosity any longer. "What has you in such high spirits today, Gwen?" she asked with a smile of her own.

Gwen looked fairly ready to combust with excitement as her eyes filled with tears. "I received a letter from Drake this morning!" she quickly pulled out a folded letter from her jacket pocket. "Apparently, the men at Trevor's Cove are allowed to periodically send letters home." she said excitedly.

"How is he doing? Is he well?" Isabel asked, putting a hand to her heart.

"He is doing as well as can be expected. He said he missed me and the girls terribly. He mentioned that he and Luther are roommates with a young man they are meant to help teach to fight. Drake mentioned that the young man was also a prisoner of Alpha Maddox's. He asked if I could assist in delivering the young man's wife a letter." Gwen pulled a second folded letter out of her jacket with a furrowed brow. "The only problem is the letter is only addressed to Princess. I have no idea where to even start looking."

Alice gasped and covered her mouth with her hand. "Princess?" she asked as tears blurred her vision.

"Yes. Do you know who it belongs too?" Gwen was still looking down at the letter with a furrowed brow.

"Gwen, I think that letter belongs to Alison." Isabel said gently. Gwen's head shot up and looked at Alice. Her eyes taking in Alice's tear-streaked face and shaking hands. "Why don't you take your letter over there under the trees." Isabel suggested softly.

Gwen extended the letter to Alice, and she slowly took it from her. Alice ran her fingers over the writing on the front of the letter. It was Greyson's handwriting. Alice quickly got to her feet, gave a quick thank you, and moved to the tree Isabel had suggested.

She settled herself on the soft grass on the opposite side of the tree, so she was out of sight of the others. With shaky hands, Alice broke the seal and slowly unfolded the paper. There was a smudge of dried blood on the edge of the paper and Alice's heart picked up speed.

> *Princess,*
>
> *I cannot even begin to tell you how much I miss you. Life here at Trevor's Cove isn't too bad so far. They feed us like kings and do what they can to keep us happy and healthy. I spend my days training with a few of the other prisoners and have had a couple of fights so far. I just won my first fight. If I had known that winning fights would give me the privilege of writing to you, I would have tried harder to win earlier. As it is, I am glad I now know.*
>
> *My roommate asked his wife to deliver this letter to you and I hope it didn't take too long for her to find you. There was a man and his nephew that came through the slaves camp a week ago and tried to buy a few of us slaves as living punching bags for them. Lars did not seem to like the idea and sent them packing.*
>
> *Please tell me if you are well. I could not bear it if something were to happen to you, Princess. I have not forgotten my latest promise to you and no matter what you may hear, I am keeping that promise. I hope someday soon I will be able to send another letter to you. Know that I am alive and well. And I plan on staying that way.*
>
> *Forever yours, Prince*

Alice reread the letter. At first, it didn't seem to hold much information, but on the second time through, several things popped out at her. *A man and nephew* had to be Isaac and Matthew. Greyson had seen them, but they were unable to get him out. He had several fights, but had only managed to win one? What was he playing at?

He had to be doing it on purpose because there was no way he would not be winning the majority of his fights if he was actually fighting. He also made a point to let her know that he was still putting up a fight, even if it might not seem that way.

Alice wiped the tears off her cheeks. Greyson was alive and Isaac and Matthew were working on freeing him. She wondered if she was allowed to respond back. Getting to her feet, she returned to the table. Both women looked up at her as she retook her seat.

"What is the news?" Isabel asked eagerly. Alice knew that Isabel was worried about her son.

"He is alive and well. He said it isn't too bad and they are feeding them like kings." Alice gave a small shoulder shrug. "Gwen, do you know if we can send letters back?"

"The man that delivered the letter to me said he leaves first thing in the morning and any replies must be to him this evening. I was planning to write a letter once we are done here." Gwen smiled at Alice.

"Do you mind if I hide a letter within yours?"

"Not at all. Would you two like to come home with me and you can write your letter at my house?" Gwen offered.

"That sounds like a great plan." Isabel clapped her hands in excitement. "I am so glad that you both were able to hear from your husbands."

Their meal continued on a happy note as they discussed everything from the cooling weather to new fabric that was supposed to arrive later that week at the dress makers. Once they finished eating, they left together and headed for Gwen's home.

As they walked through the marketplace, the unsettled feeling of someone watching her caused the hairs on Alice's neck to stand on end. She took a casual look around but didn't see anyone. The feeling persisted all the way to Gwen's home.

Twenty minutes after arriving, Alice and Isabel left Gwen and headed back towards the castle. They were only a few steps from the dwelling when the feeling of being watched returned. Alice moved closer to Isabel's side as they continued on their way. Isabel gasped when a large figure suddenly stepped in front of them, causing them to stop. Alice's hands balled into fists when she recognized Cain's smiling face.

"My dear Alison, it is so good to see you again." Cain took a half step closer.

"I wish I could say the same." Alice said dryly. Isabel linked her arm through Alice's and Cain's eyes dropped to their entwined arms. When he lifted his gaze back up to hers, his brow was lifted.

"Might I have a moment to speak with you alone, Alison?" Cain was all manners with a charming smile, but Alice did not trust him. Without waiting for a response, he pulled her a few feet away from Isabel.

Alice glanced back and was met by a worried looking Isabel. "I am afraid Queen Isabel needs me, sir." She tried to move away, but Cain's grip only tightened. "Let go of me."

Cain stepped closer and lowered his voice. "Listen here, Alison. You will be mine. It is only a matter of time. You can willingly leave your pathetic husband, or I will force you to, the choice is yours."

"I will never be yours." Alice said calmly, even though alarm bells rang in her mind. She tried to pull her arm free again and before either one of them could say any more, Isabel was standing next to them.

"Alison is under my protection, Cain. You will let go of her or you will receive the consequences." Queen Isabel's voice was full of authority and Cain's grip loosened. Isabel relinked her arm through Alice's, pulling her farther away from Cain. After a tense moment, Isabel turned and began walking back to the castle.

"Remember what I said, Alison." Cain's voice called after them.

Neither Queen Isabel nor Alice spoke until they were back in Isabel's room. As soon as the door closed behind them, Isabel demanded to know what Cain had wanted. Alice told her everything.

Alice had begun shaking and knew that Cain would do all he could to fulfill his threat. A plan was made for Alice to remain in Queen Isabel's room or in the garden. He would be watching for her, and Isabel felt certain he would try to kidnap Alice if he had to.

Chapter 14

Greyson pushed his aching muscles. He needed to get stronger and faster if he wanted to get out of here. His lungs burned, but still he continued on. They had been at the cove for just over two weeks and Greyson had been given permission to start training earlier in the day.

Lars had been beyond angry that Greyson appeared to have no fighting skills whatsoever. He had paired him with Luther and Drake for training so that he would, hopefully, learn something. The extra training was also allowed because Lars was apparently losing money on Greyson's fights.

Before the sun rose each morning, Greyson was led to the training grounds so he could run the perimeter. He pushed himself as hard as he could each day, grateful that he could build his endurance while hiding his fighting skill.

Being stuck in small prison cells for a year had greatly reduced his ability to run for hours and that fact frustrated Greyson. A loud whistle blew, and Greyson slowed to a walk, letting out a growl of frustration. He was panting and his muscles protested but he wanted to continue. However, the whistle was not something one ignored if they did not want to get beat.

He laced his fingers behind his head as he took slow measured breaths, trying to slow his racing heart. He looked across the arena and noticed that several slaves were lined up with Lars and a few other men speaking a short distance away. A guard waved Greyson over and he reluctantly joined the others.

Now that he was no longer moving, he could feel the chill in the early morning air. His hair was drenched with sweat that dripped down his bare back and chest, causing his skin to break out in goosebumps.

The salty ocean wind blew in his face, and he took a deep breath to calm his still racing heart, but froze. There was a scent, well two scents, in the breeze that he recognized. As casually as he could, Greyson looked back over to Lars and the two men that stood with him.

Sure enough, they were there. Lord Isaac and Matthew stood speaking with Lars, looking as if they did not have a care in the world. Greyson looked back down to the ground. Footsteps approached the line of slaves, but Greyson kept his eyes trained on the ground. He rolled his shoulder forward and made himself look unsure.

"Like I said sir, we met at Alpha Maddox's pack. When I learned you dealt with slaves, I knew that I just had to come." Isaac was saying.

"And why is that?" Lars asked as he slowly headed in Greyson's direction.

"My nephew needs someone to spar with. Someone who can take a hit but cannot throw one back very well. The boy has set fires a few times brawling in not-so-great places." Isaac smiled at Lars. "My question is, do you have a slave that fits the bill? And if so, are you willing to sell him?"

"We have one that might be what you are looking for." Grey's mind whirled as the three men stopped in front of him. He could not go with them. Not without Luther, Drake, and Bear.

Greyson needed to let Matt know it was crucial that he stay for a bit longer. He looked up as Isaac and Lars discussed him. Matthew caught his eye and Greyson coughed twice. Matt scratched his left eyebrow and Greyson felt a small wave of relief. Matthew had understood his signal for more time and responded in the affirmative.

"Uncle, this one is the one we saw the other day." Matthew interrupted. "Sir, Wolf is not a very competent fighter like you are saying he is. For crying out loud, he tripped over his own feet in the match." Matthew gave Greyson a look of disgust.

"I assure you he does much better outside his formal fights." Lars laughed.

Matthew put on a thoughtful expression before moving closer to Greyson as if to get a better look. Matt slowly circled him before standing just behind Greyson.

"I need someone who can give me a bit of a challenge. This man is a disgrace." Matthew gave him a small shove and Greyson allowed himself to stumble forward. "I don't want this one."

Isaac looked between Matthew and Greyson before nodding. "Do you have any others?"

Lars shook his head and the three men walked away as they continued to converse. Greyson could not get back to his cell fast enough. Unfortunately, it took over thirty minutes for the guard to lead him back to his room.

When he walked in, Greyson found himself alone. When he was sure no one was around, Greyson lifted the paper Matt had slipped him. It was small with a simple message that caused his blood to simultaneously boil and run cold.

P stuck in pack. Man wants claim on P. Must hurry.

He crumpled the paper when the door flew open. Luther and Drake entered with Bear. Bear was the nickname they had given the guard that brought the healing salve for Greyson.

They had chosen the name because the man was bigger than most men there, but he was soft on the inside. He cared about the people around him, either slave or fellow guard, but was forced to work for Lars. Bear was also a higher-ranking guard and had assisted in getting Greyson a punching bag for his cell and arranging for his early morning training.

Usually, the man spent a minute or two conversing with them, but Greyson was relieved when he gave him a quick nod and left. Greyson reread the paper again and shook his head.

Alice was trapped in Alpha Maddox's pack, alone, and there was apparently a man trying to take her from him. Did she like the man? It didn't matter. She needed to get away from Maddox. Greyson let out a frustrated growl as he ran his hand through his hair.

"Is something wrong?" Luther's voice cut through Greyson's troubled thoughts.

"Yes." Greyson said quickly before turning to face his companions. "Ali is trapped in the pack and there is a man trying to claim her for himself. I was advised to hurry."

Drake lifted both eyebrows in surprise and Greyson handed over the slip of paper. "Where did you get this?" Drake asked.

"My brother passed it to me." Greyson explained what had happened that morning. "We need to start planning our way out."

Over the next two hours, the three of them brainstormed an escape plan. A knock on the door had them looking towards it. Bear stepped in the room followed by three lower slaves with lunch trays. They quickly left after putting the food on the table, but Bear stayed. They updated him on the urgency to leave. Bear listened thoughtfully but did not say much. He never did.

"I agree with the need to leave sooner rather than later. I have met a few other slaves that I believe would be assets both in getting out of here, and once on the outside." Bear said. "I haven't told them anything, of course. But Luther, Drake, it is time for your fights."

Without another word, Drake and Luther stood and followed Bear out. Greyson got to his feet, unable to just sit still. He had too much pent-up energy. He needed to do something. Automatically he moved to the punching bag and began his old routine.

As he threw punch after punch, Greyson thought of everything he knew about the layout of Trevor's Cove and the habits of the guards. The door opening behind him had Greyson shifting his stance and weakening his punches.

He glanced over his shoulder and watched as Luther assisted Drake to his bed. Greyson quickly moved to help. "How did your fight go?" Greyson asked once Drake was laying down. Drake's lip was split open, and his right eye was starting to swell closed.

"I won, if that is what you are asking." Drake grunted out.

Another knock on the door and Bear came in. "Since you won, Drake, you get to write home." The guard placed paper and pencil on the table before turning to them. "Wolf, you fight in an hour." Greyson nodded his understanding as Bear left.

"Gwen." Drake breathed as he sat up. He moved to the table and began writing. Luther and Greyson let him be, knowing how important this was to him.

Greyson moved back to the punching bag and began his routine again. After several minutes a throat cleared, and Greyson looked over at Luther.

"I thought you didn't know what you were doing?" Luther said a little stunned.

"I never said that." Greyson threw a few more punches. "People see what I want them to see. And at the time you asked if I could fight, I didn't trust you."

"Fair enough." Luther grumbled. "So, what would be your answer now if I asked you?"

"I've been training to fight since I was four. Well, training to be an assassin would be the more accurate description." Greyson sent Luther a crooked smile. "If you want, I can give you some pointers."

Drake laughed from the table. "Just because you can punch a bag does not mean you can fight. Sorry kid, if I am a little skeptical of your abilities considering what we have seen from you so far."

"Care to go a round with me before my fight? I could use a good practice." Greyson asked Luther. "And please, don't hold back. I really need to see where I'm a bit rusty."

"Sure, kid. But I do not want to hurt you." Luther warned.

"I've been warned. Now, no holding back." Greyson said again.

Luther wasted no time in attacking Greyson. Greyson easily dodged and deflected each attack Luther made at him. After a few minutes, Greyson could start to anticipate Luther's next move. With one quick move, Greyson jumped to the side and hit a pressure point in Luther's neck causing the older man to crumple to the floor, unconscious. To Greyson's relief he wasn't even winded. He turned to Drake with a smug smile on his face.

"Did I pass?" Greyson asked.

"If you can fight, why do you act like a complete novice out there?" Drake asked, moving to Luther's side and kneeling down. He checked his pulse before looking back up at Greyson.

"If they knew what I could do, then I would be fighting at a much higher level. I do not want to hurt anyone. I want them all to think I can't fight so when it comes to our escaping, it will be easier." Greyson explained as he grabbed Luther under his arms and pulled him towards his bed. "Help me get him to his bed. He is going to have a bit of a headache when he wakes up in a few minutes."

They just set Luther on his bed when a knock came at the door followed by Bear opening it. "Time for your fight, Wolf." Greyson nodded and followed Bear from the room.

As they walked through the halls towards the arena, Greyson turned his mind to the upcoming fight. He had purposely lost his previous three fights, but today he was planning to win. If there was a chance he could write to Alice, he would take it. He would make the fight close, but he would win.

The stands were packed with people. The noise was deafening. Greyson scanned the crowd and spotted who he wanted to see. Isaac and Matthew were in seats near the top of the bleachers, giving them a great view of the whole arena. Matthew gave him the slightest of nods and Greyson turned his attention to Bear.

Bear moved up to Greyson's side with a syringe. The Equalizer. Greyson hardly felt the needle, but the drug caused a burning sensation that spread through his body. Greyson purposely stumbled a little to appear as if the Equalizer was affecting him.

His opponent was shaking his head and moving slowly towards the center of the ring. Greyson barely heard Lars announce the competitors as he sized up his opponent. He watched the other man, Beaver, move slowly around him. Greyson held his ground in the center of the ring, waiting for the bell to ring that signaled the fight to begin.

As soon as the bell rang, Beaver attacked. Greyson fought against instinct and allowed Beaver to get in several good blows before he retaliated. He kept his punches controlled so he didn't hurt the man. The fight continued for more than ten minutes.

Greyson marked the moment Beaver started to get tired. Keeping with Beaver's energy level, Greyson slowed as well. His previous fight with Luther and his time at the punching bag had Greyson already sweaty, making it look like the fight was taxing on him.

Greyson shuffled forward and threw a punch at Beaver's guarded face. However, right before Greyson's fist connected with the man's arms, Beaver dropped his guard on that side. Greyson's fist connected squarely with Beaver's jaw, and he went down.

Beaver lay unconscious at Greyson's feet and Greyson took several steps back, putting a surprised look on his face. In all honesty, he had not expected Beaver to lower his guard at that moment. He had planned on winning the fight a different way, but this worked.

Anyone could see that Greyson's win was won by pure luck and not real skill. Bear came over to Greyson and pulled him from the arena. Just as Greyson was stepping into his cell, Bear mumbled something about bringing supplies for writing home.

Luther was glaring at Greyson when he turned around to face his companions. Greyson smiled at them and told them about his win. Bear returned and handed Greyson his writing supplies. Greyson moved to the table and sat down.

He wiped under his nose with the back of his hand and began to write. He wasn't sure if the letters were screened or not, so he kept his words simple and nonsuspicious. When he was done, he sat back and stared at the letter. There was so much he wanted to say, but didn't dare.

Greyson folded the letter and sat back in his chair. The smile slowly fading from his face. He had no idea where to send the letter. He had been so excited to send one to Alice that he forgot he had no idea where she was exactly. He turned the letter in his hands slowly before tossing it into the trash can next to the door with a muttered curse.

"What's the matter, kid?" Luther asked.

"I just remembered; I have no idea where she is." Greyson let out a heavy sigh as he moved to his bed and laid down on his back. His earlier high from the win and ability to write to Alice had quickly morphed into depression.

"Maybe my Gwen can find her for you. It won't be the fastest way to reach your girl, but there is at least a chance it will get to her. I can seal your letter in with mine." Drake moved over to the trash and removed the letter.

"Yeah, sure." Greyson mumbled as he took the letter back from Drake. He added a few lines explaining how he was having to send the letter before giving it back to Drake. He laid down on the bed and closed his eyes.

He had little to no hope that Gwen would be able to find his Princess. He kept all the names out of the letter so no one could connect her to him. He cleared his mind of everything but Alice. Her face, her smile, her laugh. He missed her.

Weeks passed and Greyson's mood had not improved much. In fact, according to Luther, his mood had only gotten worse. Greyson spent his mornings running and his afternoons at the punching bag in their cell.

Drake attributed it to not having any contact with Alice for over two months. Drake was currently at one of his fights and Greyson and Luther were trying to work out their escape plan. Greyson ran his hand through his hair in frustration. This was not working. He needed to clear his head, so he stood and moved to the punching bag.

Luther let out a frustrated sigh as he moved to the edge of the bed and watched Greyson pound out his frustrations. Greyson increased his speed as he threw plan after plan away in his head. There were too many guards. Not enough time to unlock all the doors they needed to before the alarm was raised.

The only thing that would work is if there was a massive distraction. If only he could reach Matt. The kid had a knack for coming up with creative yet effective distractions. Greyson punched the bag harder in his frustration.

The sound of sand hitting the stone floor pulled Greyson from his thoughts. He blinked several times as he watched the sand pour from a split in the fabric where his fist had connected. "Not again." He growled in frustration. How was he going to clean it up this time?

"Again? You break punching bags often?" Luther asked in surprise. "I don't think I have ever seen anyone break a bag before."

"Several times a month when I was training daily." Greyson gave up on the punching bag and sat heavily on the bed next to Luther. "We need a distraction, but the only person I can think of who could make a big enough one is my brother."

"Is your brother still around?" Luther asked.

"Yeah. I saw him in the crowd at my last fight." Greyson answered as he leaned his elbows on his knees and hung his head.

"You mentioned that someone called you an Alpha?" Greyson nodded his head. "He seems loyal to you. You should try to mind-link your brother next time you are in the arena." Luther said thoughtfully. "It won't hurt if it doesn't work, but if it does." Luther began to smile. "We might just have a chance of getting out of here."

"Don't mind-links only work between Alpha's and their pack members and between mates?"

"As an Alpha that does not belong to a pack, you could start your own. If your brother is loyal to you, he would be a part of your pack. Since you are not affected by the Equalizer, you should be able to reach him if your bond with him is strong enough."

"You are assuming he is a wolf Shifter as well." Greyson pointed out. "When he was seventeen and found out that I was a wolf Shifter he said if he were one too, he would be loyal to me. But I don't even know if he shifted."

"It won't hurt to try." Luther patted Greyson's shoulder before moving to his own bed and laying down.

Greyson thought over the possibility of actually getting to speak with Matthew. His next fight wasn't until tomorrow afternoon, and it was a group fight. Bear had suggested to Lars that Greyson might fight better if Luther and Drake were with him.

Lars liked the idea and set up a three-on-three match. If Matthew could provide the distraction during the fight, Bear might be able to release the other slaves that they had planned on liberating. He wished he could free them all, but that wasn't possible at the moment. He would come back after saving Alice and free the rest of them and take out Lars. Human trafficking made Greyson's blood boil.

The door opened and Drake walked in with a smile on his face. Blood dripped from a cut on his head, but he didn't seem to even notice. As soon as the door closed, Drake unfolded a piece of paper as he stepped towards his bed.

"What's that?" Luther asked curiously.

"A letter from Gwen." Drake beamed. He must have won his fight in order to receive the letter. Greyson tried to push down his jealousy. His friend receiving a letter from home was a good thing. Drake hadn't had any communication with his family in three years. The man deserved this. Greyson already knew that he wouldn't be getting one from Alice, but he still felt disappointed he hadn't. "I think this is for you, Grey."

Drake handed him a letter with *Prince* written across the front of it. Greyson looked down at the paper in surprise. Was this from Alice? He swallowed hard before slowly breaking the seal and unfolding the paper.

> *My dearest Prince,*
>
> *I cannot tell you how surprised and happy I was to receive your letter. I am relieved to hear that your current accommodation is better than your last. Just know that if you get fat, I will be putting you through a training program to get you back in shape when you get home. I am glad you are keeping your end of your promise and know that I fully plan on keeping both of mine. I miss you and your insufferable behavior.*
>
> *On a more serious note, my Prince, I need you to know that things here are not at all comfortable. There is a man here that has gone from annoying stalker to issuing threats. I thought about asking for my father or brother to come, but I am afraid that this man would do something drastic. I fear he will come up with a way to force my hand. Rest assured that at the moment, I am safe.*
>
> *As much as it pains me to admit this, I was wrong. Prince, I need you. I am scared and do not know what to do. Please, come back to me. Win another fight quickly so that I might hear from you again soon. Just this time leave off the blood.*
>
> *With Love,*
> *Princess*

Greyson got to his feet and began pacing. Alice needed him. She was scared. He needed to get to her. He needed to run. He moved to the door and banged on it. Luther and Drake grabbed him and pulled him away from the door.

"What has gotten into you?" Drake asked.

"I need a run. I need to think." Greyson tried to shove the two of them off but failed.

"What has happened?" Luther asked with brows furrowed. Greyson shoved his letter into Luther's hands. Luther read through the note before passing it to Drake. Greyson impatiently waited for them to finish reading it. "You thinking we need to move quickly?"

"I do my best thinking while I work out." Greyson started moving back to the door.

"Grey, wait." Drake called after him. "Gwen mentioned something about a friend of hers being pursued by Cain, Alpha Maddox's Beta. She is worried about her friend's safety. Cain is just as bad as Maddox."

"He is *worse* than Maddox." Luther corrected. "If he is the one that Ali is talking about, we need to leave as soon as possible."

Greyson pounded on the door again. A few minutes later, Bear opened the door with a concerned expression. Drake explained that they wanted to do a little more training with Greyson before the fight the next day.

Bear nodded and led them to the training arena. As soon as his feet hit the hard dirt of the arena, Greyson took off at a run around the perimeter. By his tenth lap, Greyson's anxiety began to fade to a more manageable level. Luther's advice to reach out to Matt came back and Greyson focused.

"Matt!" He called. There was a long stretch of silence. "Matt! I need you." Greyson tried again.

"Grey? How the heck?" Matt's voice came into his mind.

Greyson let out a relieved breath. "It's me. I am at the training arena where there aren't any inhibitors. I will explain the how later."

"Isaac will be relieved to know that we have a way to communicate with you. He was beyond angry that you asked for more time several weeks ago."

"I know. I have a few people here that rely on me. People I cannot leave behind. I will explain all, hopefully tomorrow."

"Tomorrow? What's happening tomorrow?" Matthew asked with a smile in his voice.

"You are getting us out of here." Greyson proceeded to explain his tentative plan to Matthew. Matt had some suggestions of his own from when he had toured the grounds several weeks before. He didn't know what kind of distraction he was going to use, but he said Greyson wouldn't be able to mistake it.

Thirty minutes later, Bear blew his whistle and Greyson said good-bye to his brother as he jogged the rest of the distance back to Drake, Luther, and Bear. Bear led them to the showers and then back to their cell.

Greyson explained the plan to everyone. This plan hinged on Matthew's distraction and Bear's ability to unlock all the doors without too much delay. Greyson tried to sleep, but his mind kept going over the plan. It had to work.

Chapter 15

Greyson decided against his normal morning run. If all went according to plan, he would be taking his run this evening with Drake, Luther, Bear and close to ten other slaves. He had never executed a mission with so many people he needed to protect. No one knew who the head of the escape plan was. Which kept the chance of a betrayal down, but Greyson was still anxious.

All training and fights were cancelled in preparation for the mega-match. At least all the prisoners would be in their cells, making it easier for Bear to free them. Breakfast was a quiet affair and Greyson moved restlessly in his seat.

"Calm down, kid." Luther laughed. "No need to fret."

"There are so many things that could go wrong today." Greyson shrugged his shoulders, trying to appear more at ease. "Once we get out of here, there will need to be one clear leader. In my experience if there is not, men tend to become disorganized quickly and people get hurt."

Drake and Luther looked at him with matching looks of surprise. They glanced at each other before Drake cleared his throat. "We've had a leader since the beginning."

Greyson furrowed his brow in confusion. Had he missed the conversation when the leader was decided? He didn't think so. The door opened and Bear stepped in and closed the door behind him.

"Lars has everything in order. He will not be permitting any slaves to leave their cells before or during the match. You three will be escorted directly to the arena an hour after lunch." Bear gave them their instructions and rules from Lars.

Luther sat forward, his attention on Bear. "Bear, if you had to point out the leader of our little pack, who would it be?" Greyson nearly laughed at the confused look on Bear's face. He was pretty sure it had matched his own when he was told a leader was already picked.

Bear visibly swallowed and glanced at Greyson. "Isn't it Wolf?"

"That's what we assumed, too." Drake said with a smile.

Greyson looked between the three men in stunned silence. He hadn't asked to be the leader. He was a soldier. He was given orders and he followed them. He had never led anything. "I'm sorry, what?" Greyson finally found his voice.

"You are the brains, the driving force, and the strongest among us. You have been leading us from the very beginning. Luther and I have only been advisors of a sort." Drake patted Greyson on the shoulder.

"Bear, how are things looking for the fight?" Luther asked, changing the subject. He tended to do so in order to prevent an argument on something he thought of as a done deal.

Greyson let it slide for now. Their first priority was escaping. He could solve the issue of who was in charge once everyone was safely away from Trevor's Cove. Bear stayed for only a few minutes more. Everything appeared to be going smoothly. Greyson only hoped it continued.

He would have loved to work out some of his tension on the punching bag, but they had not replaced the broken one yet. Needing to do something to keep himself from going insane, Greyson dropped to the floor and began doing pushups.

Greyson was sweating and his breathing was becoming more labored by the time he stopped and stretched. He met Luther's eyes, and the man just shook his head in disbelief. He had told Greyson on multiple occasions that Greyson needed to learn to relax and just sit. The only time Greyson could remember being able to just sit was when Alice was beside him. The thought of Alice brought back the night before he left for the castle.

He had held her on the couch for hours in silence. He had not wanted to let her go. Before missions, he felt like a caged animal, pacing along the bars, looking for an opportunity to break out. Alice had calmed his usual restless spirit.

With her that night, he had felt whole and at peace. But she had insisted the book in the hidden library was vital and he needed to free her from a life in hiding. He closed his eyes and took a deep breath. He could almost feel her head resting on his chest and smell her vanilla scent.

Greyson thought over the escape plan again. He was confident that they could get out of Trevor's Cove. But what would they do once they were out? Where would they go? They needed that planned out as well, otherwise they would just get captured again. He cleared his throat. Drake was rereading his letter from Gwen and Luther was staring up at the ceiling.

"What is the plan for when we escape the cove?" Greyson asked.

Luther looked over at him and squinted his eyes in thought. But it was Drake who answered. "I think we should head to the First Moon Pack. Once we are in their territory, we can appeal to the Alpha King for aid."

Luther nodded slowly. "I think that would be best. We cannot take on Alpha Maddox with only fifteen undisciplined slaves. We will need his aid and permission to eliminate Alpha Maddox."

"First Moon Pack? Isn't that where you said my mother was from?" Greyson asked.

"It is. Your grandfather, Alpha Lawerence, is the Alpha King at present." Drake sent him a smile. "I am sure he will be more than excited to meet you, Grey."

Greyson shook his head and resumed going over their plan in his mind. It was still weird to think he had family other than Matt and Alice.

Before Greyson felt fully prepared, Bear opened the cell door. It was time. They were led to the arena through an alternative route. Apparently, Lars didn't want to risk the two groups coming into contact with one another before being put in the fighting ring. Once they were lined up on their side, Greyson expected Bear to approach with the Equalizer, but he didn't.

The crowd was louder than normal. The thought of a three-on-three fight had drawn more spectators than Greyson expected. He scanned the crowd but could not see Isaac or Matthew.

"Matt?" Greyson asked through the mind-link.

"We're here." Matt answered. "Grey, Lars announced that this is a match to the death." Matt said anxiously.

"Luther, Drake, did you hear that?" Greyson asked.

"Yes." They said in unison through the mind-link.

"My distraction should still work for the most part. I will need you guys to create a bit of chaos in the ring for me to implement my main attraction." Matt said. "Where is our rendezvous spot?"

"We will get you your distraction, Matt. Rendezvous at the First Moon Pack." Greyson said as he eyed the three men who entered the arena on the other side.

Their opponents carried themselves with confidence. Greyson hadn't seen them before, so he assumed they were part of Trevor's Cove before he had arrived and fought at the top levels. The way they moved and eyed Greyson, Luther, and Drake gave Greyson the impression they knew that it was a death match. Greyson could sense them sizing them up from across the arena.

"What's the plan, Grey?" Luther asked through the mind-link as he stretched.

Greyson glanced up at Lars to see him grinning down at him. Greyson knew that Lars was trying to force him into fighting. It was as if he knew Greyson had been holding back. "I'm going to kneel down and not fight."

"Are you mad?" Drake yelled in his head. "If this is a death match, you are going to get us all killed."

"When Lars announces the death match. I am going to kneel down. Before the match can begin, you and Luther start yelling at me. One of you will try to attack me while the other holds him back. They will not start the match when a team is fighting against themselves." Greyson explained. "Matthew will have his distraction to allow him to implement his plan."

"Brilliant, Grey. Just like in Smithfield." Matthew's laughing voice said.

"Ladies and gentlemen. Thank you for coming to such a grand event." Lars's voice boomed around the stadium causing the crowd to quiet down. "This match is unique. We have decided to spice things up. We will have a three-on-three match. Not only that, but each man will have the ability to shift if they so choose. Our first team is made up of our veterans Boar, Dove, and Stag. Our second team is made up of Drake, Snake, and Wolf. Competitors. This match is to the death. The last team standing will be our victors." The crowd roared with excitement.

Greyson walked two steps forward. Lars's eyes trained on him. Greyson held his gaze as he slowly lowered himself to his knees. Lars's eyes narrowed as he watched Greyson, and a hush fell over the crowd. A quiet conversation started behind him, but it quickly became louder. There was the sound of shuffling feet and a growl of frustration.

"If he wants to die today, then I might as well do it myself." Luther yelled. "After all the time we have put into helping him train, the least he could do is fight for us."

"You know the kid is not a fighter. Snake, hold on." Drake yelled back.

"No!" Luther said. "He is going to get us killed, Drake. You cannot pretend that he isn't." More shuffling behind him and Lars broke eye contact to stare behind Greyson.

Greyson glanced at the three men on the other side of the arena. They watched Drake, Luther, and Greyson with confused expressions. "Enough!" Lars yelled as he got to his feet.

Greyson returned his attention back to Lars just as a loud explosion shook the ground. Greyson whipped his head around. On the far side of the arena, thick black smoke rose in the air followed by screams from the crowd.

Greyson got to his feet and took a few steps back. Another explosion. Greyson turned to see Lars's podium engulfed in smoke. Chaos rang through the air as guards and spectators ran in all directions.

"I think that's our cue." Greyson said as he turned and ran for the door that led back through the compound.

He didn't need to look behind him to know that Luther and Drake were hot on his heels. They ran through the hallways pulling previously locked doors open with ease. They were just about to the last set of doors when a noise behind them caused Greyson to stop. He turned around to see Lars standing in the hallway with murder in his eyes. He moved slowly towards them with a whip in one hand and a knife in the other.

"Keep going." Greyson whispered as he stepped in front of Luther and Drake. "I will catch up."

Luther gave Greyson's back a pat before he and Drake disappeared through the door. Greyson mirrored Lars's approach, reading his every move. The whip was nearly pointless in such a small space, but the knife would be useful. Greyson finally stopped five feet from Lars.

"You have destroyed everything! I should have killed you weeks ago." Lars spat. Greyson did not reply, just waited. "No matter. I will just do it now."

Lars lunged, and Greyson easily deflected the attack. It did not take long for Lars to drop the whip and focus his energy on trying to stab Greyson. With each minute that passed, Greyson became more and more aware of his waisted time.

Soon more guards would come, and his window of escape was closing fast. Lars let out a frustrated growl as Greyson once again deflected the knife. This time, however, Greyson managed to get the knife from Lars.

Seeing that he was outmatched, Lars took a step back. His eyes were blazing with hatred as he glared at Greyson. Five guards rounded the corner behind Lars and Lars's scowl turned into one of victory.

Lars continued to back up until he was nearly fifteen feet away. Greyson weighed his options. He had only one knife and had not practiced throwing in over a year.

He could attempt to end this here and now. If he killed Lars, the head of the slave trade in the area would be eliminated. But would the guards see it as liberation or an attack on their leader? He could turn and run, praying he made it into the forest before they caught him. If he did run, Lars would hunt him down, which would put Alice in more danger.

Making his decision, Greyson squared his shoulders and fixed his stance. "You don't have to do this."

"You will regret this, Wolf." Lars sneered. "You will..." Greyson did not let Lars finish. He threw the knife and hit his target. Lars cut his threat off midsentence and looked down at his chest.

Time seemed to freeze as Greyson watched Lars pull the knife from his chest as he sank to his knees. The guards looked at Greyson in surprise. He didn't wait to see what would happen next. He sprinted through the door and down the vacant hallway.

Greyson burst through the door at the end of the dim tunnel and out into the sunlight. He blinked several times as he glanced around, heart pounding. He took a deep breath and caught the scent of Luther. Without hesitating, he followed it into the forest.

Chapter 16

Alice sat in her window seat as she reread the books that she had brought with her. She had not opened them up since she became Queen Isabel's companion and she needed to figure out where the burial place of Queen Mara and Alpha King Tyson was.

Alice turned her attention out the window. It had to be somewhere close. As soon as Queen Isabel returned from her lunch with Gwen, Alice would ask her. After all, she was their descendent.

Rain pattered the window and Alice leaned her forehead against the cool glass. She hoped that Gwen had another letter from Drake and Greyson today. It had been nearly four weeks since she sent her letter to him. Four weeks of being couped up in her room. She was ready for fresh air and ready for Cain to disappear.

He had shown up to Queen Isabel's room several times asking after her. Queen Isabel had been gracious in her responses. Refusing to let him in, and at the same time, claiming that Alice was busy and refusing to interrupt her.

Over the weeks, Cain had become more and more angry over not seeing her. He started coming by when Queen Isabel was gone. Alice refused to answer the door. At least she had her punching bag and knives.

She spent a lot of her time training. The time she wasn't training, she was helping Queen Isabel with whatever she needed help with. Well, as long as it could be done from their rooms. Alice had grown stronger over the weeks. Her accuracy with her knives had also gotten better.

She had even started teaching Isabel how to throw daggers. The Queen was not half bad. There was usually a considerable amount of laughing compared to when Matthew taught her.

Alice recognized how crazy she had been the nine months Greyson was missing. She had been in a very dark place. She was barely living. Her family had been right to be concerned about her. If she had stayed in that state, Alice could picture herself slipping more and more away, until she lost her will to live. She might have even tried to take the fight to Sasha herself.

Alice shook her head. She wasn't there anymore, and she knew Greyson was alive. He would come for her and together they would destroy the stupid stone that had caused her family so much trouble. Alice pulled the amulet out of her shirt and looked down at it. This little thing was the reason for so much death and suffering.

"What's that?" Isabel's voice caused Alice to jump. She had not heard her come in.

"Oh, it's just a trinket that my great grandmother had given me for my birthday." Alice tried to tuck it back into her shirt, but Isabel had sat down on the bench next to her and extended her hand.

"May I?" Alice hesitated but slipped the chain over her head and handed it over to Isabel. Alice watched anxiously as Isabel examined the necklace. After several moments, a small smile spread on Isabel's lips.

"It has been a long time since I have seen this." She reverently touched the amulet before handing it back to Alice. "Well, I have not actually seen it in person. There is a painting at my childhood home of Queen Mara. She is wearing this necklace in it. I had always found the necklace beautiful."

Alice blinked at Isabel in surprise. She had seen the Guardian's Stone in a painting at her home? Alice didn't know what to say. "How did you say you came to have the Guardian's Amulet?"

"You know of the Guardian's Amulet?" Alice asked quietly.

Isabel softly laughed. "The amulet protects its wearer. It can even suspend one's life for up to an hour in case of an emergency. Queen Mara had worn it until her eldest daughter's wedding day, when she gifted it to her."

Alice's brows furrowed. What was Isabel talking about? This necklace held the Stone from Alpha Tyson, didn't it? "I think you might be mistaken." Alice said slowly. "This amulet holds the stone from Alpha Tyson."

Queen Isabel shook her head. "No, my dear. That necklace is indeed the Guardian's Amulet that is used for protection. The Guardian's Alpha Stone is something different entirely."

Alice felt her breath rush from her lungs as if she were punched in her stomach. "That can't be." Alice looked back down at the necklace in her shaking hands. If this wasn't the Guardian's Stone, where was it?

Isabel gently took the necklace from Alice's hands and put it over Alice's head. "Keep this on at all times." She gave Alice a kind smile before reaching for her hand. She twisted Alice's hand so that the wolf pendant was visible. "This is quite unique." Isabel gently touched the wolf's head's smooth surface.

Alice blinked at the sudden change in topic. "Yes. Greyson gave it to me when I was eleven." Alice told her.

"Why did he give it to you?" Isabel asked. Her gaze moved from the pendant to Alice's face with an intense look as if the answer mattered a great deal to her.

"We had had a bit of an argument. He said he was sorry. He said it was given to him a long time ago and that he was giving it to me to show his dedication to keeping me safe. I turned it into a bracelet and have worn it ever since." Alice explained as a blush heated her cheeks.

"I gave this to Miss Mary the day I took him to the orphanage. I asked her to give it to Grey when he was old enough and to explain that it was from his mother." Isabel wiped a tear from her eye before it could fall. "This, Alice, is the Guardian's Alpha Stone."

Alice gasped as she looked down at her bracelet. All this time she had already had the Stone. Her great grandmother had been wrong about the necklace. "Do you know how to destroy the Stone?" Alice asked as she gently ran her thumb over the smooth surface.

"It first has to be activated, which I believe it has." Isabel rotated on the bench so that her back rested against the window.

"What makes you think that it has been activated?" Alice's curiosity made her unable to remain silent.

Isabel gave another soft laugh. "Greyson is your mate, correct?" Alice nodded in confirmation. "He gave you the Stone to show his dedication to you when he had nothing else to give. That is a token if I ever heard of one." Alice remained in stunned silence. Is that why he was able to communicate with her father and brother in wolf form without being in a pack?

Alice rubbed her forehead. "Okay, so it has been activated. Now what? It needs to be destroyed so no one can use it to hurt others."

"From what I remember from Queen Mara's journal, the Stone's ability is removed from the Stone when a sacrifice of love is made."

"What does that mean?" Alice asked. How was she supposed to sacrifice for love? "I thought that its power could be removed only at the resting place of Queen Mara."

"The power within the Locket of Estell can be removed at Queen Mara's and Alpha King Tyson's tomb. A sacrifice of love is needed for the Stone's power to be removed. I am not sure how. You and Grey will need to figure that out." Isabel patted Alice's hand.

"Why would my great grandmother think that the Guardian's Amulet was the Guardian's Alpha Stone? The Guardian Matron also thought the same thing."

"The Guardian's Amulet was given to Mara's oldest daughter, Lisa. Lisa and her husband moved to Arlania. Over the years, Lisa discovered more and more girls with gifts. She created a sanctuary for them to live in. The Guardian's Alpha Stone was passed down to Mara's second daughter, Bethany. Bethany passed the Stone down to her daughter and so on. Until it was given to me."

"I don't understand how the Amulet was thought to be the Stone?" Alice shook her head.

"The information on both were put into a book. It was written in such a way that only those in which the knowledge was passed to, would be able to read it. Lisa and her husband passed away without having children. If she didn't tell anyone about the differences between the two, a person could easily confuse the two objects when reading the book."

Alice furrowed her brows as she thought over everything Isabel had told her. "If the Stone was passed down to the daughters, why did you give it to Grey and not one of your daughters?"

"My daughters were the bright spots in my life. I was able to give them everything. When Grey was born, I could give him very little. I gave him the Stone so that Maddox could never discover it and what it could do. As my girls grew, I was able to make sure that Hailey, Faith, and Ivy were married to decent men. They live in various packs around Valencia, but they never visit because they are afraid of Maddox."

"I am so sorry, Isabel. I hope that you can see them someday soon."

"As do I." Isabel sighed heavily before rolling her shoulder's back and putting a smile on her face. "Are you ready for our lesson?"

Alice nodded distractedly and Isabel moved to the other side of the room to set up the target and gather the daggers. Alice slowly joined her. *Please, come home Grey. I can't do this without you.* she said in her head.

Alice pushed thoughts of the Stone and Amulet from her mind. If Greyson did not come, Alice didn't know what she would do. She shook her head to clear away thoughts of Greyson. Taking a deep breath, she focused on helping Isabel with her knife throwing.

Chapter 17

Greyson continued to run away from Trevor's Cove as several more explosions happened. How many explosions did Matthew rig up? Greyson followed the scent for several miles before slowing his pace. He listened for any sound of someone following him but heard nothing. He was unfamiliar with the area and had to rely on following Luther's scent in order to regroup with the others.

"Matt?" Greyson opened the mind-link.

"We made it out. Isaac took flight and I'm following him." Came Matt's response. "He is circling, so I think he found you."

Greyson looked up, and sure enough, a hawk circled overhead. "Hurry up. I'm not sure what kind of lead we have, and we need to catch up to the others." Greyson stopped and waited for Matthew.

The hawk landed not far from him, and Isaac shifted. "You are a sight for sore eyes." Isaac said with a smile as he pulled Greyson into a tight hug. Greyson returned his embrace, patting Isaac on the back. Isaac was the father Greyson never had and he had missed him terribly.

"Where's my hug?" Matthew's voice sounded from behind Greyson.

Greyson turned to face his brother with a large smile. "How many explosions did you set off?" The brothers hugged.

"Twenty." Matt said with a laugh. "No one will get hurt. They were nothing but giant smoke and stink bombs."

Greyson laughed before he pulled Matthew in for another hug. "I have missed you guys, but we should probably keep moving. I was separated from the others back at the Cove."

"I'll scout for them from the air while you both track them." Isaac said as he shifted and took flight again.

"Luther's scent leads this way." Greyson gestured with his head and began jogging in that direction.

Matthew fell into step beside him as they ran through the trees. Greyson kept an eye on the sky as he followed the scent of Luther. Several more miles passed, and Greyson slowed their pace. They should have created a big enough lead at their previous pace. They continued forward at a fast jog. The sun was beginning to sink lower in the sky, creating deeper shadows.

"How much of a lead do you think the others still have over us?" Matt asked.

"I'm not sure. I think we are getting closer." Greyson shrugged. He opened the mind-link. "Drake, Luther."

"We all made it out." Drake answered.

"How far did you make it?" Greyson asked.

"We made it a good distance. We are taking a rest near a river before crossing it and then continuing. Bear was able to release several additional slaves with that distraction your brother created." Luther said. "Where are you?"

"We are following your scent, Luther. Stay where you are, and we should reach you soon." Greyson instructed as he picked up his pace again.

"I think you should hurry. There is a Beta here that thinks he is in charge. He is wanting to make camp here." Drake piped in again.

"On our way." Greyson cut the mind-link and pushed faster.

Ten minutes later, Greyson could hear the sound of the river and angry men. He and Matthew slowed their steps to a walk as they listened to the argument. They approached slowly, not wanting to startle anyone. Greyson took a minute to slow his breathing to a more normal rate before stepping out of the trees.

No one noticed that Matt and Greyson had joined the group. That was incredibly dangerous. What if Greyson and Matt were guards from the Cove. Greyson shook his head as they slowly made their way through the crowd until they reached the center of the group.

Luther, Drake, and Bear stood close together as they faced a man that had two men that flanked him. The man's face was red with anger as he continued to argue with Luther.

"I am the highest ranking here. We have put plenty of miles between us and Trevor's Cove. This is an ideal spot to camp for the night!" The man yelled.

Matthew scoffed loudly, drawing attention to him. A look of relief flashed across Luther and Drake's faces. "This is a terrible place to camp." Matt retorted.

"And who are you to have an opinion?" The man growled at Matthew.

"Why don't we all just calm down." Greyson said stepping forward.

"Why don't you butt out of this and let the adults talk." The man took a menacing step forward.

"I didn't risk my life so that you could try to get us all killed or recaptured because you want to make camp in the worst place possible." Greyson matched his condescending tone. The man looked to be in his late thirties with a muscular build. "We do not have time for your power trip. So, why don't we just jump to the end? If you want to take control of this group, challenge me."

"Challenging you will be easy. You are the prisoner who trips over his own feet during his fights." The man laughed.

"Man or wolf?" Greyson asked, moving further away from the group.

The man rolled his shoulders. "We can start as men and then we can move to wolves."

Greyson nodded and then turned his back to him. "Matt, keep an eye out for Isaac. He should be spotting us soon." Greyson began as he heard footsteps approaching behind him. He pretended not to notice as he turned to Drake and Luther. "We should probably have a few of the men try to cover up some of the tracks."

"Uh, Wolf?" Bear said hesitantly, but Greyson ignored him. He knew that the man was close.

Greyson continued dishing out assignments, and just as the challenger was within striking distance, Greyson stepped to the side. He spun and kicked the man's feet out from under him. He landed flat on his back hard with a whoosh of air.

Greyson hid his smile as he looked down at the man, as he gasped for air. He rolled onto his hands and knees as he struggled to suck in a breath. As soon as he straightened up, Greyson delivered several quick punches to his midsection and a final blow to his jaw.

The man stumbled back several steps. He wiped the corner of his mouth and growled in frustration. He and his two buddies shifted into their wolves. Luther and Drake started to step forward, but Greyson motioned for them to stay put. Matt, however, moved to his side.

"Are we going to shift too, or are we going to take them out like old times?" Matt said loudly enough for everyone to hear.

"You can shift?" Greyson turned to Matthew with a smile.

"Alice said I'm nearly as big as you are." Matt puffed his chest out with pride.

"Well, let's see what you are made of." Greyson shifted into his large black wolf. It felt good to shift after so long and he couldn't help stretching.

He looked over to Matthew's wolf and laughed. Matt's wolf's ears were black as well as his legs, but his body was a dark grey with white sprinkled throughout. He was a very unique color, but it fit Matthew's fun personality.

Greyson turned his attention to the three wolves across from him. The two wolves on the sides shrank back with their tails tucked while the wolf in the middle seemed frozen. The middle wolf was bigger than the other two, but still quite a bit smaller than Matt and Greyson.

Greyson took a step closer to them and the wolf on the right whimpered. Greyson noticed that all the men watching went silent as well. He turned his attention to Luther and Drake. They were staring wide eyed at Greyson and Matthew. Greyson turned his head back to the three troublemakers and noticed that they all had shifted back into human form. Matthew followed their lead and then Greyson shifted.

"Are we done?" Greyson asked, crossing his arms over his chest.

"Yes, sir." The man in the middle ducked his head and mumbled.

"Good. Those of you who wish to make your own way home, by all means, go. But I am heading for the First Moon Pack to speak with Alpha Lawerence. I am hoping to gain his assistance in challenging Alpha Maddox and putting a stop to his reign." Greyson did not wait for any responses before turning to Drake. "Lead the way, Drake."

"When were you going to tell us that both you and your brother were Alphas?" Luther asked.

"Does it matter?" Greyson said as they followed Drake to the river's edge. They moved carefully through the water. Once on the other side, Drake began to jog east. "Plus, I didn't know Matt could even shift till a few minutes ago."

"It is just unusual for two Alphas to be born in the same family." Drake commented.

"Since both of you are Alphas, who is going to be the leader?" Bear asked from right behind them.

Greyson glanced back and was pleased that nearly fifteen men followed them. They all seemed to be listening with interest to the conversation. "I have no desire to be in charge. My loyalty is to Greyson. I will follow him anywhere." Matthew stated without hesitation.

"I too pledge my loyalty to Alpha Grey." Bear said firmly.

The rest of the men followed suit, declaring their loyalty to Greyson. With each declaration, he felt a new bond form in his mind. Almost as if he could sense each and every one of the men. Not as clear as he could with Alice though.

He couldn't sense their emotions, just the fact that they were there. Luther moved to Greyson's left side and Greyson glanced at him. He didn't say anything as they continued, but Greyson knew that the older man wished to discuss something later.

They travelled for several more hours. The sun was down, and they had slowed to a walk. The men let out a collective sigh of relief when Greyson called a stop for the night. Everyone was exhausted.

Greyson assigned four men to take up sentry posts with a change in men every hour. No one complained, which made Greyson glad. He didn't know what had changed the attitude of the men, but something had definitely made them more willing to follow his orders.

A hawk's cry broke the silence of the night just before Isaac landed and shifted. Several of the men jumped to their feet in surprise. But when Greyson embraced him, they relaxed. Greyson introduced Isaac to the group before settling back against a tree.

"Took you long enough." Greyson teased Isaac.

"I found your group by the first river early on, but I saw you and Matthew there, so I didn't see a need to land. I flew back to Trevor's Cove to see if there was any search party being launched." Isaac explained as he sat close to Greyson. "It seemed they were concerned with something else for several hours. By the time they regrouped, it was getting too late in the day to send out a party. They are planning to start out at first light."

"Very good. We have a good lead on them then." Matthew commented.

"It looks like you have less men here than you did at the river." Isaac said as he glanced around.

"Someone challenged Greyson, but as soon as your boys shifted, the challengers backed down. I don't think they expected such big wolves." Luther chuckled.

"I know that they are bigger than several of the other wolf Shifters, but isn't it normal to have wolves of various sizes?" Isaac asked.

"Wolves come in all shapes and sizes. But there are a few general rules. Betas tend to be slightly bigger than the average wolf. Betas are typically second in command within the pack. Alphas are bigger than Betas. And then there is Greyson's wolf." Drake explained.

"What's special about my wolf?" Greyson asked, keeping his voice down. "Matthew's wolf is just as big."

"Matthew is definitely an Alpha. However, he is still smaller than you by a few inches and you are much thicker than he is." Luther said.

"You are both royal by blood. It would not surprise me if you were the next Alpha King." Drake said quietly.

"You can't be serious." Greyson shook his head. "I am not king material. All I want to do is get to the Howling Meadows Pack as soon as possible so that I can get Alice back."

"Whether you like it or not, you are now the Alpha of this small pack of freed slaves." Bear joined in the conversation. "These men have already declared their loyalty to you. The only thing that is left for you to do is declare your Beta."

Greyson looked at the men around him. He felt protective of the whole group. That is why he had pushed them so hard today. He wanted to make sure that they were as far away from the threat as possible. He turned his attention to the five men directly around him. He studied each and every one of them. He caught Matt's eye, and he knew that he needed him by his side.

"Matthew Hunt, I declare you as my Beta." Greyson said loudly. The men who had not fallen asleep yet, looked their way with smiles.

"You do realize I am barely eighteen, right?" Matthew asked in disbelief.

"As I recall, you have been by my side since you were four. You have more experience than all of these men because of the way we were raised. I couldn't think of anyone better." Greyson smiled at his brother. "Plus, it is too late now. I already did it." Matthew chuckled as he rolled onto his back and closed his eyes.

Silence fell among the men. Greyson was aware of each of the sentry shift changes throughout the night. He was pleased with the men's willingness to change shift so frequently.

By morning, everyone seemed relatively well rested. Drake had told them it would take two more days to make it to the First Moon Pack's territory.

Two men, Jarom and Linus, volunteered to hunt and bring back food. Both men weren't much older than Matthew but had a gift for hunting. They were gone less than an hour before they dragged in a rabbit for each man. With the size of their lead on the search party, Greyson allowed for a small fire and quick meal.

Once they were travelling again, Greyson told Drake to keep this current pace and dropped back to talk with several of the men. He wanted to get to know each of them better, so he knew how to best use them.

He learned that several of the men had families within the Howling Meadows Pack. Others came from nearby packs that were just as bad. Every last one of them had someone waiting at home for them. Drake held the record for being the longest away from home with most being gone close to a year and a half. Luther was arrested not long after Drake.

Greyson also learned that both Luther and Bear had a talent for tracking. They could pick up on the slightest of smells when they are in their wolf forms. Seven of the men were great fighters. Drake was a diplomat as well as a fighter. Jarom and Linus were great hunters but were still young and needed a bit more training in staying quiet. Matthew quickly became friends with them, and Greyson smiled at the stories Matthew told. The two boys were enthralled with everything Matthew said.

"Your brother is sure to be a favorite." Luther chuckled.

"He usually is." Greyson smiled. "He could never pass up an opportunity to tell a good story."

When Matt finished telling several of the men about Harrisburg, Greyson called him over. "What's up, Grey?" he asked cheerfully.

"Before we get to the First Moon Pack, I would like you to hear a story from Luther and Drake." Greyson nodded to Luther.

Matthew listened intently without interrupting. When Luther was done, Matt seemed to be deep in thought for a long time. Luther and Greyson allowed him time to process everything he had heard. Greyson nearly tripped when Matthew broke out laughing.

"So, when you call Alice 'Princess', she actually is a princess?" Matt laughed even harder.

"That is what you took from all that?" Greyson chuckled. "Not the fact that you and I are both royal princes by birth? Or the fact we are headed for our maternal grandfather's pack to gain assistance to take over our father's pack?" Greyson glanced over at Matthew to gauge his reaction.

"That's pretty cool, too." Matt's face lost its smile. A deep scowl marred his face. "Grey, Alice is livid. She is so mad at you."

"How is she? I vaguely remember you saying she wasn't doing very well after I disappeared."

"When Isaac brought her back, she was so withdrawn. We didn't realize she wasn't eating until she passed out in the drawing room. After that, Rowan made sure she ate. About a month in, she started putting everything she had into training. She was like a machine. She would not stop, and it got to the point she was practically falling asleep at the dinner table." Matt shook his head as if he were there at that moment. "We were all worried about her.

It got to the point that we made sure someone was with her at all times." He took a deep breath. "Grey, it was bad."

Greyson ran a hand through his hair. "I need to get back to her."

"She followed Isaac and me to the Howling Meadows Pack. Isaac looked ready to throttle her and then take her back home. But she seemed to be coming back to life with the chance that you might still be alive. When she saw you on your way to the boat, it was like…I don't know. It is hard to describe. When you were gone all her color was muted and then it all came back. Does that make sense?" Matt turned to Greyson.

"I think so." Greyson looked down at his feet as he stepped over a large rock. They were both quiet for several minutes. Greyson swallowed hard before turning back to Matthew. "I love her, Matt."

Matthew smiled at him. "I know. I could see it from the window when you were in the garden."

"That can't be possible." Greyson shook his head.

"To be honest, I think you have been in love with her since you were fourteen. When you came back to the compound, you told me about the girl that irritated you, remember? And you refused to even look at the girls that practically threw themselves at you. Then in the barn I could see the attraction between you two. The garden just kind of confirmed my hunch." Matthew said with a shrug.

Luther laughed. "I miss judged you, kid. Even though you are a much livelier man than our young Alpha, you are quite observant and smart."

Greyson let out a growl which caused both Matt and Luther to laugh harder. Greyson would have been madder if Matt didn't have a good point. Maybe he had been in love with Alice since they were kids.

He had given her his only connection to his mother on that trip. He still could not explain why he would give up such a priceless trinket to a girl that did nothing but irritate him. Greyson sighed in frustration. Regardless of when he fell in love with her, she currently had his heart, and he planned to win hers in return.

Chapter 18

The group moved quickly. Greyson was grateful that the men were all in good shape from the training they did at Trevor's Cove. Luther and Bear would periodically fall back and cover their trail as they went. They only had to make it to the First Moon Pack before their pursuers reached them. That was the most important step.

Once there, they would be Alpha Lawerence's problem and no one else had jurisdiction there. Drake had assured Greyson that the Alpha King would meet with them once he was informed that Drake and Luther were among the group.

They were on day three of their freedom and the forest was beginning to thin. Drake and Luther's energy seemed to increase as they drew closer to their previous pack's borders. It was almost midday when Greyson noticed a change in the air. His senses went on high alert. They made it another mile before he felt eyes on him.

"Eyes and ears open gentlemen. We are being watched." Greyson said through the mind-link. "Keep our current pace and do not act nervous. Whoever is watching us will eventually make themselves known."

"We are within the First Moon borders. It is probably the patrol keeping tabs on us until back up can get here." Drake commented.

As they continued, Greyson slowed his pace slightly until he was at the back of the group. From this position, he could keep an eye on each of his men. He heard a stick break behind him, but he kept his attention forward while he listened more closely. There! Another snap of a twig, this time closer. Greyson fought against his training to turn and fight.

"Six o'clock." Greyson mind-linked the group. "We should stop and wait. Move into a tight group." He ordered. "Remember we are the trespassers and seeking sanctuary."

His men did as he ordered. Greyson could tell that the men behind him were moving to surround them. Matthew commented on that fact as well. In less than ten minutes after they stopped, a man stepped out in front of Drake.

"Who are you and what are you doing on our pack lands?" The man barked out.

"You will need to address our Alpha." Drake said firmly.

"And who is your Alpha?"

Greyson stepped away from the group with his head held high. "I am."

The man laughed as he moved to the back of the group, closer to Greyson. "Why are you in the back of your pack, little Alpha? Afraid to get hurt?"

"On the contrary. I am back here so that I might keep an eye on each of my men. With a potential threat coming up behind us, I figured the best place for me to protect my pack was back here." Greyson took up a relaxed stance.

The man narrowed his eyes at Greyson, and he gave the man a smile in return. "Why are you on our pack lands?" The man asked Greyson.

"We seek an audience with Alpha Lawerence." Greyson stated.

The men around them laughed. "You can't trespass on our land and then demand an audience with the Alpha King."

"Two of my men were previous members of the First Moon Pack. They have assured me that the Alpha King would, indeed, wish to meet with me." Greyson said coolly.

There was some noise from his right and Greyson glanced in that direction. An older man with grey hair stepped from the trees. He moved slowly at first, but then ran the last several steps to Luther and pulled him into a hug.

There were hushed words spoken between the two of them as they embraced. The man next to Greyson watched with a furrowed brow. When Luther pulled back, he had a smile on his face. The older man looked over at Greyson with wide eyes.

"Why don't we all shift and head back to the castle. We will move faster that way." The old man called.

"But..." The first man began to protest.

"Jerry, I said shift and head back to the castle." The old man interrupted him.

"This is my father." Luther said through the mind-link. "I told him that you are the son of Queen Isabel."

Greyson nodded. Their escorts had all shifted to their wolves and waited for Greyson's men to do the same. Greyson hesitated. With the reaction of the group last time he and Matt shifted, he didn't want to show the First Moon Pack his wolf just yet. Matt also needed to keep his Alpha size a secret for the time being.

"How far to the castle?" Greyson asked Drake as he walked up to him.

"We are about five miles from the castle, Alpha." Drake said with a small smile. Greyson rolled his eyes at the formal title Drake used.

"Matt, you think you can run in human form with me while the others are in wolf form?" Greyson mind-linked.

"Absolutely, brother." Matt responded as he rubbed his hands together. "It has been a long time since we had a foot race."

"Men, shift. Follow our escorts." Greyson called in a loud voice.

His pack shifted quickly, leaving Greyson and Matthew the only two in human form. Greyson nodded to Luther's father to lead the way. The brown wolf nodded and turned northeast. As soon as all his pack wolves were on their way, Greyson nudged Matthew's shoulder. Matthew gave him a smirk before sprinting off in the direction the others had disappeared, Greyson hot on his heels.

Matthew was faster than Greyson remembered. Granted, the last time they raced was several years ago. Greyson ignored the urge to run faster and overtake Matt. If he did, he would burn out before they reached the castle. Matt on the other hand, seemed to have forgotten this was a long-distance race.

Greyson smiled to himself as he noticed Matt's pace slacken slightly. Greyson pulled even with Matthew for a few miles. As the grey stones of the castle started to appear through the trees, Greyson pushed himself faster. This was the time to put all he had left into the race.

By the time they reached the wolves at the front side of the castle, Greyson was several feet in front of Matthew. He skidded to a stop on the loose gravel. He bent over, bracing his hands on his knees as he gasped for air. Matthew threw himself flat on his back with a frustrated growl.

"Still too slow, Matt." Greyson panted.

"How did you do it? You were in prison for nearly a year. I thought for sure that would have slowed you down." Matt grumbled.

"You burn your energy too fast out of the gate. You have been running on your reserve for the last mile." Greyson laughed. "You need to pace yourself at the beginning."

A throat cleared and Greyson turned to see nearly forty men watching him and Matthew. Greyson offered Matthew a hand and pulled him to his feet. They were still breathing hard, but Greyson straightened to his full height and walked towards Drake and Luther.

"I hope we didn't keep you waiting." Greyson said, not knowing what else to say.

Luther coughed as he covered his mouth with his hand. Greyson saw the corner of his mouth turn up before he was able to cover it. Luther was trying not to laugh. "Not at all. I am impressed you got here so quickly on foot." Luther managed to say.

Luther's father shook his head and turned to the large doors at the top of a wide set of stairs. Greyson turned to the large structure and took it in.

The exterior was made of large grey blocks with big windows every few feet. The doors were twice as tall as a normal door and made of a rich dark wood. Greyson slowly made his way up the stairs and through the entry doors with Matt and Luther right beside him.

Drake fell into step behind with Bear close on his heels. The rest of Greyson's men followed silently. They were led to a large room at the back of the castle. In the center of the room sat a long rectangular table with at least thirty chairs.

Greyson gestured for his men to take a seat. After all were seated, Greyson took his seat between Matthew and Drake. Luther sat on Matt's other side while Bear sat on Drake's. His men all sat on the same side of the table as he did, leaving the other side free for the Alpha King. Greyson noticed that several guards stood in the hallway to keep an eye on them.

Drake leaned close to Greyson with a smirk. "A foot race?"

Greyson shrugged, but he could not stop the smile that spread across his face. It had felt so good to let go for a moment. Matthew always helped Greyson branch from his normally serious temperament. It was even more fun when Greyson won after Matthew pushed and pushed for Greyson to compete with him. Greyson's smile grew when Matt started to grumble.

"You are really out-of-shape, how did I lose?" Matt hissed under his breath.

"Our Alpha is out of shape?" Bear asked in disbelief.

"Before he was fool enough to give himself over to the enemy and thrown into prison, I doubt Grey would have been winded after such a race." Matt leaned forward so that he could see Bear.

"In Alice's letter she threatened to put me through training if I got fat." Greyson chuckled.

"Alice wrote you?" Matt asked, surprise written all over his face.

"If you won your fights, you could write a letter home. Another win and you could read the reply." Drake explained.

A commotion in the hallway drew their attention. Luther's father stepped into the room. "We have a man here that says he is with Alpha Grey. He said his name is Isaac Young."

Greyson got to his feet and nodded. "He is with us. He is my uncle."

Luther's father nodded before stepping from the room to return a moment later with Isaac. Isaac moved to an empty chair down the table and sent Greyson a quick nod. Instead of retaking his seat, Greyson began walking down the length of the chairs before turning around and walking to the other end. Thus began his pacing as he waited. He hoped this meeting with the Alpha King would go well. He needed to get to Alice. There was a rising urgency to get to her.

He had walked the length of the table four times before he heard Matthew's voice. "Don't worry, Grey could never just sit still. He always has to be in motion."

Greyson ignored Matthew's comment. How were they going to get into the Howling Meadows Pack? Was Alice still safe? Would Alpha Maddox recognize him? Greyson let out a frustrated growl. Maybe he should sneak in by himself and extract her. There was no need to endanger anyone else. Once he knew she was safe, he would go after Sasha and Bradley and then Maddox.

Bradley. Greyson hated the man. The castle faded from his vision, and he was back in a dark rocky cave-like room. There were candles all around him to light the circular room. The ceiling was low, and Bradley had to duck his head in order to keep from hitting it.

In the center of the room was a stone table with its top slightly askew. Greyson's arms were tied behind him and chained to the wall. His feet were tied out in front of him. Greyson's abdomen was on fire. Looking down he saw a white bandage around his torso.

Snatches of memories surfaced of the fight at the cabin where Greyson was winning, throwing a dagger and hitting Bradley in the stomach with it, and then the gunshot. Alice in the bunker. Bradley started to laugh. He asked Greyson where she was. When he refused to say anything, Bradley had gone into detail about everything he was going to do to Alice.

Greyson's blood began to boil at the rage he had felt combined with the helplessness of not being able to stop Bradley. A hand touched Greyson's shoulder and he whirled around throwing a punch. His attacker ducked out of the way and Greyson continued to defend himself. He punched the attacker in the gut, and he stumbled back a step.

"Grey!" A voice growled. It took several more moments before Greyson's surroundings started to come back into focus. "Grey!" The voice came again.

Greyson blinked several times and Matthew came into focus. Greyson took several deep breaths as he looked around the room. Not only was his fifteen men sitting at the table, but ten men sat across from them. All eyes were on him. Greyson shook his head and rubbed the back of his neck. "Sorry, Matt. Got caught in a memory."

"No harm done. Come on." Matthew led the way back to their seats as if nothing had happened. As if Greyson hadn't just attacked his own man.

Greyson took his seat and took a deep breath before looking across at the men that sat there. In the center, sat a man with greying hair and amber colored eyes. Greyson blinked. The man had to be Alpha Lawerence.

Clearing his throat, Greyson adjusted in his chair. "I must apologize." The other Alpha raised a brow. "First for trespassing into your territory without permission, and for my resent display. I am afraid I am suffering from residual effects of my recent captivity."

"Are you really okay, Matt?" Greyson asked through the mind-link.

"You do far worse to me when we spar. Seriously man, don't sweat it. But I do expect you to tell me where your mind was later." Matt answered.

"I do have to admit I was intrigued when Samuel informed me that his son had returned with someone who claims to be the son of Queen Isabel." The Alpha King sat back in his chair and studied Greyson and Matthew.

"I have claimed no such thing. However, Luther and Drake were with Queen Isabel when she gave her two sons to an orphanage. They are under the assumption that I am one of those sons." Greyson explained. He could see Luther and Drake shake their heads out of the corner of his eye.

The Alpha King continued to watch them for several long moments. He turned his piercing gaze to Luther and then to Drake. Greyson took the time to observe the Alpha King. Not only did he have their same eye color, but Greyson could see some of Matthew in the older man's features. Silence continued to fill the room and a cough sounded from down the table.

"As fun as it has been to stare at one another. My men are hungry, and we could use some clothes." Greyson crossed his arms over his chest.

The man that laughed at Greyson in the forest got to his feet quickly. "You dare speak to the Alpha King in such a way?"

Greyson slowly got to his feet and stared at the man. He could feel the familiar presence of his wolf rising to the surface. He continued to glare at the man, and Greyson was pleased to see the man's aggressive posture begin to slip.

Greyson's wolf pushed a little more and the man swallowed hard before lowering his eyes and retaking his chair. Greyson blinked twice before retaking his own chair. He glanced around the table and noted that everyone, but Isaac and the Alpha King, had bowed their heads.

"Your Alpha presence is impressive." Alpha Lawerence commented. "You are right, I should have at the very least, had the kitchen send up some food. Nolan, why don't you go make sure that we get food here in the next few minutes." The man that yelled at Greyson stood up with a quick nod to his Alpha and left. "So, tell me, what is your name?"

"My name is Greyson Hunt." Greyson answered.

"Hmm. Are you at all familiar with Queen Isabel's family?" The Alpha King asked.

"I am not. I grew up in Arlania and only came to Valencia about a year ago. All my time here has been spent either in Alpha Maddox's dungeon or at Trevor's Cove." Greyson leaned back in his own chair.

"My wife's maiden name was Hunt." The Alpha King said softly.

"Is that where she got it from?" Matthew asked. "I was wondering about that."

"And who are you?" Alpha Lawerence moved his gaze to Matthew.

"This is my younger brother, Matthew Lawerence Hunt." Greyson introduced.

"I spoke to Queen Isabel for about an hour while we were in the Howling Meadows Pack. She confirmed that both Grey and I are her sons." Matthew leaned forward, resting his elbows on the table. "Since she is our mother and your daughter, does that make you, our grandfather? Do we get to call you gramps or grandfather or papa?" Matthew's normal rambling kicked in and Greyson elbowed him to get him to stop.

Matthew's comments were followed by silence for the space of several heartbeats before Alpha Lawerence started to laugh. When his laughter finally faded into a wide smile, he rose to his feet. "Young Matthew, you are just as talkative as your mother was when she was young. But you, Greyson, have your mother's hair." He smiled sadly at them. "Why don't you, Matthew, Luther and Drake accompany me to my office while your men are fed and taken to their rooms to rest."

Greyson stood as well and turned to look at his men. "Bear, you are in charge." Bear gave him an acknowledging nod. Greyson opened the mind-link "Men, behave yourselves. I expect you to show respect and watch out for one another." Once he was assured that all understood, Greyson began to move towards the door. Matt, Luther, and Drake followed him silently. He stopped behind Isaac's chair and laid a hand on his shoulder. "Come on Isaac, you are with me."

Alpha Lawerence raised a brow but didn't say anything as the five of them followed him from the room. No one spoke as they walked through the halls. Unlike Alpha Maddox's castle with halls that were cold and had no life, this castle had family pictures, art and other nicknacks that made the space feel like a home and lived in.

The study was not any different. On the desk was a picture of a woman and a little girl with amber eyes and dark reddish-brown hair. There was a large window right behind the desk. Bookshelves lined the wall with some of the shelves displaying pictures while others held books.

Greyson moved over to the shelves and picked up one of the pictures. A young woman with long dark hair stood next to Alpha Lawerence. The woman was in a wedding dress. Both had forced smiles on their faces, and Greyson knew the woman was his mother on her wedding day.

He replaced the picture before turning to face the room. Alpha Lawerence was taking a seat behind his desk while Isaac, Drake, and Luther were sitting in chairs against the wall opposite of where Greyson stood. Matthew was examining a few pictures on a nearby shelf.

"I heard you boys had a foot race back to the castle." Greyson turned his attention back to Alpha Lawerence as he broke the silence. "Was there a reason you did not shift? Matthew, are you able to shift yet or just do not have the ability?" he asked curiously.

"No, sir. I can shift." Matthew answered as he continued looking at the pictures. "Grey didn't want to freak your men out."

"All of my guards are Shifters. Why would shifting freak my men out?" Alpha Lawerence asked confused.

"Sir, if I may?" Drake sat forward. The Alpha King motioned for him to continue. "The Hunt brothers have unique shifts. Both are Alphas."

Alpha Lawerence's eyes went wide as he turned his attention back to Greyson and Matthew. "Both Alphas?" he asked quietly. Greyson shrugged as Matthew turned around.

"That's what we have been told. The truth is, in Arlania wolf Shifters are not common. Those that are wolf Shifters are all about the same size. We are bigger than they are, but I'm not really sure what all the fuss is about." Matthew moved to one of the two chairs in front of the desk and sat comfortably.

"Alphas are not very common. It's usually passed down through families. To have two born within the same family has never happened." Luther explained.

Greyson's earlier feeling of urgency returned. He needed to get going. "As good as it has been to catch up with lost family members, I am in a hurry." Greyson moved to stand behind the empty chair next to Matthew. "Drake and Luther convinced me to stop here first to ask for your assistance."

Alpha Lawerence sat forward with interest. "What do you need my help with?"

"Alpha Maddox's Beta has taken an interest in Greyson's wife. He has ordered all the guards to prevent her from leaving the Howling Meadows Pack. She had made it clear to Cain that she was married and uninterested in him, but he has not taken the hint." Matthew answered.

"In her letter, she said he went from annoying stalker to making threats." Greyson ran a hand through his hair. "I need to get to her as quickly as possible."

"You came here to ask for my army to save your wife?" The Alpha King asked.

"No, I came here to ask for any assistance you are willing to give." Greyson shook his head before meeting Alpha Lawerence's eyes. "My goal is to remove Alpha Maddox from power, rescue my wife, and liberate all those who are suffering under Maddox's command." Greyson paused for a moment. "However, my first priority is getting my wife to safety. Once she is safe, I will take out Maddox."

"I see." Alpha Lawerence said. "What makes you think you can remove Maddox from power? Many have tried to in the past. I have even tried, but with my daughter's life at risk, I haven't been able to do much."

"Greyson has a unique skill set." Matthew laughed. "With a distraction, he could probably get into the pack, eliminate Maddox and Cain, and leave with his wife without an issue."

"You are ridiculous, Matt." Greyson smacked the back of his brother's head.

"Greyson is very skilled in combat and spy work." Isaac spoke for the first time since entering the castle.

"I would be happy to have you host my men while I go on alone if need be." Greyson said, ignoring Isaac. "But I wouldn't complain if you were willing to send some men with me."

"We can't just walk in and demand they give Alice back." Isaac said, shaking his head.

The office went silent for a few minutes. All lost in their own thoughts as they tried to think of a plan. "Why couldn't we?" Matthew asked with a smile.

Chapter 19

Matthew's plan was ridiculous. Greyson stomped up the stairs following one of the maids, as she led him to his room. Greyson and the others had been hashing out a plan for hours in Alpha Lawerence's office. The maid opened a door and stepped aside for Greyson to enter.

Once inside, he took a quick look around. The room was big and spacious. Thick, heavy curtains were pulled across the window. A large four poster bed sat against the wall to his left. A bathtub was sitting in the middle of the room full of steaming hot water.

Greyson made sure the door was locked before taking a quick bath. He found clean clothes sitting on the end of the bed. Once dressed, He paced around the area. A knock came at his door, and he wondered who was there. It was getting late, and he figured everyone would be winding down for the night.

He pulled the door open and was surprised to see all his men waiting in the hall. Greyson took a step back and gestured for them to come inside. "I would have thought you all would be resting, considering the last several days." Greyson said as he closed the door.

"We want to know what the plan is." Bear said as he crossed his arms over his chest.

Greyson took in all his men. Matthew had plopped down on Greyson's bed, tucking his hands behind his head, and crossing his ankles. Isaac was sitting in a chair near the window while the others spread themselves throughout the room. All were listening intently.

"We will be leaving for the Howling Meadows Pack in two days. Alpha Lawerence has agreed to assist us." Greyson's announcement was met with smiles and cheers. "Tomorrow we will be gathering supplies and preparing for travel. It will take us three days to get to Howling Meadows from here. So, rest up, men. I will need you at your best."

The men nodded before leaving his room. Isaac and Matthew stayed behind. Greyson let out a heavy breath and ran his hand through his hair. He knew that tomorrow's preparation was needed before they traveled with such a large group, but he still didn't like it. The extra day, on top of the three days to get there, seemed way too long to get to Alice.

"She is fine, Grey." Isaac spoke softly. "She has become an incredible fighter over the last two years." Greyson nodded but did not say anything as he clenched and unclenched his fists.

"Alice really has become quite the little warrior." Matt said from the bed. "When she made it back to the Talford's and started training again, I could tell you had been working with her. Her first spar with Luke ended with his broken nose." Matthew chuckled. "I don't know who was more surprised, Alice or Luke."

"She was good even before I started working with her." Greyson mumbled.

"Yeah, she was good before, but she can almost best me now." Matt got to his feet. All traces of his normal teasing gone. "Alice has taken what you taught her and has put everything into perfecting it over the last year. She will be fine until we get there."

"I cannot shake this overwhelming need to get to her as quickly as possible. I am tempted to leave in the morning and meet everyone there." Greyson admitted.

"You know that you have to be here tomorrow, Grey. Our plan depends on it." Isaac pointed out. Greyson sighed and sank down on the edge of the bed. He leaned forward so that his elbows rested on his knees. "Grey, Alice's best chance is for you to follow the plan."

"I know, Lord Isaac. I know." Greyson said in defeat.

"You will see your lady love in no time." A mischievous glint entered Matthew's eye. "If I were you, I would prepare for a scuffle. She is so mad at you. You should have heard her cursing you for not making it back to the bunker and leaving her behind. And then when she found out you were alive, she was cursing you for making her think you were dead for so long."

"It is not like I stayed away on purpose. The dungeons have something in the walls that prevent Shifters from being able to shift. Their cuffs and chains are the same way." Greyson shook his head. "After I was shot, I blacked out. When I woke up, I was in a cave with Bradley. He tried to get me to tell him where Alice was. When I refused, I was drugged and transported to Alpha Maddox. Not only was I unable to shift, but they made sure I was unable to fight back."

"Your torture?" Matthew asked.

"Yeah, I was given the privilege of frequent trips to have information extracted. For months, I was not able to get up or move around. That is when I was assigned two guards, that I assumed, were there to keep them from killing me. After another couple weeks, I was able to do some pushups to try to get back into shape." Greyson clarified and he stood back up. He made his way to the window, pulled back the curtain, and looked out into the darkness of night.

"We know that, and I think she does too. But she is still upset with you." Isaac moved to his side and patted his shoulder. "It really is good to have you back, Grey. I am going to bed so that I can leave at first light. I will fly to check on Alice and report back as soon as I can."

"Thank you, Lord Isaac." Greyson gave him a small smile.

He watched as Isaac and Matthew left for their own rooms. Greyson blew out the candles around his room and laid down on the bed. He hoped that Isaac could get to Alice quickly and find her well.

Greyson needed to be patient. Isaac was right. Tomorrow was crucial in their plan to overthrow Maddox and save Alice. He had waited a year to see her, he could wait four more days.

Greyson tossed and turned all night. He was too restless to fall asleep. He gave up on trying to rest as the sky began to lighten. He made his way through the halls silently and slipped through the front door. The cool morning air calmed him a little. Taking a deep breath, Greyson began jogging around the perimeter of the castle. With each lap around the building, he increased his speed. Greyson was lost in his thoughts as he rounded the fourth corner, once again at the front of the castle. He nearly collided with someone, but quickly dove to the side, rolling to his feet.

Isaac stood there with both brows raised. Greyson glanced at the sky and noticed that the sun was just peaking over the horizon. "You off?" he asked, slightly winded from his run.

"Yes. I should get there late tonight or early tomorrow morning. With luck, I should meet you along the way in two days." Isaac nodded.

"You haven't left yet?" Matthew's voice called from the top of the stairs.

"I am leaving now." Isaac smiled over at Matthew. "You two take care of each other and I will see you in a few days." Isaac did not wait for them to respond as he shifted into his hawk and took flight.

Greyson watched until he could no longer see Isaac, feeling jealous that he couldn't leave at that moment. "Luther told me where their training grounds are. Let's go work off some of your anxious energy." Matt said as he came up beside Greyson.

He nodded and followed Matt down a path through the trees. They walked for a mile before the path stopped in a large clearing. It was set up similar to the training grounds at Trevor's Cove with multiple sparring arenas, punching bags and other equipment. Without having to say anything, they moved together to the punching bags and began warming up. Greyson smiled as he, for the first time in over a year, started his old routine. The familiar actions helped calm him.

"Before the others arrive, we should spar for old times' sake. I am curious to see how much captivity has deadened your skill." Matthew chuckled.

Greyson rolled his eyes but followed him to the nearest ring. "Are we pulling punches?"

"We better. Especially since you are wanting me fit enough to help rescue Alice." Matt shook out his arms with a grin. "Knock out to win." Greyson smirked at his brother. He needed this.

Both Matthew and Greyson were dripping sweat as they broke apart again. Greyson had no idea how long they had been at it, but neither was willing to concede. Matthew had a split lip from Greyson's attempt to knock him out. Greyson's nose was bleeding from Matt's last kick to his face.

Greyson could tell that Matthew's stamina was beginning to fade, which meant he was going to try to take Greyson to the ground. Sure enough, Matt charged, and Greyson let himself be tackled to the ground. Before Matt could recover, Greyson grabbed Matt's right arm as he threw his leg over Matt's head. He used his other leg to hold his first leg in position and squeezed. Matt struggled against the triangle hold, but after a few seconds his body slackened.

Greyson released his hold and scooted back. He chuckled as he rolled Matthew onto his back and checked his pulse. It was beating strong. Greyson sat back, breathing hard, and wiped the blood off his face. Clapping sounded and he looked up to see dozens of men watching them.

Greyson got to his feet as he scanned the assembled men. When had they gotten there? Alpha Lawerence stepped up to the side of the ring followed by Luther, Drake, Bear, and Samuel.

"You two are quite competitive." Alpha Lawerence chuckled. "Have you two always been like this?"

"Not always." Greyson looked back at Matthew who was beginning to come back around.

Matthew swore as he sat up and shook his head slowly. "You let me tackle you on purpose. I walked right into your trap. Again." He looked up at Greyson with a glare before realizing they had an audience. "Oh, good morning."

Greyson reached a hand down to help Matthew to his feet. "Alpha Lawerence was just asking if we have always been so competitive." Greyson brought Matthew up to speed on what had happened while he was out, when he saw Matt's confused expression.

"No. This was probably the closest I have ever been to besting Grey." Matthew dusted the dirt off his pants. "He has gotten slow over the last year or so."

"That is impressive. I would bet either one of you could beat any man here." Alpha Lawerence chuckled. "How about in your wolf forms?"

"I can hold my own." Greyson said.

"I haven't fought in wolf form." Matthew said at the same time. "But I have fought Shifters before."

"Hmm. Then you had better get some training done now and as we travel, Matt. Your fighting skills as a wolf are crucial." Alpha Lawerence reminded them.

Matthew nodded his head. "I was just going to ask Grey if he would work with me. But why are so many people here?"

"When neither of you showed up for breakfast, Luther remembered telling you about the training grounds. And knowing Greyson's habit of working out, we came looking for you. Word spread about a fight taking place between the new Alpha and his Beta. More and more showed up to see your skill levels." Drake answered with a smile. "To say you were holding out on us at Trevor's Cove, is an understatement."

"If Lars had known you could fight like that..." Bear's voice trailed off as he shook his head.

"I am aware." Greyson said dryly. "Now, why don't we get the men working on preparations to leave at first light." Greyson gave Luther and Drake a pointed look and they gave quick nods before disappearing into the crowd.

Alpha Lawerence, too, turned to the crowd and began issuing orders to several men. Greyson turned back to Matthew, who was dabbing at his lip. "I can't believe I still can't beat you."

Greyson laughed. "Let's shift and get you ready for the Howling Meadows Pack."

Matthew quickly shifted, shaking out his salt and pepper fur and wagging his tail. Greyson glanced around, noting that many of the men were still lingering. They were not doing a good job at concealing their curiosity over Matthew and Greyson. Refocusing on Matthew, Greyson shifted into his wolf. He immediately felt all eyes focused on him and he growled softly.

"Let us start with just sparring. I need to see where you are at, so we know where to go from here." He said through the mind-link to Matthew.

"You cannot blame them for being curious, Grey. We are the grandsons of the Alpha King, and your wolf is quite large." Matthew commented as he lunged at Greyson.

"Just focus on training." Greyson growled back.

Greyson was impressed with Matthew's natural fighting instinct. Charlie had helped train Greyson as a wolf. He had told Greyson much the same. His wolf instincts were strong, and he required little training in his wolf form.

After an hour, Greyson wanted to see how Matthew faired in a skirmish with another wolf. He mind-linked Bear to join them. Greyson stayed in his wolf form as he watched Matthew dominate the match.

Drake sparred with Matthew next, with Matthew once again pinning his opponent quickly. "Very good. I don't think you will need much help, Matt."

They all shifted back to their human forms. The three of them walked back to the castle to get something to eat. Matthew had a big smile on his face and his eyes were bright with excitement. Drake offered some advice to Matt, who listened intently.

As they entered the entryway, Samuel, Luther's father called out to Greyson. Grey motioned his brother and Drake to go ahead without him, before walking over to Samuel. "What can I do for you, Samuel?" Greyson asked the older man.

"The Alpha King wishes to speak with you. He is in his office." Samuel bowed before moving down the hall that led to the dining room.

Greyson let out a sigh as he headed for Alpha Lawerence's office. When he got to the heavy wood door, he paused and took a deep breath before knocking. When he heard the call to enter, he turned the knob and stepped inside. Alpha Lawerence looked up from his desk and smiled at Greyson.

"Come in." He gestured to the chairs in front of his desk.

Greyson closed the door before crossing the room to a chair. He took a seat and leaned back. He eyed the man across the desk expectantly, but Alpha Lawerence did not speak immediately. The silence continued to stretch on, and Greyson decided he was not going to speak first. The Alpha King asked him here, so he could break the silence.

After several minutes, Alpha Lawerence let out a heavy sigh. "Greyson, I am going to be honest with you. I am getting old." Greyson raised a brow in question but did not say anything. "I have been impressed with your men's loyalty to you and your character."

"We have known each other for less than a day, sir. There is no way you can know my character." Greyson cut in.

"I have spoken quite a bit with Drake and Luther. I trust them completely. Not only are you a good man, but you possess the skills needed to protect and serve a pack." Alpha Lawerence continued.

"What are you getting at, sir?" Greyson crossed his arms over his chest as he scowled at the man.

"What I am trying to say, Greyson, is that I want to pass my title and pack down to you." Silence followed Alpha Lawerence's statement.

Greyson laughed without humor. "You cannot be serious. I didn't ask to be Alpha of the pack I am in charge of now. I have no aspirations to be an Alpha, let alone the Alpha King." Greyson got to his feet and began pacing. "I am sorry sir, but I think you need to think of someone else."

"You being humble and not wanting power makes you the best choice, Greyson." Alpha Lawerence stood as well. "Matthew can still be your Beta." Greyson continued to shake his head. "Look, the title of Alpha King can only be passed on to a descendant. If not you, it will be passed to my daughter's husband by default upon my death. Alpha Maddox would assume the throne."

Greyson stopped his pacing and looked at Alpha Lawerence. "What about Matthew? He too is your grandson and is an Alpha."

"Matthew too would work splendidly, but you are the eldest. If you wish, we can call him in here and ask his opinion." Greyson nodded while swallowing hard.

He did not want to be the Alpha King. All he wanted was to get Alice. He mind-linked Matthew to come to the Alpha King's office immediately. They waited in silence, Greyson continued to eye the King while he observed Greyson from his spot behind the desk. It felt like an eternity before a knock sounded at the door and Matthew walked in. As soon as he saw his brother, Greyson let out a sigh of relief.

Matthew moved to the chair Greyson had been sitting in with a curious expression. "You have the same look you had when Lord Isaac and Sir

Lance suggested you marry Alice and be her bodyguard." Matthew said with a half-smile. "What now?"

"As Alpha King, I can only pass the title down to a descendant. That leaves my daughter's husband or one of you two." Alpha Lawerence said while glancing between the two of them.

Matthew sat quietly for a moment before laughing. "Congratulations, Grey. You will be perfect!" Matt jumped to his feet with a wide smile. "You have no desire for power, and you are fiercely protective of those under your care."

"No, Matt." Greyson said firmly. "You."

"Me? Don't be ridiculous. I am far too young to take on such a role. Plus, I pledged my loyalty to you. I will follow you wherever you lead, big brother." He paused, thinking for a moment. "You were asked to be the Alpha King, but are trying to pass it off to me, aren't you?" Matthew narrowed his eyes at Greyson.

Alpha Lawerence laughed, and Greyson scowled. "I don't want it." Greyson said firmly.

"That is why you will take it." Matthew said as he moved to stand in front of Greyson, putting a hand on his shoulder. "I know you do not like being put in these positions, Grey. But that is why you are perfect for them. All you ever want to do is protect those around you. You are loyal and just. Your wolf is bigger than any I have seen, which I hear is a big deal." Matthew gave Greyson a teasing smile. "You can't expect Gramps to live forever."

Greyson looked away from Matthew to Alpha Lawerence, who watched them closely. Greyson's shoulders sagged in defeat. He knew he could not say no. Matthew was right, the King would not live forever. He hung his head as the weight of the responsibility of being the Alpha King started to settle on him. He felt out of his depths being placed as Alpha over fifteen men, how would he ever manage the First Moon Pack and all of Valencia.

"Fine. You win. But you will be my Beta, Matthew." Greyson finally grumbled.

"I can live with that." Matthew said, squeezing Greyson's shoulder. "And as your Beta, I suggest Gramps be kept on as an advisor. His knowledge will be invaluable."

"I accept those terms." Alpha Lawerence moved around the desk and extended his hand to shake Greyson's with a smile. Greyson slowly took the proffered hand, and the two men shook on it. "Now, we need to gather the pack together so that I can formally hand down the title. After the exchange of power, it is tradition to shift and take a run with the pack. However, with the current circumstances, I think we could get away with shifting and allowing the pack members to greet you."

Greyson listened dumbly. What had he just agreed to? And he didn't give Alice a say in this. Not that he really had one either. He and Matt left the office and headed for Greyson's room. They cleaned themselves up from training and Matthew encouraged Greyson to eat. If anyone asked what he ate, he would not have been able to tell them. An hour later, Greyson followed Matthew back downstairs and out onto the porch.

Alpha Lawerence, Drake, Luther, Samuel, and three other men were waiting. Alpha Lawerence gave him a nod before leading the group down the steps and down a path that led away from the training grounds. Greyson followed wordlessly at the back of the group. He was tempted to sneak off and head for the Howling Meadows Pack, get Alice and disappear. He was not at all prepared for such a huge responsibility.

Before he could take off, they arrived at a large open field. Greyson stopped when he saw the number of people gathered. Matthew noticed his hesitation and moved to his side. He grabbed his arm and started to drag him forward.

Greyson swallowed hard as Matthew tugged him up two steps onto a wooden stage. Greyson had not noticed that Alpha Lawerence was already addressing the crowd. Matthew gave him a small shove forward so that he was standing next to Alpha Lawerence.

"Do you, Alpha Greyson, accept the responsibility to provide, protect and guide the First Moon Pack? And to take on the responsibilities of the Alpha King?" Alpha Lawerence spoke loudly.

"I do." Greyson managed to say. Just like when his men had sworn their loyalty to him in the woods, Greyson felt the connection of hundreds of people in his mind. He stumbled back a step and grabbed his head.

Alpha Lawerence was at his side in a flash. "Block them, Grey." He was saying. "Put up a mental block around your mind." Greyson did and the presence of so many people in his head faded. "You can have the mind-link closed so that only you can use it if you wish. You can also allow for free mind-linking among the pack so that anyone can use it."

Greyson nodded in understanding. "I want my pack to be able to communicate with one another, but still have their privacy."

"I will explain how later. But now, my King, it is time for you to shift and meet your pack members." Lawerence smiled at Greyson.

Greyson took a deep breath as he moved away to get more space. He shifted and there was a collective gasp. Greyson looked out over the crowd.

Lawerence shifted next, followed by Matthew. Greyson looked over at them. Lawerence was a dark brown wolf that was slightly bigger than Matthew. Matt's tail wagged as he moved closer to Greyson.

"Why so happy, Matt?" Greyson grumbled. He was not feeling particularly happy about his new position.

"You are even bigger than Gramps." Matt's laughter reached through the mind-link.

Greyson looked back at Lawerence's wolf. Lawerence bowed his head to Greyson. Greyson looked out over the crowd and noticed that all the assembled pack members had shifted into their wolves as well.

The rest of the evening went by in a blur. Greyson greeted each member and talked with them through the mind-link. Not one person seemed unhappy with the change of King. By the time he had spoken with each person and retired to his room, Greyson felt even more inadequate. He was now responsible for close to two hundred people. He let out a puff of air as he lay down on his bed.

He was leaving the previous Beta, Samuel, in charge of the pack while the rest of them left first thing in the morning. He needed rest before they started the long journey. Greyson closed his eyes and tried to sleep.

Chapter 20

Alice sat on her window seat and watched as the lights around the pack turned on one at a time as day turned to night. Queen Isabel and Alice had spent time practicing throwing daggers after lunch before studying the books Alice's great grandmother had given her.

They had gone over the books each day for the past week. They both felt confident that in order to break the power trapped within the Guardian's Stone, Alice and Greyson needed to be together and a sacrifice that proved their love had to be made.

Alice cracked open the window to allow the breeze to filter into her room. She closed her eyes and took a deep breath of the ocean breeze. She had grown to love the salty air of this area. She had never seen the ocean until she traveled here and found she had a connection to it.

She only wished she could visit the beach and step into the rolling waves. To feel the power of the sea and the sand under her feet. Gwen told her that there is no other feeling like it. Alice leaned her head out the window to try to catch the faint sound of the surf.

An owl hooted and Alice smiled sadly as she opened her eyes. There was an owl at Greyson's and her home. Alisha had found the night bird fascinating and they had spent several nights in whispered conversation as they listened to its hooting. Her nightmare of the kids' abduction resurfaced causing Alice's heart to beat painfully in her chest. She prayed it was just a dream and not a vision.

A hawk's cry cut through the night air. Alice cocked her head as she listened. She must have been mistaken. Hawks do not hunt at night. The cry came again, and Alice rotated on her bench to peer more intently out the window.

A hawk landed on the outside windowsill, startling Alice. She gasped as she studied the bird as it watched her. It tried to walk into the room, but Queen Isabel's magic barrier prevented its entrance.

"There is a magic barrier." Alice said quietly. The bird cocked its head at her, and she smiled. This hawk had to be Uncle Isaac. "Stay here." Alice ran from the room to find the queen.

Queen Isabel, unfortunately, was not in her room and Alice felt a wave of disappointment. Without Isabel allowing her uncle permission, he would not be able to cross the barrier. She wouldn't be able to know if they were able to free Greyson yet. With slumped shoulders, Alice returned to the window bench and sat down slowly.

"Queen Isabel is not in her room. Without her, you cannot cross the barrier." Alice gave an apologetic smile. The bird cocked its head again and Alice realized that he could not hear her. Leaning her head back out the window, Alice tried again. "It is good to see you again."

The bird rubbed its head against her cheek. Alice gave the hawk a kiss on top of its head. "There is a protective barrier around my room. Only the queen can allow your entrance." Alice whispered. There were no windows close by that would allow for any eavesdroppers, but she still kept her voice low anyway. "How is Matthew?" The bird dipped its head. Alice took that as Matthew was fine. "And..." Alice swallowed. "Have you seen...him?" The bird dipped his head again.

Alice let out a relieved sigh. "I am guessing you have come to check on my well-being?" The hawk gave a small chirp and rubbed her face again. She smiled, wishing she could have her uncle wrap her in a hug. She missed his familiar comfort. "I am fine for the most part. I am now having to stay in my room. Cain has become..." She paused, searching for the right word. "Possessive." She finally settled on. "As long as I stay in here, he can't get to me." She paused and bit her lip. "Please hurry back, Uncle. I am concerned that Cain will not be put off much longer."

The hawk froze as he watched her. He gave her another quick squawk before taking flight. Alice quickly lost her uncle in the darkness of the sky. She prayed her uncle and Matt would come and get her soon. Even if Greyson was still stuck at Trevor's Cove. She knew he could take care of himself, but she was starting to feel helpless. A noise behind her pulled her attention from the window to the connecting door. Queen Isabel stood there with her characteristic smile.

"Good evening, Alison." She greeted as she moved farther into Alice's room.

"Good evening, Isabel." Alice returned her smile. "I had a visitor while you were down at dinner." Alice pulled the window closed before turning and facing Isabel. Isabel's progress halted as her eyes widened in surprise and worry. "My uncle is a hawk Shifter. He came to the window." Alice glanced behind her.

"Oh." Isabel blinked a few times before she continued to cross the room and sat next to Alice. "What did he have to say?"

"I'm not sure what he planned on saying, but as it stands, he said nothing." Alice answered.

"He flew all the way here to you, but said nothing?" Isabel asked, confused.

"The barrier prevented him from entering the room and there was no room for him to shift on the ledge." Alice explained. "I am positive that he came to make sure that I am doing okay. If they had freed Greyson, the three of them would have come together. I told him I was safe for the time being, but to hurry their return. I feel an urgency to get away from here."

"Cain was asking about you again at dinner. He once again tried to get permission to visit you, but I denied him." Isabel grabbed Alice's hand. "I agree we need to get you away from Cain and Maddox as soon as possible. I will speak with Gwen tomorrow to see if she has any ideas on how to smuggle you past the gate." Alice nodded.

The mood in the room was heavy and Alice searched her mind desperately for something to say to lighten it. She hated the depressive feelings that always came with talk of Cain. She could not stand the man. Isabel put her arms around Alice in a quick hug. She kissed Alice's temple before getting to her feet. "Do not worry, dear. We will figure this out. Go to sleep and get some rest. I will see you in the morning."

Isabel's maternal behavior caused a lump to form in Alice's throat. She watched as the matriarch left the room, closing the door behind her. Alice changed into Greyson's shirt and climbed under the covers. Greyson's scent on the shirt was no longer detectable, but wearing it still brought her comfort. It was almost like having his arms around her.

A tear escaped her eye, but she didn't bother to wipe it away. It had been three months since she had seen her family and she missed them terribly. She missed her mother and her comforting words, but having Isabel's loving presence eased the ache a little.

Alice rolled over, pulling the blankets tighter around her. She hated sleeping alone. Back at her parents' house, Alice had started having one of the dogs join her in her bed. Greyson's strong, protective arms had ruined sleep for her. Without him next to her she felt cold and alone, making it nearly impossible to get a good night's sleep.

Alice gratefully welcomed the sun. It had been three days since her uncle had visited her and she was becoming more and more restless. Why hadn't Isaac and Matt come back yet? Alice shook the question from her mind and got dressed in a light blue dress.

This was her favorite dress the Queen had purchased for her. The color matched her eyes perfectly. Not only that but the skirts wrapped around her in a way that allowed for a lot of movement. She could even fight in it if she needed to. Alice wore her training pants under the dress just in case. She sheathed her daggers as she moved to the connecting door.

Queen Isabel was sitting in front of the fireplace reading a book when Alice walked in. She did not hesitate as she moved quickly across the room and sat next to Isabel on the couch. They had become so comfortable with one another that Isabel didn't even look up from her book as she mumbled a greeting. Alice smiled as she picked up her own book off the side table where she had left it the day before. Breakfast came and went in comfortable silence.

A knock sounded at the door, and they looked at each other with furrowed brows. After a brief pause, Alice ran to her room as Queen Isabel slowly walked to the door. Alice waited just out of sight, straining to hear who was at the door. She heard nothing. After several minutes, Queen Isabel came into Alice's room. Isabel's face was slightly pale as she looked at her.

"We have been summoned by the Alpha to the main field." Isabel said quietly. Her posture was full of anxiety.

Alice's heart rate accelerated, and she swallowed down the lump in her throat. "He asked for me as well?" Alice asked as she tried to cover her rising anxiety.

A nod from Isabel and she closed her eyes for a brief moment. Steeling herself, Alice gave Isabel a reassuring smile. They headed out the door and twenty minutes later they approached the main field.

Alice looked around with wide eyes at the sheer number of people gathered. What was going on? It was a beautiful clear day, maybe there was some sort of festival. But she quickly shook the thought away. Queen Isabel would have known about a festival.

At their approach, the crowd slowly parted allowing them to pass. It took a few minutes, but they finally made it through the crowd, emerging into the clearing. Alpha Maddox and Cain stood speaking with an older man. Queen Isabel gasped, and her steps faltered.

The men turned as they heard Alice and the Queen approach. Cain's sickening grin spread on his face as his eyes landed on Alice, and she shuddered. Alpha Maddox's smile was forced as he gestured them forward.

As they approached the men, the older gentleman's eyes remained on Queen Isabel.

"Hello, my daughter." He said, his voice thick with emotion when they finally reached him.

Isabel took a quick step towards him, and he hugged her tightly. Pulling back, he kissed her cheek. Queen Isabel moved back to Alice's side, wiping her cheeks.

"Now that the ladies have arrived, Alpha Lawerence, what brings you to the Howling Meadows Pack?" Alpha Maddox's gruff voice broke the tender moment.

"Yes." Alpha Lawerence cleared his throat. "We are here for several items of business, but the Beta of the First Moon Pack has asked if his business can be addressed first."

Alpha Maddox's brows lifted. "I thought Beta Charlie retired years ago and you never filled the position."

"Charlie had been battling a sickness for a long time." Alpha Lawerence nodded. "I did get a new Beta shortly after he left, but this Beta is newly appointed."

"What business does your new Beta have here?" Cain asked, crossing his arms over his chest.

Alpha Lawerence turned his body and focused his attention fully on Cain. "Beta Matthew of the First Moon Pack is here to challenge Beta Cain of the Howling Meadows Pack." The Alpha's voice rose loudly so that everyone could hear the declaration.

Cain sputtered, but Alpha Maddox was the one to speak. "What has Cain done to Beta Matthew that would warrant a formal challenge?" Alpha Maddox asked surprised.

"He has refused to allow my sister to leave this pack, even with the proper paperwork. He has essentially held her prisoner here." Alice watched as Matthew stepped away from the crowd behind Alpha Lawerence. He stood tall with an angry expression.

"I have heard of no such thing." Alpha Maddox spat. "Who is your sister?"

Matthew pointed to Alice, and Alpha Maddox's face jerked in her direction. His eyes widened when he focused on her. He then looked at Cain who glared at Matthew. "I am here to challenge Beta Cain for the release of my sister." Matthew growled, his eyes flashing slightly before returning to their solid amber color.

"Is this true, Cain?" Alpha Maddox whispered harshly. Cain did not say anything as his face reddened and he became more and more angry with the situation. His silence seemed to tell Alpha Maddox all he needed to know. "Very well. The challenge shall take place. Ready yourselves."

Cain stepped up close to Alice and grabbed her before she could step back. He roughly shoved something hard in her hand as he leaned forward. "You will marry me regardless of the outcome of this challenge." He growled close to her ear. He stepped away from her and stalked to the other side of the field.

Alice was shaking slightly as she looked down and opened her hand. A small wooden horse lay on her palm and her breath caught in her throat. Her head snapped up to look at Cain. He was watching her with a satisfied smile on his face and he winked. She looked back down at the horse. Asher's horse. It was so hard for her to draw in a breath.

A hand touched her arm, and she jerked back in surprise. She looked up to see Matthew standing in front of her. Alice threw her arms around his neck, and he hugged her in return. She knew he could feel her trembling because he tightened his hold on her.

"Matt, he has my kids." Alice whispered urgently. "Cain kidnapped my kids."

"What do you mean?" Matthew asked quietly.

"He handed me Asher's favorite toy. He must have them. He said he would force me to marry him if I did not agree to willingly." Alice rushed out.

Matthew pulled back and looked into her eyes. She could tell he was trying to understand what she was talking about. He kissed her forehead and stepped back. "All will be well, Alison."

Alice watched as Matthew moved over to Alpha Lawerence. Queen Isabel grabbed Alice's arm and led her back towards the crowd to clear the field. Alice kept her eyes on Matthew. He talked with Alpha Lawerence for a moment before both men looked over at Alice. Matthew sent her a reassuring nod as Alpha Lawerence stepped back to the side of the field where Matthew had previously been.

"Are you ready, Beta?" Cain's mocking voice called across the field.

Matthew turned to face Cain. "Beta Cain, I am ready if you are."

Cain nodded. Matthew smiled at him and shifted into his wolf. Matthew's wolf shook out his salt and pepper fur. Murmurs echoed through the crowd. "What is this?" Cain yelled looking around. "He isn't a Beta; he is an Alpha."

"I assure you, regardless of his size, he is the Beta of the First Moon Pack." Alpha Lawerence called with a smug smile on his face.

"Continue." Alpha Maddox roared.

Cain shifted into a light brown wolf. He would have been close to her father's wolf's size, but compared to Matthew's wolf, Cain was much smaller. The wolves approached one another, and Alice held her breath. A hand gently touched her elbow and she turned to see two men standing close. Alice was tempted to reach for Isabel but stopped when one of the men spoke.

"Our Alpha and Beta sent us to you." The man said softly. "Please, we need the horse." Alice shook her head as tears began to burn her eyes. The man moved closer to her and spoke even quieter. "Beta Matthew and our Alpha sent us to use the toy to track your kids. We will retrieve them and bring them safely back to you."

Alice observed the men more closely. She did not want to give up her only connection to the kids. She was desperate to keep them safe. She would do anything. Looking into the two men's eyes she could see their sincerity.

She grudgingly handed them the horse. They gave her quick nods before disappearing into the crowd, heading for the pack gates. She prayed they were who they said they were.

Chapter 21

"We have a problem, Grey." Matthew's voice sounded through the mind-link.

Greyson watched from the shadows as Matthew hugged Alice. Jealousy reared its head as he watched them. "What problem?" He growled back.

"Alice is claiming that Cain has her kids. Whatever that means."

Greyson's blood ran cold. "What?" he asked as anxiety grabbed at his chest.

"She said that Cain gave her Asher's favorite toy. He threatened her that he would force her to marry him if she did not willingly do so." Matt's voice became tense as he realized Greyson was shaken by what Alice had said.

Greyson opened the mind-link to Luther and Bear. "My wife was given a toy horse that belongs to our son. Cain gave it to her with a threat. Can you two use the toy to track down our child?" Greyson asked desperately.

"Should be easy enough." Bear answered. Greyson watched from a distance as Luther and Bear began making their way towards Alice. "There will be three children: Two girls and a boy. Alisha, Avery, and Asher. Once you find them, bring them back here."

"Yes, sir." They answered in unison.

Matt shifted and Cain became flustered, but eventually shifted as well. The two wolves began circling each other. Lawerence reminded Greyson to get to the Queen's Garden while the majority of the pack was distracted by the fight. He quickly moved deeper into pack lands. He immediately recognized the tall glass building that Lawerence had told him about.

"Alpha, we have caught the scent of the boy." Luther informed Greyson. "It leads outside the pack lands."

"Find them." Greyson commanded. "I need my kids safe."

Greyson peeked around the corner of the building. Two guards stood next to a metal door. He could easily take them out. He crept along the building. The man closest to him turned and their eyes met. The man's eyes widened in surprise before a smile spread on his lips. "The Silent Prisoner has returned." The man said quietly.

The second man turned quickly. His expression matched the first man's. Greyson moved away from the wall and closer to them. "John, Phil. How are you doing?" Greyson said conversationally. He watched them closely for any sign of either of them being upset to see him.

"Better now that you are here." Phil commented. "You need access to the garden?"

Greyson squinted his eyes as he watched them for a moment. He did not sense any sign of them lying to him. He gave a small nod and Phil quickly unlocked the door. John stepped inside. Phil gestured to him to follow. Hesitantly, Greyson stepped through the door. He was startled at the sudden loss of sound, and he shook his head. A chuckle had his head snapping up. John was smiling at him.

"Disorienting, isn't it?" John asked and Greyson nodded.

The sunlight disappeared and Greyson whirled around to find Phil standing right behind him. The hairs on the back of his neck stood on end. He shifted his body so that he could keep an eye on both men at the same time. John lifted his hands in a gesture of peace.

"Don't get us wrong, we are glad to see you are still alive, but what are you doing back here?" Phil asked.

"I am here for my wife and if I can manage it, remove Alpha Maddox from power." Greyson responded honestly.

"What makes you think you can beat Alpha Maddox?" John asked.

Greyson shrugged. "I have the support of the First Moon Pack and their Alpha." They did not need to know that Greyson was the Alpha now.

It was quiet for several minutes before John stepped closer to Greyson. "A young woman asked a question a few months ago. She asked if I would side with Alpha Maddox or the Silent Prisoner if he came back to challenge the current Alpha." John paused as he locked eyes with Greyson. "I pledge my loyalty to you." He said, and Greyson felt the connection.

"I too, pledge my loyalty to you." Phil said firmly, behind Greyson.

Greyson was taken aback. "You do not even know who I am. Why would you pledge yourselves to me?"

"Queen Isabel saw fit that we protect you and we have come to know your wife. If a woman like her can be so concerned over you, that is enough for me." John said.

Greyson glanced between the two men, not knowing what to say. He cleared his throat. "Well, you should probably know that you have just pledged your loyalty to the Alpha of the First Moon Pack." Greyson said with a crooked smile.

Both men's mouths fell open. Phil was the first one to recover. "Come Alpha, let us get you inside the garden. We need to get back to our post before anyone notices us missing." That snapped John from his surprise, and he unlocked the door behind him.

"Thank you." Greyson said as he stepped from the antechamber. His gaze took in his surroundings.

The garden was filled with so much natural light that Greyson momentarily forgot he was in a building. There were trees, flowers, walking paths, birds and butterflies everywhere he looked. He moved slowly deeper into the garden.

Greyson paused under a large tree near the center and took a deep breath. A swing hung from a tree to his left and he smiled. The kids would love playing in the garden. His smile quickly faded as he remembered his kids were currently being held captive.

After a while, voices pulled him from his thoughts, and he turned around to see who else was in the garden. Two women were stepping away from the door he had entered the garden through. His heart tripped as he recognized Alice. He watched as they moved in his direction, neither one noticing him. His eyes were trained on Alice. Her face was pale, and she looked upset. She shook her head at something the woman said.

Alice stopped suddenly and her head whipped in his direction. Their eyes met, and time seemed to freeze. He took a small step forward. She rushed towards him, and he was prepared to take her in his arms and never let her go. But instead of throwing her arms around him, Greyson got a fist in the face.

He stumbled back a step, taken by surprise. He regained his senses as another one of her fists flew at him. He deflected each attack until he managed to grab her wrists. He gave them a quick tug and she fell against his chest. He wrapped his arms around her, trapping her to him.

She struggled against him and pounded on his chest. "I hate you!" She cried. "I hate you!" She continued trying to hit him.

"I know." He whispered. "Alice, I'm so sorry."

A sob broke from her lips as she sagged against him, and he held her tighter. "I hate you." She whispered again.

Greyson held her until her sobs turned to hiccups. He leaned back but did not let her go. He wiped her tear-streaked face before pressing a kiss to her forehead. "I'm sorry, Princess." He murmured with his lips still touching her skin.

"We should probably get you back up to your room, Alice." A woman said from several feet away. Greyson had forgotten she was there.

Alice rotated in his arms so she could see the woman and nodded. "Okay. You can tell Queen Isabel that I am fine. Thank you, Gwen." The woman nodded with a smile.

Gwen? Drake's Gwen? The woman turned to leave. "Gwen?" He called after her as he let go of Alice only to grab her hand. "Do you know a man named Drake?"

The woman whirled around and stared at him with wide eyes. "He- he is my husband, sir." She stammered out.

"He is at the main field with the First Moon Pack. He is very anxious to find you." Greyson said with a smile. The woman's tears immediately began to flow as she turned and rushed for the door.

Greyson turned his attention back to Alice. She was watching him. Without saying a word to him, she turned and started for a different door. He kept a tight grip on her hand as she led the way up multiple staircases to a pair of large doors.

She opened them and they entered a large bedroom. She did not stop, but continued to another door and led him into another bedroom. Once they were both in, Alice closed the door and locked it. She turned to him with a glare.

"I am still angry with you." She said as she tried to pull her hand from his grasp, but he only tightened his hold.

"Alice, I understand you are angry with me. You have every right to be." Greyson said calmly as he pulled gently on her hand. "But please give me another chance." He stepped a little closer to her.

"You purposely made that man angry enough to shoot you." Alice accused as tears brimmed her eyes.

"I could not risk Bradley finding the hatch door. He had been too close to it. Your safety was too important." Greyson cupped her face with his hand. "And in my defense, I didn't know he had a gun." Alice's chin quivered and Greyson would do anything to take away her pain.

"You have no idea how it felt, Grey." Her voice was soft as she closed her eyes. "I could feel the pain of the bullet in my stomach and then there was nothing. I could not feel anything." A tear escaped and Greyson wiped it away with his thumb. "Then came the dreams."

"What dreams?" Greyson asked confused.

"They started about a month after you disappeared. The first one was of you tied to a post while you were whipped. Then, the next one came a few days later, you were on a table."

"Please tell me you are joking." Greyson said painfully as he squeezed his eyes closed and bowed his head. "Please tell me you didn't see it."

"I had the dreams every few nights for eight months, until I got here." Alice said softly.

"Oh, Alice." Greyson said around the lump in his throat. "I wish I could have prevented you from seeing any of that."

Alice's hand covered the one he still had cupping her face, and he opened his eyes. Sadness filled Alice's eyes and he tried to step away. He couldn't believe she had witnessed the torture he had gone through, and he couldn't bear to see her hurt because of him. Alice wrapped her arms around his torso and buried her face in his chest.

He returned her embrace. They stood there for a long moment. Without thinking, Greyson lowered his face to her neck and breathed deeply. The scent of vanilla filled his nose and he let out a sigh. Oh, how he had missed that smell. Alice squirmed.

"Don't Grey, it tickles." Alice tried to push him away, but he held her firm.

"I missed you." Greyson breathed in her heavenly scent.

"Greyson, please." She giggled. "You can't ask for a second chance and then tickle me." Alice pushed against his chest.

Greyson straightened. "You're right, Ali." He tucked a strand of Alice's hair behind her ear. "I should have asked this in the garden, are you okay? That Cain guy hasn't hurt you, has he?" Greyson studied Alice's face carefully.

Her lips pressed into a thin line. Worry filled her eyes. "Greyson, the kids. He has our kids! We need to find them." She tried to pull away from him again, but he pulled her back to him.

"Everything will be okay. I have my best trackers on their trail now." Greyson soothed.

Alice took a step back, her brows pinching in confusion. "Your best trackers? Those were your men?"

Greyson released Alice and took a few steps towards the window before turning back to her. "It is a very long story, one that I can't wait to tell you. But that will have to wait until later. Right know all you need to know is that Luther and Bear are great at what they do. I would have gone with them, but I must be here for the banquet."

"What banquet?" Alice asked as she bit her lip.

"The Alpha King has come with an announcement. Rumor has it, he is stepping down as Alpha." Greyson gave her a crooked grin.

"Rumors, huh? I am assuming you came here with Matthew who is somehow the Beta of the First Moon Pack." Alice raised her brow and Greyson took a step toward her as he gave a slow nod. "Then wouldn't you know what the announcement would be?" When Greyson only shrugged, Alice stuck her lip out in a pout. "Fine, keep your secrets for now. I didn't sleep well the past year, so I am going to take a rest until said banquet happens."

Greyson watched as Alice headed over to a dresser along the far wall. She pulled out a large black shirt. She turned around with her cheeks pink and cleared her throat. Greyson smiled and gave her a wink before turning his back to her.

Laying down in bed and cuddling with Alice sounded like heaven on earth. He crossed his arms over his chest. He hoped that she would allow him to. He could really use some sleep after the year he had.

"I'm done." Alice's soft voice reached him, and he turned around. She was leaning against the bedpost watching him. Greyson took her in as well. She was wearing a man's shirt. Jealousy burned in his veins. "What's wrong?" Alice asked, taking a small step towards him.

"You are wearing a man's shirt." He said through clenched teeth. He opened and closed his fists, trying to calm himself.

Alice glanced down at the shirt before looking back at him with a coy smile on her face. "I am. Since the owner of the shirt wasn't here, I have been using it to feel the comfort he would bring me. It is almost like having his arms around me."

Greyson's nostrils flared. Who was this man? He couldn't be mad at Alice for moving on, he had been gone for a year, but he still couldn't stop the fierce possessiveness that flooded his system. Alice was his.

Alice watched him closely with amusement in her eyes that only made him more irritated. With a small shrug she turned away from him and climbed into the bed. Greyson stood fuming as he watched her for several minutes.

"Are you going to come lay down or are you going to glare at me while I sleep?" Alice asked with a laugh in her voice. Greyson grumbled under his breath as he settled next to her on the mattress. He lay on his back, careful not to touch her. As soon as he was settled, she spoke again. "I hadn't noticed how important he had become to me until he had to go." She sounded like she was facing away from him.

"I'm glad you found someone you could care so much about." Greyson said stiffly.

He was jostled a little as Alice turned to face him. She propped herself up on one elbow and looked at him with searching eyes. Greyson glanced at her and when their eyes met a smile spread across her face. "I love him."

Greyson's jaw clenched painfully. He struggled to find something to say that was not him yelling or threatening to rip the man's head off. He sat up, and moved so he was sitting on the edge of the bed. "He's a lucky man." He finally grounded out.

Alice remained silent for several minutes as she watched him with her brows raised in surprise. She scooted closer until she was sitting next to him. She ran the back of her hand along his cheek. There was a red mark where she had punched him. Greyson had his eyes closed and she could tell he was trying to remain calm. Alice took her other hand and placed it on his arm.

She concentrated on Greyson, and she sensed multiple injuries. She healed his cheek, his raw and bruised knuckles, and his back. None of the injuries were deep, to her relief. When she was done, Alice laid her head on Greyson's shoulder. He was still tense, and she could feel his anger and frustration.

A laugh finally bubbled out of her. Greyson glowered down at her. When her laughter died down enough to speak, she finally asked. "You don't recognize your own shirt, Grey?"

Greyson's head snapped to the side to look at her fully. Her eyes still sparkled with humor as she watched him. His shirt? She was wearing *his* shirt? Greyson twisted toward her as he continued to study her. "My shirt?" he asked dumbly.

Alice laughed again. "Yes, Grey. I am wearing your shirt. It used to have your scent on it but that faded weeks ago. It was the only way I was able to get any sleep." She admitted as her cheeks reddened in embarrassment at her admission.

Greyson scooted closer to her, still trying to wrap his head around what she had said. "You love me?" he asked slowly.

Alice's eyes filled with tears, and she nodded. "Yes. I love you."

Greyson pulled her into his lap and pressed his lips to hers. She kissed him back as she wound her arms around his neck. Greyson pulled back just enough to look into her eyes. "Alice, I love you. Since the day I saw you sitting on that rock above the river." Alice smiled. She pulled his head back down and pressed her lips back to his.

Chapter 22

Alice lay with her head on Greyson's chest. He had a large scar that ran along his ribs and she slowly traced it with her finger. Greyson had his arms wrapped around her, holding her close. One of his hands was combing through her hair. She had never felt more at peace than she felt at this moment.

He pressed a kiss to her forehead. He gently grabbed her hand that was tracing the scar and brought it to his lips. He froze for a second before speaking. "When did you get a ring?"

"Matt bought it for me." Alice turned and rested her chin on his chest as she looked into his eyes. "We really didn't have enough time to get one, and women can't walk around without an escort here, unless they are married. So, I thought it best if I had one." She smiled.

"If you want, we can get a different one." Greyson brushed the hair back from Alice's face.

Alice rolled more on top of Greyson before pressing her lips to his. Greyson's arms wrapped around her. "Not a chance." She whispered against his lips. "Sapphires are my favorite stone and I love this ring."

He gently removed the ring off her finger and Alice pulled back in surprise. "If you are wanting to keep this ring, I at least get to put it on you." Grey smiled before kissing her again. Alice couldn't help but laugh as Greyson slowly slid the ring back on her finger. She pressed her lips back to his. Grey tangled his hand in her hair as he deepened the kiss while his other ran down her back.

*   *   *

Alice was once again laying with her head on Greyson's shoulder. His breathing was starting to deepen as his body became more relaxed. Alice bit her lips as she debated, should she disturb him or let him rest?

"Grey?" she asked softly.

"Hmm?" His chest rumbled under her head. He pressed a kiss to her forehead.

"A month ago, I had a dream about the kids." She said and he pulled her closer. "It was late at night and there were several men in the trees outside the Finn's store. I heard breaking glass and then the bottom floor was on fire. I ran to the stairs at the back that led to the living quarters, but I stopped as the door opened. Two men were forcing the kids from the building. Alisha was carrying Avery. All of them were crying. Alisha was screaming and begging for them to go back in to save their grandparents." Greyson's arms tightened around her. "The men laughed and one of them said that the flames couldn't hurt what isn't alive."

Alice buried her face against Greyson as he held her tight. "We will get them back soon, Love." He kissed her temple. "Tracking them down might take a few hours, but once they are found, Luther and Bear will be able to bring them back quickly."

Alice nodded but didn't say anything. Greyson's faith in his two men boosted her confidence that they would find the kids. She began to relax again as she cuddled with Greyson. His fingers slowly ran along the length of her spine. His palms were rough compared to the softness of her skin, but she loved the feel of it. A knock sounded at her door, and she jumped.

"Alice?" Matthew's voice called tentatively through the door.

"Yes?" Her voice squeaked. Matthew could not see her like this. What would he say if he saw her in bed with Greyson. She tried to scoot away from him, but Greyson held her to him as he chuckled softly.

"Is Greyson in there?" Matt asked.

"I'm here, Matt." Greyson called as he rolled over so that he was laying on top of her. "You are my wife, Alice. We are doing nothing wrong." He whispered close to her ear.

"Grey, we can't." Alice's protest was cut off as he kissed her. She ran her fingers through his hair as she kissed him back.

"Good. You haven't been responding to my mind-links." Matt fell silent and Alice tried her hardest not to giggle as Greyson's attention moved from her lips to her neck. "Can I come in?" Matthew asked.

"What do you need, Matt?" Greyson asked between kisses.

"Queen Isabel has sent me up here to escort Alice down to the banquet."

Greyson let out a groan as he lifted his head. "We are getting up now. Give us ten minutes and you can take her down." He pressed one last kiss to Alice's lips before getting out of bed and putting on his pants. Alice lay there as she watched him pull on his boots. He glanced over his shoulder at her, and grinned. "Come on, Alice. You need to get dressed, too."

"I was actually thinking of going like this." Alice said without moving. She hid her smile as she saw Greyson's eyes flicker. He slowly crawled over to her. He caged her between his arms and lowered himself to just before kissing her.

"Please get dressed, Love." He whispered. "You are mine and I am not sharing."

Alice lifted herself up until her lips touched his for a brief kiss. "Fine, but you should know that I hate having to wear dresses."

"When this is over, you can put my shirt back on." Greyson kissed her again before locating his shirt on the floor.

Alice got out of bed and began gathering her clothes. She felt Greyson's eyes on her, and she smiled at him. She dressed quickly, pulling the blue dress back on. She had Greyson button up the back of her dress before she started sheathing her daggers. Greyson gave her a crooked grin as she tucked one up in her hair. When she finished, she turned fully to Greyson.

"You look stunning, Princess." Greyson pulled her close and kissed her. "But we need to get going. I have to get down there soon."

He pulled her from her room and into Isabel's. Matthew sat waiting on the couch and stood as they entered. He looked between them a few times before smiling. "Glad to see she didn't kill you, Grey. When you didn't respond to the mind-link, I got worried."

Greyson laughed. "I was busy."

"I can see that." Matthew said with a smirk as he touched his neck just below his ear. "You both have a little something right here."

Greyson turned to face Alice with furrowed brows and then he blushed slightly. His reaction to Matthew's teasing made her nervous. Why were they both looking at her like that? Greyson moved to her side and leaned close to her ear. "Sorry, Love. I may have left a mark on your neck."

Alice gasped as she covered her neck where she knew Greyson had favored kissing her over the last couple of hours. "Greyson Hunt." She complained as her face heated.

"Don't worry sis, it's just another sign that you are off limits." Matthew laughed. "And you can't really be mad when Grey has one too."

"Okay, Matt. That's enough." Greyson put an arm around Alice and pulled her up against him. She could feel his protectiveness kick in. "How was the fight?"

"Easier than some of my sparring matches with Bear. Cain was so freaked out by my wolf that I practically won before it began. I pinned him down just like you had done to Alice right after she shifted. It only took me a few minutes." Matt shrugged.

"Wish I could have seen it." Greyson said.

"No, you don't. You would rather have been up here with Alice." Matt laughed.

"Can't argue with you there." Greyson shrugged before kissing Alice's temple. "For the banquet, Alice, you will be escorted by Matt. He will be introducing you to Drake, Gwen's husband. He is assigned to protect you throughout the night. Unfortunately, Matt and I have our assignments that we need to complete. Please stay with Drake. If you get separated from him for any reason, mind-link me."

Alice looked between the two men before settling her gaze back on Greyson. "Where will you be?"

"Grey has to stay in the shadows for a bit. Until we know that Cain and Maddox won't recognize him as their previous prisoner, he will need to stay close to Alpha Lawerence." Matthew explained. "Don't worry Alice, all will be well. I will be next to Alpha Lawerence as well if you need me." Alice nodded her understanding and gave Greyson a kiss before Matthew offered his arm and they left the Queen's rooms.

Alice hesitated before stepping into the throne room. There were so many people in attendance that the massive room felt crowded. Matthew guided her through the throng until he stopped by a tall man.

The man was clean shaven with short hair. He stood next to a beaming Gwen, and she knew that this man was Drake. Introductions were made and Matthew quickly got lost in the crowd. Gwen linked her arm through Alice's as she told Alice about how happy their girls were to see their father again.

Hours passed and Alice had yet to catch even a glimpse of Greyson or Matthew. She could tell he was close by though, which was a comfort. Drake and Gwen were talking with a friend when Alice felt a strong grip on her elbow.

Before she could say anything, she was yanked away from the group, and she stumbled several steps. She looked up to see who had grabbed her, only to come face to face with Cain. His face was twisted with rage.

"Who is he?" He growled at her. Alice tried to take a step back, but his grip only tightened, and an involuntary whimper escaped her lips. "I asked you who touched you, Alison? His scent is all over you."

"Let go of her." Came a deep threatening voice from behind her. Alice turned to see Drake's stoney expression. He was very intimidating as he stood there, compared to the smiling and joking Drake from a few minutes ago. Another man was flanking him with his arm's folded.

Cain did the opposite and pulled her closer to him. "This has nothing to do with you." Cain practically snarled.

"Do I need to come step in?" Greyson's voice sounded in her head.

Alice immediately felt calmer. "No, Love. I can manage."

"If he doesn't come away with a broken finger at the very least, I am going to be coming over." Greyson warned and Alice smiled.

"See she is happy to be with me." Cain smirked at Drake who only raised a brow.

"I'm smiling because I know what I am going to do." Alice clarified as she grabbed one of Cain's fingers and bent it back swiftly. A snap sounded and he howled in pain.

He let go of her elbow and she took three steps back before Drake shoved her behind him. Eyes began to turn in their direction as Cain continued to yell while grabbing his injured hand. "You little..." He rushed at her. Drake's fist connected with his face, sending him stumbling backward.

"What is going on?" Alpha Maddox's booming voice caused all the other noises to cease in the great hall.

"Your previous Beta didn't get the hint." Matthew said as he stepped out of the crowd. "He once again assaulted my sister." He turned to Drake. "Drake, report." Matt snapped.

"She was standing with us one minute and the next she was gone. I spotted her several feet away with him grabbing her arm. She tried to pull away, but he refused to let her go." Drake pointed to Cain's hand. "Ali defended herself and he ran at her. I stepped in then."

Alpha Maddox was fuming. He glared down at Cain. "Cain Micheals is at your mercy, Beta Matthew. He broke the conditions of the challenge."

Cain got to his feet and tried to lash out at Matthew but stopped just shy of him. A heavy presence pressed on her, and she could tell it affected everyone around her. Cain dropped to his knees as the presence became stronger.

Alice glanced over at Matthew, and even he seemed to be affected by it. Just as suddenly as it came, it was gone. Several men approached Cain, but Alice's arm was grabbed again. She turned to see the tense face of Drake behind her. He gestured for her to follow him as he tugged on her arm.

As they cleared the thick crowd, Alice noticed Gwen standing with another man. Drake nodded to him and the four of them left the room through the same door that Alice had entered.

Drake moved quickly and Alice had to practically jog to keep up. Alice noticed another man standing outside Queen Isabel's door. He acknowledged their approach with a nod.

"We were asked to bring you back to your room. Linus, Jarom and I will stand guard in the hall until our Alpha has given the all clear." Drake informed her. "Gwen, you need to stay with Queen Isabel and Ali."

Gwen nodded as she turned the doorknob and Alice followed her inside. Isabel stood from the couch as they entered. Her whole body radiated with tension. Alice quickly moved to her side and reached for her hand, giving it a gentle squeeze.

"What is going on? Why were we brought here?" Alice asked.

"I'm not entirely sure. When Cain grabbed you and Beta Matthew stepped in, a young man approached me and said that the Alpha of the First Moon Pack asked that I return to my room, and he was to stand guard. He gave me a keyword that my father had used in the past, so I followed him. He brought me here." Isabel said in a rush. "I was hoping you would have more information."

"Drake asked me to follow Linus and wait for him by the pillar." Gwen rung her hands.

"Maddox turned Cain over to Beta Matthew for breaking the stipulations of the challenge. Drake pulled me away before I could see what went on after that." Alice explained what she saw.

With them not knowing much about what was happening and the three men refusing to allow them to leave, Isabel suggested they wait in the small sitting area near the fire.

The Queen was sure that someone would be coming to let them know what was happening. So, Alice sat next to Isabel on one couch while Gwen took the other couch and they waited, the only sound coming from the crackling fire.

Chapter 23

Greyson watched the crowded throne room from the shadows of a pillar. From his vantage point he could see Alice as she stood with Drake and Gwen on one side of the room. On the other side of the room, he could see Matt and Lawerence talking with Alpha Maddox.

Several people had come up to him to start up a conversation. He recognized several of the guards from the dungeon, but they didn't seem to recognize him. As the night wore on, Greyson began to relax little by little as the possibility of him being recognized seemed less likely.

"Cain pulled Ali away from us. I'm making my way to her now." Drake's voice said in his head.

Greyson straightened up to his full height as he scanned the crowd for Alice. On his second scan, he spotted her. Drake and Jarom stood close, and Greyson could see their threatening stance. Alice didn't seem to be in any immediate danger, but he still didn't want that man anywhere near her.

"Do I need to step in?" Greyson mind-linked Alice.

"No, Love. I can manage." Alice responded. Greyson could see Alice stumble closer to Cain as if she had been yanked.

Greyson's anger started to rise. "If he doesn't come away with a broken finger at the very least, I am going to be coming over." He warned. If he was over there, he would definitely do more than break the man's finger for touching Alice.

"Drake, I need you to get Alice back up to her room. Get Queen Isabel and Gwen up there too. Take Jarom and Linus with you." Greyson ordered. "Matt, Cain is harassing Alice. You will need to step in."

Greyson watched as Matthew abruptly turned away from Alpha Maddox and pushed his way through the gathering people as a cry of pain rose above the noise of conversations.

The people directly around Alice had turned all their attention on what was happening. Cain tried to grab Alice, but Drake punched him, sending him stumbling backwards. Matthew finally reached them with Alpha Maddox and Lawerence right behind him.

Greyson clenched and unclenched his fist as he watched the group carefully. It was killing him to keep back. All he wanted to do was charge forward and show Cain what happened when he messed with another man's wife. Greyson could feel his anger building in him as Cain lunged for Matthew.

Just before he reached him, he stopped and dropped to his knees. Greyson watched as many people's heads bowed while others dropped to their knees. The air in the room grew thick.

"Greyson, you need to retract your Alpha presence." Lawerence said through the mind-link. Greyson blinked several times and took a deep breath. The heaviness in the room disappeared. He saw several people shake their heads while others looked at Lawerence.

"Maddox put me in charge of Cain's punishment." Matt said. "What do you want me to do?"

"We should take him back to First Moon so that he doesn't get let off easy." Lawerence advised.

Greyson thought for a moment. "Have Maddox's men put him in the dungeon until we can transport him back to First Moon. Have him put in my old cell." Greyson lips turned up slightly in a small smile. Cain had been the one to move him into that cell shortly after he first arrived. He said it would help in breaking Greyson.

Movement at the far side of the room drew Greyson's attention. Jarom was guiding Queen Isabel from the room. Greyson returned his attention to Alice. Drake was guiding her through the crowd as he headed for Linus and Gwen. The four of them followed the path that Queen Isabel and Jarom had taken. Greyson let out a sigh of relief knowing that Alice and Queen Isabel were safe. He wasn't sure how well Cain would take to being arrested.

As Greyson had suspected, Cain started to fight the guards that tried to grab him. Unsurprising, several of the Howling Meadows' men shifted and began fighting to protect Cain. The First Moon pack men didn't waste any time in shifting as well. Women screamed and ran for the exits as the fighting broke out. Greyson ran into the fray, heading towards Matt and Lawerence. By the time he reached them, Greyson noted the absence of Alpha Maddox.

Cain had shifted as he tried to fight his way towards the closest exit. Greyson gave Matt a look before they both headed towards Cain's wolf. Cain snarled and snapped at Matthew who jumped back out of reach. Greyson used Cain's moment of distraction and moved closer. He delivered a hard punch to the wolf's side and then quickly moved out of reach. Cain whirled in Greyson's direction and Matt moved in to take a shot.

Before Matt could reach Cain, another wolf tackled him. Greyson heard Matt's cry of pain, distracting him. Cain took off towards the doors. Greyson did not even look at Cain as he rushed towards Matthew who was laying on his back with the wolf biting his shoulder.

Greyson rammed into the wolf's side with his shoulder causing him to release Matt. Greyson and the wolf rolled a few times before stopping. The wolf recovered quickly and as Greyson got to his feet, the wolf swiped at Greyson with its paw. Greyson felt the burn as the wolf's claws raked across his chest. Ignoring the pain, Greyson pulled one of his daggers from its sheath and stabbed it into the wolf's neck. The wolf let out a yelp before it dropped to the floor.

The chaos around him continued for several more minutes as Greyson moved to Matthew's side. He dropped to his knees to examine his brother. Matt groaned as he sat up. His shoulder was a mess. Blood was everywhere and his face was pale. He looked over at Greyson and wrinkled his nose.

"You look terrible." Matt said through clenched teeth.

"You don't look much better." Greyson retorted. The pain in his chest grew with each passing minute. "Looks like we are out of practice." Greyson rotated and sat next to Matt.

Before Matt could respond, Lawerence and Jonah, one of Greyson's men from Trevor's Cove, knelt next to them. "What happened to you two?" Lawerence asked, concern written all over his face.

Ignoring his question, Greyson looked around. The fighting had stopped. "Are any of our men injured?" Greyson asked as he pressed a hand to his chest only to feel wetness.

"Yes. You and Matt. Everyone else is fine." Lawerence said. "Let's take a look at your injuries."

Jonah helped Greyson take his shirt off. Greyson was surprised to see four deep gashes starting at his left shoulder and traveling diagonally to his right hip. Immediately, Jonah pressed Greyson's shirt over as much of the wound as he could. Lawerence was looking at Matt's shoulder with a grim look. Matt lay still on the floor with a pain filled expression on his face.

Lawerence called out to a man not far away. "Where is your hospital?"

"No." Greyson growled out. "Take us to Queen Isabel's room." Lawerence and Jonah exchanged worried looks and didn't move. "Take us there. Now." Greyson said again, this time more forcefully. Each moment they sat there the more Greyson could feel his strength leaving him.

Following his orders, Lawerence assisted Matthew while Jonah helped Greyson stand. By the time they reached the hallway that led to Queen Isabel's room, Lawerence and Jonah were practically carrying both Matthew and Greyson.

Seeing the state they were in, Jarom and Linus ran down the hall to get help. Drake banged on the Queen's door with a look of concern. Greyson barely registered being dragged into the room and put on the floor.

"What happened?" Alice's voice reached through his muddled brain as a hand touched his face.

"Help Matt first." Greyson pushed through gritted teeth as he squeezed his eyes shut.

Greyson groaned in pain as someone pressed something on a part of his wound, only for a second later to have another part of his wound pressed on. He didn't know how much time had passed before he felt a gentle hand touch his cheek. Slowly the pain in his chest receded little by little until he felt no more pain. He let out a sigh of relief and opened his eyes.

He was met with Alice's light blue eyes that were blazing with anger. "Thank you, Sweetheart." He said quietly only to get a punch in the gut. He curled in on himself and rolled to his side. "Alice." He whined.

"Do not 'Sweetheart' me." Alice said angrily. "What were you thinking?"

"He saved me, Alice. A wolf had me pinned down and biting my shoulder. If Grey hadn't tackled him, I probably would have been dead." Matt said from not far away.

Greyson got to a sitting position and looked around. Drake, Jonah, Lawerence, Isabel, and Gwen were staring wide eyed at Alice. Matthew was covered in drying blood, but his wounds seemed to have disappeared. He looked down at his chest and noticed that his too, had been healed.

"You are an angel, Alice. What would I ever do without you?" Greyson said with a crooked smile.

"You would have already been dead." Alice growled back. "Saving your brother or not, Grey. I am still mad at you. You could have been killed."

Greyson moved so that he could lean his back against the couch. Then he reached for Alice and pulled her onto his lap. She didn't fight him but sat rigidly. He pressed a kiss to her forehead. "I know. I am sorry. I will be more careful in the future."

Alice let out a sigh before relaxing against him. "I can live without Matt, but I can't live without you." she said softly.

"Hey!" Matt said in mock horror, and Greyson chuckled.

"Seriously, Alice. Thank you." Greyson kissed her cheek as he held her close.

"What just happened?" Lawerence's voice cut through the little bubble around them.

"Cain apparently had some supporters. They attacked when we tried to take Cain into custody." Greyson explained.

"I know that." Lawerence rolled his eyes. "I meant that." He gestured from Matt to Greyson.

"She is a Guardian." Isabel said with a smile. "A healer. But I thought you were a Seer?"

"I am both." Alice responded. "My mother, has multiple gifts, too."

"That is unheard of." Isabel's brows drew together in thought. "The prophecy. The White Wolf?"

"Yes." Was all Alice said.

Lawrence, Drake, and Jonah all looked thoroughly confused. "I will explain later. But first, what are we going to do about Alpha Maddox and Cain? He got away when Matt was attacked." Greyson asked.

"I will find Alpha Maddox and set up a meeting for tomorrow. We will hunt down Cain after." Lawerence started moving to the door. "You two boys should get a bath or something to clean all that blood off and rest. Tomorrow is not going to be easy." And then he slipped out the door.

Greyson sent Jonah with Lawerence. He didn't want anyone in his pack to be alone. Matt began giving orders for their men to buddy up and instructed everyone to be extra cautious.

Drake was sent home to spend time with his family while Linus and Jarom stood guard in the hallway outside Queen Isabel's room. Once Alice, Isabel, Matt, and Greyson were alone, Greyson turned his attention to his mother. He studied her as she began picking up the bloodied rags and tossing them into the fire.

Greyson moved Alice off his lap and got to his feet. He moved to his mother and pulled her into a hug. She startled, but after a moment returned his embrace. When he pulled back, he saw tears in her eyes. He wiped a tear off her cheek and gave her a smile.

"Thank you for sending John and Phil to protect me while I was in the dungeon. And I do not know how you did it but thank you for having Lord Isaac attempt to free me."

"I wish I could have done more. Knowing that you were stuck in there and unable to do anything was...difficult." Isabel whispered.

"You did everything you could have, and that is all I could have asked for." Greyson smiled.

"We really should get some rest, Grey." Matthew cut in. "We can continue catching up tomorrow. I will sleep on the couch in here with mother, you can keep an eye on Alice." Greyson glanced over at Matt and saw the twinkle in his eyes.

Greyson didn't respond to his brother's teasing as he grabbed Alice's hand and led her to her room. He made sure to lock the door before heading over to the wash basin. He cleaned the blood off the best he could as Alice changed for bed. They climbed into bed together and Alice cuddled close. Greyson let out a contented sigh. It did not take long for Alice's breathing to deepen. Greyson smiled as he savored the feel of Alice next to him.

Just before he fell asleep, he felt someone trying to mind-link him. He opened his mind and Luther spoke. "We found where they are keeping the kids. We have been watching the cabin for about an hour trying to see how many guards are here and where the kids are, exactly. Something must have happened because they are suddenly on high alert."

"How many guards are there?" Greyson asked, fully awake.

"We have only seen two." Bear responded.

"Take out the guards and get the kids as quickly as possible." Greyson said. He then gave them a brief rundown of Cain's escape.

"We will let you know as soon as we are headed back." Luther said before the mind-link closed.

Greyson laid in bed fully awake for an hour. He was going out of his mind. For the hundredth time, he wished he could be there with Luther and Bear. Worry filled him as he waited. Had Luther and Bear been able to get the kids? Were the kids alright? Finally, Greyson felt the now familiar pull of someone trying to mind-link him.

"Tell me you have good news." He growled out. His anxiety colored his tone.

"Of course we have good news." Bear said in frustration. "We have your three kids. They are safe and unharmed."

"You could have warned us that they are fighters." Luther accused.

"What do you mean?" Greyson asked. Knowing the kids were unharmed and in safe hands was a huge relief.

"The little guy has done nothing but kick, bite, punch and call us names since we got them. The older girl will not let us hold the baby who has cried nonstop since we showed up." Luther explained.

"How long till you get back?" Greyson ignored Luther's unhappy tone. "With Cain on the loose, don't take the shortest route back. He has supporters and you will most likely be outnumbered."

"It will take us longer to get back since they won't let us carry the baby, but we should be back within six hours. Maybe a little less." Bear said.

"Tell them that Alice and I sent you to get them." Greyson suggested.

There was a pause. "The boy has stopped trying to attack us, but they don't seem to fully believe us." Luther said.

"Tell Alisha that I said she was right, Alice and I are fated mates."

Another pause. "That only made her cry. Thanks for the advice, boss." Luther said sarcastically.

"But they seem to trust us now." Bear laughed in disbelief.

"Hurry back. And keep them safe." Greyson sighed in relief.

"Yes, sir." Luther and Bear said.

Now that the kids trust them, they should be able to move quicker. And the quicker they get here, the quicker they will be out of Cain's reach. Greyson knew that Alice would be relieved once the kids were here with her. And Greyson couldn't deny the excitement he felt at the prospect of seeing them again. Even with his mind in high gear, Greyson's exhaustion finally caught up to him and he fell asleep.

Chapter 24

Voices in the other room pulled Greyson from his sleep. He squinted his eyes against the light of the sun streaming in through the window as he looked around. He relaxed back into the pillow when he turned his head and saw Alice snuggled up to him.

A smile touched his lips as he closed his eyes again. For the first time in a year, Greyson actually woke up feeling well rested. He pressed a soft kiss to the top of her head, but she did not stir.

"You look like Greyson." a small voice said. It was slightly muffled through the closed door.

"Is that so?" Matt's laughing voice easily reached through the closed door.

"Yeah, but he is bigger than you." The little voice spoke again. Greyson ran a hand down his face as he tried to shake the sleep from his mind.

Greyson recognized that little voice. Asher. The kids were here. Not wanting to wake Alice up, he carefully extricated himself from the bed. He moved quietly across the room and cracked the door open. He slipped through quickly and closed the door behind him.

Alisha stood nervously next to Isabel. Isabel's back was facing Greyson so he could not see what she was holding. Matthew crouched next to Asher who was studying Matt with a furrowed brow.

"That's because he is older than I am." Matt commented. "But I am the fun one."

"Don't let him fool you Asher, Matt's fun usually leads to trouble." Greyson said with a smile.

Asher spun around and when he saw Greyson standing only a few feet away, he launched his little body at Greyson. Greyson leaned down and caught him to his chest in a tight hug. Straightening back up he kissed the boy's head as he lifted him in his arms.

Asher had grown some since the last time he saw him. Asher's arms went around Greyson's neck in a vice like grip. Arms wrapped around his middle and Greyson looked down to see Alisha's tear-streaked face. He let go of Asher with one arm and wrapped it around Alisha, holding her close to him.

"Let's move to the couch." Greyson suggested as he moved them in that direction. Alisha's hold on him slackened until they were sitting on the couch. Asher still hadn't loosened his hold on Greyson's neck. Alisha sat next to him, and he pulled her close to his side. Greyson closed his eyes against the sting of tears that started. He had missed them terribly. "Are you both okay?" he asked, his voice thick with emotion.

"They threatened to kill Avery like they did grandma and papa if we didn't keep quiet." Asher said as he leaned back. "And they took my horse." The boy's bottom lip pouted.

"Where is Avery?" Greyson asked looking around.

Matt was watching them with a crooked smile on his face. He pointed with his chin to someone behind Greyson. He turned to look and saw his mother holding the little girl.

Greyson sat Asher on the couch and stood up. He moved quickly to his mother and gently took Avery from his mother's arms. Greyson ran a hand over the little girl's soft hair and pressed a kiss to her chubby cheek. She was no longer the baby girl he had known. Avery had grown so much. He cleared his throat as he held her close. He moved slowly back to the couch with the other kids. Asher immediately climbed back onto Greyson's lap and Alisha laid her head on his shoulder.

"Is she walking yet?" Greyson asked softly while continuing to study all the changes in Avery.

"Yeah, but she doesn't say words yet, only babbles." Alisha answered. It was quiet for several minutes as the four of them sat together. "Why did you leave? Alice was so sad when you left." Alisha asked, turning her face up to him.

"I was not given a choice. Some bad men forced me to go with them. I only got away from them a week ago." Greyson explained simply.

"You were taken like we were." Asher said with a frown.

"Yes, like you were." Greyson pressed a kiss to the top of Asher's head. "Did they hurt any of you?"

"They threatened to stab Avery if we didn't cooperate." Alisha said quietly. "They killed grandma and papa, so we did what they told us to."

"Where are we going to live now?" Alisha asked as tears filled her eyes again. "First mother and father, and now grandma and papa."

Greyson looked at each of the kids before returning his attention to Alisha. "You will be staying with me and Alice."

Asher began to bounce on Greyson's lap. "Does that mean you are going to be my new dad?"

"If you want me to be." Grey said with a smile.

"Da, da, da, da." Avery began patting Greyson's face and his heart nearly burst.

"I think the baby is in favor of that." Matt laughed.

"Would you like that Alisha, to live with me and Alice?" Greyson asked. She sat quietly as she looked from her brother to her sister and then back to him. Nervousness began to sneak its way into him.

"I would like that a lot." Alisha finally answered with a smile. Greyson let out a relieved breath and returned her smile.

"When can we see Alice?" Asher asked, sitting up straighter.

"Alice is asleep but if you want, you can go wake her up." Greyson laughed.

Asher jumped from his lap and stumbled. Greyson immediately handed Avery over to Alisha and picked up the boy. Asher sniffled as he once again wrapped his arms around Greyson's neck.

"The boy's ankle pains him when he walks on it." Luther said. Greyson snapped his head up. He had not noticed Bear and Luther standing near the door to the hallway.

"Why don't I carry you in and set you on the bed. After you wake Alice up, she can look at that ankle." Greyson rubbed Asher's back. "Come on Alisha, why don't you and Avery come too."

Greyson moved to Alice's door with Alisha right behind him. He glanced back at Bear and Luther, and they gave him a nod. They would wait until he was done with the kids.

Alice was still curled up in the blankets when Greyson reached the bed. She looked so peaceful as she lay there. Asher began to squirm in Greyson's arms, so he set the boy gently at the bottom of the bed before taking Avery from Alisha.

Greyson couldn't help smiling as he watched Asher slowly crawl up the bed. Matt stepped up next to Greyson with a smile of his own. "They are cute kids." He whispered. "Fatherhood looks good on you, brother."

"They are great kids." Greyson agreed.

Asher paused next to Alice's head. He looked back at Greyson as if asking permission. Greyson gave him a nod and the boy smiled. Greyson watched as Asher leaned down as if to give her a kiss on the cheek but instead blew as hard as he could, giving her a raspberry.

Alice jerked awake. Matt laughed loudly as Asher giggled. Alice looked around disoriented. She looked at Greyson in surprise before turning her gaze to Asher. A sob broke from her as she pulled the boy to her. She smothered him in kisses as he clung to her. After several moments, Alice's head turned, and she looked at Alisha. Alisha threw her arms around Alice's neck and the two continued to cry.

"Did I surprise you?" Asher asked with eagerness.

"You sure did. When did you get here?" Alice turned to look at Greyson.

Greyson moved to the bed and sat down next to Alice. "Not too long ago." Alice leaned against Greyson as she pulled Asher onto her lap.

Alisha scooted up to Alice's side and Alice's arm draped over the girl's shoulders. Greyson pressed a quick kiss to Alice's temple. Avery started reaching for Greyson's face again while blowing spit bubbles. Alice reached over and brushed a few whisps of hair off Avery's forehead.

"Greyson said that you can help my hurt ankle." Asher said.

"You have a hurt ankle?" Alice's brows knitted in concern as she looked down at Asher. "Which one?" Asher showed her his left ankle. His whole ankle was purple and blue and three times the size it should have been. Alice put her hands on it and a soft blue glow started. A minute later, Asher's ankle looked completely normal. "How does it feel, now?" Alice asked gently.

"It doesn't hurt anymore!" Asher yelled in excitement. He jumped off the bed and ran around in circles before stopping at the bottom of the bed. His grin stretched from ear to ear. "Greyson said he could be my new daddy since the bad men killed grandma and papa. Does that make you my new mommy?"

Alice looked over at Greyson with wide-eyed surprise. "He did, did he?"

"He did." Asher began to jump around the room again. "Which is amazing because I love you both so much. And Greyson, I mean dad, can teach me to ride a horse."

Laughter echoed from the other room and Greyson couldn't help his smile. He was so glad that the kids were happy to live with him and Alice. It was hard to only see them once a week while they lived with their grandparents.

A pang of regret and sadness washed over Greyson as he thought of the loss of Mr. and Mrs. Finn. They were both great people and did not deserve to die. Anger replaced the sadness as he thought of the men that had killed them and taken the kids hostage.

"Grey, Lawerence said the meeting with Alpha Maddox is in an hour." Matthew cut into his thoughts.

He gave Avery another kiss on the cheek before standing up and handing Avery to Alice. "I need to get Luther and Bear's report and then meet with Matt and Lawerence before the meeting with Alpha Maddox." He leaned down and pressed a kiss to Alisha's head. "Linus, Jarom, and Jonah will stay to help guard you while I'm gone." He kissed Alice on the lips. He started to straighten up, but Alice pulled him back down for another kiss.

"Why are you involved with all these things? Can't Matt and Alpha Lawerence meet with Alpha Maddox while you stay here?" Alice asked, confusion written all over her face.

"I wish I could, but I can't, Alice." Greyson scooped Asher up as he ran by. He kissed the squirming boy's cheek before setting him back down. "You be good and mind my men." Asher nodded and Greyson mussed up his hair.

Greyson followed Matt from Alice's room. Luther and Bear were eating while sitting on the couch. Before Greyson could say anything, Alice grabbed his arm. He looked down at her and her eyes flashed with irritation. He wrapped his arms around her as he smiled. She was so beautiful when she was irritated.

"Don't smile at me like that, Grey." She scolded him as she tried to push him back. "That was not a good enough answer. Why do you have to go?"

"Just tell her." Matt said as he moved over to sit in a chair near Luther and Bear. "She is going to start swinging if you make her angry enough."

"Tell me what?" Alice glared at Greyson and he let out a sigh.

"I tried to get out of it, Alice. I really did. This is all Matt's fault." Greyson pointed at Matthew before returning his hand to her waist. Alice only raised one of her brows as she continued to glare at him. "Lawerence is our grandfather. He needed to pass his pack down to a descendant and he refused to give it over to Maddox. That left me or Matt." Greyson tried to explain but stopped as he tried to find the right words. He still did not think he was right for the position of Alpha King.

"Greyson doesn't think he is good enough to be the next Alpha of the First Moon Pack, let alone the Alpha King. Lawerence thinks he is perfect for it. Greyson tried to pass it off to me, but you know me, Alice, I have no desire to be in charge of anything." Matt explained from his chair with a smirk. "Greyson made me the Beta without giving me much choice."

Isabel gasped as she placed a hand over her mouth and tears were in her eyes. Alice was still confused about what they were trying to tell her.

Greyson transferred his weight from one foot to the other as he became uncomfortable but his hold on her never slackened. She looked up into his face, but he would not meet her eyes. "I am Alpha King Greyson, Alpha of the First Moon Pack."

Alice studied his face and saw what Matthew was trying to explain. Greyson was definitely uncomfortable with the responsibility that had been placed on him. But he would be amazing at it. He was loyal, protective, caring, and fair. If only Alpha Maddox was half the man Greyson was. Alice laughed at Greyson's reluctant confession.

"Alpha Lawerence couldn't have chosen a more perfect successor." Alice said, and Greyson groaned as he let her go.

"Not you too." He grumbled.

"Grey, look at me." Alice said sternly. "You were made for this."

"That's what I said." Matthew laughed and Greyson glared at him.

"Alice, as my wife, you will be expected to be Alpha Queen." Greyson pointed out.

"So, I'm not your Princess anymore?" Alice teased.

"You will always be my Princess." Greyson pulled her back to him and kissed her.

"Now you see why he has been ignoring us." Matt said in a loud whisper, causing Bear and Luther to laugh. "As disgustingly sweet as it is to watch you two, Grey, we really need to get the day going." Greyson pulled back away from Alice. Her cheeks were bright red, and Greyson could not help his chuckle. He gave her a wink before joining the men in the sitting area.

"All right men, I trust that Matt filled you in on what has happened since you left yesterday." They nodded as they continued to eat. "I want to thank you for rescuing my kids and bringing them back safely." Greyson gave them a half smile.

"I don't think I have ever seen you the way you are with them." Luther said before taking a drink. "All I have seen from you is a restless man that is more of a machine. Training, fighting, and more training. It is nice to see you actually looking happy."

"And those kids love you." Bear spoke up. "They were not happy with us when we first found them. They knew we weren't the men that kidnapped them, but they didn't trust us either. Not until Luther told Alisha what you told him to say."

"What did you tell Alisha?" Alice asked as she sat in Greyson's lap. He automatically put his arms around her as she settled back against him. "I told

Luther to tell her that I said she was right about us being fated mates." Greyson kissed Alice's neck.

"Are we?" Alice asked rotating to face him. "When did you figure this out?"

"It was not long after we got to Trevor's Cove. Drake and I had to practically spell it out for him." Luther laughed.

"Yeah, he didn't seem to catch on before he was shot and taken to Alpha Maddox either." Alice laughed as well.

"Wait, you knew?" Greyson asked in disbelief.

Alice smiled at him. "I figured it out the night you were so angry that you couldn't stop your shift and then couldn't shift back to human for a few hours." Alice raised her shoulder.

"All that talk about finding your mate by having me take you around kissing men," Greyson said slowly.

"Was me trying to get you to realize that you were actually my mate." Alice finished for him with a smug smile on her face.

Greyson growled at her as he tickled her. She squeaked as she tried to get away, but Greyson's hold on her was unyielding. He continued to tickle her until she screamed out an apology. He finally stopped his assault on her, and she glared at him for a moment before she smiled.

Greyson pulled her until her back rested against his chest again. He kissed her temple before turning back to Matt, Luther, and Bear. They all were watching them with amused smiles on their faces.

Luther told them how they tracked Asher's scent and found a remote cabin several hours away in no man's land. Greyson tightened his arms around Alice as he explained about the previous evening and the upcoming meeting. He dismissed them to go rest, since they had been up all-night bringing Asher, Alisha, and Avery back.

More food was brought up for the kids. Alice helped Asher dish up a plate while Greyson held Avery as she chewed on a pancake. Matt joked with Asher as he ate and laughed. Isabel sat next to Alisha and the two of them were having a quiet conversation.

Greyson caught Alice's eye from across their makeshift breakfast table and winked. She blushed prettily and Greyson couldn't help the flip of his stomach as he watched her. He sat comfortably in his chair, content as his gaze swept over those around him. Isabel and Alisha, Matt and Asher, Avery and Alice. His whole family, together.

"Greyson, it's time." Lawerence reached out through the mind-link. "Alpha Maddox is requesting the presence of Queen Isabel and her companion. We are to meet in the Council Chambers."

Chapter 25

Greyson and Matt entered Queen Isabel's Garden to meet with Lawerence before the big meeting. Greyson immediately spotted him near the center of the walking paths. He was speaking with Drake in hushed tones. Both men turned at their approach and bowed their heads briefly in acknowledgment.

"How is your wife?" Lawerence asked with a kind smile.

"She is doing better now that the kids are safe." Greyson answered. By the puzzled expressions on both Lawerence's and Drake's faces, he guessed Matt had not spread the news of the kids' retrieval to the whole pack. Greyson updated them on Alisha, Asher and Avery's rescue and Alice's relief to have them returned safe and sound.

"Don't let him fool you, Grey was just as happy to see the kids as Ali was. And the kids absolutely adore him. I have never seen him actually just sit before. But when he was holding the baby, he literally just sat. It was weird. No pacing, no tapping, or any other restless behavior that he normally does." Matt said as he shook his head.

Greyson reached over and smacked Matt on the back of the head, causing Drake to laugh harder than he already was. "Back to business. How is this meeting with Maddox going to play out?" Greyson asked.

"The Counsil room is quite big. I was thinking we should have at least twenty of our men in the room with us. Maddox is most definitely thinking that I am stepping down as Alpha King and I am here to do that. That is why he requested Isabel's and Ali's presence. He does not currently have a Beta, so his Queen will need to be there as his second in command." Lawerence explained. "I will be sitting in the center on our side, and I want both of you to sit on either side of me. We will remain silent until Alpha Maddox speaks. I will bring up concerns about Trevor's Cove, like we discussed earlier. After that, I think we need to play it by ear to see what Maddox does." Lawerence's gaze locked with Greyson's. "Before the end of the meeting, I will address you as the Alpha of the First Moon Pack."

"Won't it be weird to have you running the meeting instead of Grey?" Matt asked. "After all, he is the Alpha."

"As a member of his council, I can be tasked with meetings like this." Lawerence answered. "But we should probably get going, we don't want to be too late."

The four of them exited the garden near the market. John and Phil were standing at their post and only gave small nods as they passed. A wave of anxiety hit Greyson as they approached the main doors of the castle. Flashes of the torture room and the whipping post assaulted him. His skin began to feel clammy, and his heart rate ratcheted up several notches.

"Is everything okay?" Alice's voice broke through his memories. He glanced around quickly, but realized she had mind-linked him.

"I am now that I can hear your voice." Greyson took several slow, deep breaths as he followed behind Lawerence and Matt. Twenty of the First Moon Pack warriors surrounded them as they moved through the castle halls.

"What's wrong, Grey?" Alice sounded more concerned than before. Blast the mate bond.

"Just dealing with some memories of this place. Nothing to worry about, Love." Greyson entered the room and scanned it quickly. His eyes found Alice's bright blue ones. He sent her a wink before pulling his gaze from hers and settling in the chair to Lawerence's right. "You look beautiful." Greyson hid his smile at the blush that colored Alice's cheeks.

Greyson took stock of the room's occupants. Next to Alice, was his mother and then Maddox on his mother's other side. On Maddox's side of the long rectangular table were ten men. Only four of the men looked to be warriors, the others looked like councilmen.

At the amount of force that Lawerence brought with him, Maddox's eyes widened in surprise. It took several minutes, but everyone eventually found their seats and silence filled the room.

Greyson mind-linked everyone to remind them to remain as still as possible and to remain silent. He was impressed when five minutes went by, and there was no sound made. He would have thought Maddox incapable of patience. Greyson kept his gaze trained on Maddox, even though he desperately wanted to watch Alice instead.

She mind-linked him with comments about how big of a change it was to see him so intimidating instead of how he was yesterday, bare-chested and holding her close. Greyson's face and neck heated. He told her he loved her before cutting the mind-link. Alice coughed before clearing her throat. The woman was a blasted distraction.

Maddox adjusted in his seat before lacing his fingers and resting his hands on the table. "Alpha Lawerence, you have come to my pack and asked to speak with me. What is it that I can do for you?" Maddox finally broke the stalemate.

Lawrence's posture relaxed slightly. "I have become aware that Trevor's Cove is being used by slave traders as a fighting ring." Lawerence's voice was devoid of emotion as he spoke.

"I have heard the same thing." Maddox sat back in his chair with a half-smile. "What is it you wish me to do about it?"

"According to Valencia law, what they are doing is illegal. Slave trading is also against the law." Lawerence pointed out.

"Slave trade in Valencia has been around for quite a number of years." Maddox chuckled softly. "I still fail to see what that has to do with me."

"Now that the First Moon Pack has a young and active Beta, the pack is determined to put an end to all slave trade in Valencia and arrest the key players." Lawerence's posture straightened back up. "We have come to see if you are in favor of such a plan."

"To round up all major players in the slave trade would be nearly impossible. And I have heard that those that are to fight are criminals. What is the difference in sending them to fight or just killing them for their crimes?" Maddox countered.

Greyson clenched his fist in his lap and directed his gaze down. He took a deep breath, catching a whiff of vanilla. His rising anger ebbed slightly with Alice being nearby. He hadn't been happy that Alice had to be there, but now he was beyond glad she was. He needed her calming presence.

Of course, Maddox did not see the difference. He tortured his prisoners, and they lived in far worse conditions than Trevor's Cove had to offer. In order to remain in control, Greyson blocked out the conversation about the slave traders for a while. He could not wait to unleash his anger on Maddox.

After a good half hour, Greyson tuned back into the conversation. "Is that all you wished to talk about?" Maddox was asking. "You travelled quite the distance for a conversation that could have been handled by a councilman."

"You are right, a councilman would have done a fine job handling this meeting. I don't get out nearly as much as I should." Lawerence chuckled.

Maddox's smile grew. "You are getting up there in years. Maybe it is time someone younger took up the mantle and allowed you to retire."

"Actually, I have been thinking quite a bit about retiring." Lawerence said but didn't elaborate. Greyson noticed Maddox's barely restrained excitement. He truly thought that Lawerence would name him the Alpha King. "It was almost painful to realize how old I am getting as I watched my Beta and some of my pack spar. A few outshone me, which doesn't bode well for a king."

"No, it doesn't." Maddox agreed with a laugh. The room fell back into silence for several minutes as Maddox tapped his fingers restlessly, a gleam of excitement in his eyes.

Lawerence sighed as he got to his feet. Greyson and Matt did the same, followed by Maddox. "I guess I should name the new Alpha King and Alpha of the First Moon Pack." He paused and Maddox beamed. "I am pleased to introduce. Alpha King Greyson, my grandson. He has been Alpha of the First Moon Pack for almost a week now. He made his brother, his Beta." Maddox's jaw dropped in shock. "I feel confident that between the two of them, Valencia will prosper once again."

Once the shock wore off, Maddox's face began to turn purple with rage. "Your grandsons? You have no grandsons!" Maddox roared.

"Do you not see the resemblance to yourself, Alpha Maddox?" Lawerence said with a smirk.

Before anyone knew what was happening, Maddox turned to Isabel and grabbed her by the throat. Her eyes bulged and her face started to turn red. Chaos erupted all around him. Greyson leapt over the table to get to Alice. Greyson watched as Alice jumped to her feet and slammed her fist into Maddox's face twice before he let go of Isabel and lunged towards Alice.

Maddox had managed to punch her a few times before Greyson got to him. He slammed Maddox up against the wall hard enough that he let out a cry of pain. Greyson glanced over at Alice. Matt was helping her to her feet, and she gave him a reassuring smile even with blood dripping from her nose.

Greyson turned back to Maddox with a glare. "I, Alpha Greyson of the First Moon Pack challenge Alpha Maddox, of the Howling Meadows Pack." Greyson growled.

"You have no grounds to challenge me." Maddox spat.

The men of the First Moon pack growled. "You attacked Queen Isabel for no reason and then attacked the Queen of the First Moon Pack. Your illegal dealings with the slave traders and wrongful treatment of prisoners. Do I need to go on?" Greyson pushed Maddox harder into the wall.

"Isabel lied to me about the death of my own flesh and blood. She must pay for her deceit." Maddox countered.

"As Alpha King, I decide the consequences of Alphas and Queens." Greyson said coldly. "Living for twenty-two years without her sons is payment enough. You on the other hand can either accept my challenge or be put to death for your crimes. Which will it be?"

The room fell deathly still as Greyson waited for Maddox's answer. "I accept your challenge." He finally grounded out.

Drake and another warrior from Greyson's pack grabbed Maddox and hauled him from the room. The rest of the men began filing out after them. Greyson, however, turned to Alice. She had wiped the blood off her face and her previous red and swollen face looked normal. Greyson pulled her into his arms.

"Are you all right?" He whispered.

"I'm okay, Grey. I healed Isabel and Lawerence took her back to her room." She pulled back to look up into his face. Concern filled her eyes as she studied him. "You cannot really fight him, Grey. What happens if you lose?"

"Have some faith in me, Love." Greyson pressed a kiss to her forehead.

"But you have been in prison for a year." Alice protested.

Greyson cut her off with a kiss. When he pulled back, he cupped her face. "I will be fine. But I want you to go back up to the room, too."

Alice looked ready to protest when Matt cut in. "They are waiting on you, Grey."

Knowing that fighting with Alice was a lost cause, she would just end up down at the fight anyway, Greyson grabbed her hand and pulled her from the room. Matthew led the way back outside to the main field. A growing crowd was assembling.

Maddox was on his knees being held in place in the center of the ring that had formed. Lawrence was standing several feet away glaring at him. Greyson stopped walking at the edge of the open space and turned to Alice.

"You will stay with Matt. No exceptions." Greyson glanced over Alice's head briefly and made eye contact with Matthew, who nodded his understanding. "If you can't do this, you will be taken back to the room, do you understand?" Greyson said sternly, holding Alice's gaze.

"I promise to not interfere in the challenge." Alice said, and then bit her lip.

Greyson gave her one last kiss before crossing the field to stand next to Lawerence. Maddox growled at him as he approached. Greyson could already feel his wolf stirring, ready for a fight.

"What are the terms, Alpha Greyson?" Lawerence asked.

"If I win, Alpha Maddox is to be judged by his people and the people of Valencia for his crimes." Maddox struggled against the men holding him. "If he wins, he will be stripped of his Alpha title, but allowed to live." Greyson said loudly. "Shifting is allowed."

Maddox's glare held nothing but hatred as he stared at Greyson. Lawerence backed up towards the spectators as the men holding Maddox released their hold on him and jogged out of the field. Greyson rolled his shoulders and tuned into his wolf's senses as Maddox slowly got to his feet.

"Do you remember me?" Greyson couldn't help asking. Maddox's lips pulled back over his teeth in a sneer. "No? I was the Silent Prisoner you enjoyed torturing." Greyson supplied.

Maddox's eyes flashed with recognition before returning to a glare. "Your eyes are the same as your mothers." He growled out before shifting into his sandy blonde wolf. He was as big as Matt's wolf.

Knowing he could not take on an Alpha wolf in human form, Greyson shifted into his black wolf. He was several inches taller than Maddox and quite a bit thicker. Maddox froze for several seconds as he took in the size of Greyson's wolf. A growl came from Maddox as he rushed at Greyson.

Alice grabbed Matthew's arm tightly as the two wolves collided in a flash of teeth and claws. She tried to tamp down her anxiety and worry so that Greyson could concentrate on the fight, but she was failing. Matt pulled his arm from her grasp and draped it over her shoulders, giving them a gentle squeeze. Greyson's wolf was notably bigger than Alpha Maddox's, which gave her some comfort.

Alice squeezed her eyes shut as Maddox bit into Greyson's back leg, coming away with bloody fangs. Greyson returned the blow with one of his own, causing Maddox to yelp before creating distance between them. The fight continued on like this, each wolf trading blow for blow.

Maddox's wolf lashed out with no mercy while Greyson's wolf seemed to try to subdue the smaller wolf. Matthew grew stiff beside her, and she turned to look up at his face.

"What's wrong?" Alice whispered.

"Maddox is not going to stop until one of them is dead. Greyson is going to have to kill Maddox if he wants to end the fight." Matt explained without taking his eyes off the two wolves.

Alice could tell that Matt had mind-linked Grey by the change in Greyson's fighting style. Each one of his blows was harder and he moved faster than before. Greyson turned, exposing his belly for a few seconds. Alice watched in horror as Maddox lunged for the vulnerable spot, going for the kill shot.

Just before he could sink his teeth in, Greyson's jaw clamped down on Maddox's neck. He pinned him to the ground just like he had done to Alice the night she shifted for the first time. Maddox thrashed and tried to break the hold Greyson had on him but could not. He refused to submit to Greyson and Alice felt a wave of regret right before Maddox's wolf stopped struggling.

All was deathly still for several moments as the crowd held their breath, waiting to see if Maddox's wolf would get up. Greyson shifted back to his human form and hung his head. It was plain to see that he didn't take any joy or satisfaction in what he had to do. A movement out of the corner of Alice's eye drew her attention.

Cain stood next to a slightly older man with jet black hair. They both were glaring at Greyson. The man she didn't know moved and the sun glinted off a shiny object in his hand. A gun. Alice's breathing quickened as she looked between the two men and Greyson. Greyson had not looked up yet as he observed the lifeless wolf laying in the grass.

Without thinking, Alice sprinted out onto the field. Her only concern was getting to Greyson before the man shot him. She didn't know how she knew that was his plan, she just did.

She jumped in front of Greyson just as a shot rang out. She slammed into him, and they both fell to the grass. Pain exploded across her stomach as she gasp for air, but she could not seem to draw in a good breath.

She closed her eyes against the bright sun directly overhead. A hand touched her cheek, and she opened her eyes to see Greyson's face close to hers. Tears were in his eyes as his shaking hand moved from her face to her abdomen.

"What have you done, Princess?" Greyson cried as he returned his hand to her face.

Besides the pain, Alice was beginning to feel cold and heavy. She tried to open her mouth to say something but couldn't. She squeezed her eyes closed and felt hot tears run down past her ears and into her hair. Greyson's lips pressed against her forehead, and she could feel that his own cheeks were wet.

"I'm sorry, Grey." She mind-linked him. Her awareness of the world fading. "I'm sorry."

"Please, don't leave me." Greyson was begging her, but Alice could not muster any more fight. "I love you, don't leave me."

Chapter 26

Alice first heard the sound of a page turning in a book. She slowly opened her eyes, but immediately shut them. The room was way too bright. The sound of a book being closed and footsteps drawing closer reached her before a cool hand touched her forehead and then blackness.

Alice opened her eyes again. This time the room was dimly lit, and she blinked several times as she attempted to sit up. Hands pressed her firmly, yet gently back onto the mattress. She turned her head to see Greyson sitting in a chair next to her bed. "Alice." He breathed a sigh of relief as tears filled his eyes.

"Grey?" Alice's voice was scratchy. Greyson grabbed a cup from the bedside table and helped her drink. "What happened?" She asked once he returned the cup to the table.

Greyson reached for her hand and raised it to his lips, kissing her knuckles. "You, my dear Alice, were shot." He squeezed his eyes closed for a moment before looking back at her. Anger flashed in his eyes. "You practically died on the field. What were you thinking?"

"I saw Cain and a man with a gun. Their full attention was on you, and I knew…" Alice moved a little and then groaned. "I knew they were going to kill you. I lost you once, Grey. I couldn't do it again."

"So, you took the bullet instead?" Greyson growled. A knock on the door stopped what Greyson was going to say next.

An old man with thinning hair walked in. "You sent for me, Alpha?" The man crossed to Greyson. "Awe I see our patient is finally awake." He smiled at Alice. "I just need to check the incision site to make sure that all is healing properly."

Greyson stood from his chair and moved to the other side of the bed where he grabbed hold of her other hand. The doctor pulled up her shirt enough to reveal a thick white bandage on her stomach. Greyson's hand tightened on hers and he pressed another kiss to her knuckles. She had never seen him so undone before.

"You are a very lucky young woman." The doctor said as he carefully started to pull the bandage back. "The bullet hit several vital organs. Honestly, I have no idea how you stayed alive. It was a miracle that you lived long enough to remove the bullet and suture you up." He finally removed the bandage and froze.

"What is it?" Greyson asked anxiously.

"The incision?" The man said paling.

"Infection?" Greyson moved closer as tension rolled off him in waves.

"It's gone." The doctor's cold finger touched her skin before pulling back quickly as if he was burned. "I don't understand." He breathed.

Greyson's head dropped as he drew in a shaky breath. "Thank goodness." He looked back up at the doctor, his eyes glowing. "This is between you and me. No one else will know of this." Greyson's voice was hard. When the doctor nodded, Greyson let out a sigh and his posture sagged as if he carried the weight of the world. "Alice has the ability to heal herself."

The doctor blinked in surprise. "If she heals herself, why did she need me?"

"My guess is the bullet caused enough damage that it would have killed her before she could heal herself. You also had to fish out the bullet." Greyson shook his head. "But I'm not fully sure."

"How did she not die then?" The doctor asked as his thick white eyebrows drew together. "Her heart rate was far too slow. It appeared to have stopped for almost an hour."

Alice's mind spun. Her heart had almost stopped for an hour and yet she was alive. She sat up quickly, startling both Greyson and the doctor. She tugged her shirt back down as she faced Greyson. "Where is Isabel?" She asked.

"She is sleeping in the other room with the kids and Matt. Alice, you should be lying down and resting." Greyson said as he tried to get her to lay back down.

"I feel fine." Alice argued. "Thank you, doctor, for your role in saving my life." Alice gave the doctor a smile as she dismissed him. He gathered his things and then left the room. "I need to speak with Isabel." Alice turned back to Greyson.

Greyson ran a hand through his hair, clearly battling whether to force her to rest or to do as she asked. In the end, he quietly slipped into the next room. A few minutes later, he returned with Isabel and Matt. Isabel sat next to Alice on the bed and grabbed her hand.

"What is it, Alice?" Isabel asked, clearly concerned.

"Where is my necklace?" Alice gave Isabel a pointed look, hoping she understood what Alice was really asking.

"After your surgery and you were stable, I removed the necklace." Isabel explained.

"Your necklace? As in the Guardian's Stone?" Greyson asked as he stepped towards the bed. A muscle ticked, as he clenched his jaw.

"The necklace wasn't the Guardian's Stone, Greyson." Isabel turned to look at him.

"Of course it is. It said so in the book I retrieved from the hidden library at the castle." Greyson began to pace.

"No, the necklace was a protection amulet called the Guardian's Amulet. If mortally wounded, the wearer's life is preserved for one hour. After Alice's surgery, the glow faded. She used up all the power left within it." Isabel patted Alice's hand before standing.

Greyson took Isabel's vacated spot. "So, without that necklace, Alice would have died?" Matt asked in disbelief.

"I believe the necklace kept me alive long enough for my natural healing ability to repair the damage." Alice squeezed Greyson's hand.

"Why Alice? Why would you risk sacrificing yourself for me?" Greyson sounded pained. "You shouldn't have done it. You could have died." Greyson had rotated to face her.

Slowly Alice maneuvered until she was sitting in his lap. She wrapped her arms around his neck as his arms went around her waist. Guilt filled Greyson's eyes and she knew he was blaming himself for her injury. "Because I love you, Grey. I would willingly sacrifice my life for yours, just like you would for me."

Alice's wolf pendant grew hot, and she yanked it off. It began to emit a purple glow. Alice gasped and dropped it on the bed. Greyson set her on the chair that he had been sitting on when she woke up, and positioned his body in front of hers. Alice stood and clasped the back of Greyson's shirt as she peeked around him to see what would happen next.

After several tense moments, the purple glow faded, and the wolf pendant returned to its normal black color. "Well, that was interesting." Matt said slowly.

Greyson moved forward and slowly picked it up. His brows furrowed in confusion. "It's cold." He said as he glanced at Alice.

Alice grabbed it from his hand to examine it for herself. "Aren't all stones cold?" Matt asked confused.

"This one always seemed to be warm." Alice explained. "But Grey is right, it's cold now."

"I think you did it, Alice." Isabel said softly.

Alice looked over at Isabel. She sank down onto the bed as Isabel's words sank in. She dropped her gaze back down to the wolf pendant. "A sacrifice must be made. Proof of love conveyed." Alice whispered. Still in a bit of shock, Alice raised her eyes up to Greyson's. He was crouched in front of her with a concerned expression on his face. "We did it. We removed the magic from the Guardian's Stone."

"What? I'm not following. I thought you said the necklace was a protection amulet." Greyson stated as he continued to watch her. Alice explained what Isabel had told her about Isabel giving Greyson the stone as a baby. And that him giving it to her when they were teens probably activated the stone's ability. "All this time, we had the Stone." Greyson cupped Alice's cheek. "The Stone knew what I didn't at the time." He kissed her gently. "You were already mine back then." Alice smiled before putting her bracelet back on.

"We should all get some rest. It was a long day yesterday, and tomorrow might prove to be just as chaotic." Isabel said after she yawned.

Matt agreed and the two went back to the other room. Greyson climbed into bed next to Alice and pulled her close to him. He buried his face in her neck and took several deep breaths. Alice bit her lip to keep from squirming as his breath tickled her neck.

"What happened after I was shot?" Alice asked.

Greyson shook his head. "Not tonight, Love. You aged me ten years with your little stunt, and I need rest. We will explain everything to you later." He kissed her temple.

"I'm sorry I scared you." Alice whispered.

"I understand why you were so angry with me for making you think I was dead." Greyson kissed her forehead. "On the field, I was ready to kill you myself if you lived. You should never have risked your life for me."

"Grey, I would do it again if I had to." Alice said gently.

"I know." His arms tightened around her. "Get some rest." After several minutes, Greyson's soft snoring had Alice smiling. His familiar scent and sounds lulled her back to sleep.

Chapter 27

As Greyson woke, he looked over at his sleeping wife. Her head rested on his shoulder and her hand gripped his shirt in a soft fist. Carefully, he scooted out from under her and out of bed. He pressed a gentle kiss to her head and pulled the blanket more fully around her before getting dressed and slipping out the door. He checked on the kids and stepped out into the hall.

Luther, Matt, Linus, and Jonah were in the hall waiting for him. "How is she doing?" Linus asked, keeping his voice down.

"She woke up for a few minutes last night with questions but is resting right now." Greyson looked back at the door. He hated having to leave her so soon after she nearly died.

"Hopefully, this goes quickly so you can return soon." Luther gave him an empathetic smile. "Linus and Jonah have volunteered to stand guard while the rest of us go to the trial." Greyson nodded his thanks to the two men before turning and heading down the hall, Matt and Luther following.

The throne room was filled with pack members from both the First Moon and Howling Meadow packs. Lawerence saw them enter and gestured Greyson over. Taking a deep breath, he met with Lawerence at the front of the room where Alpha Maddox had sat. Matt stood at his side and scanned the room on alert. As he turned to face the room, a hush fell over the crowd.

"Alpha King Greyson, of the First Moon Pack." Lawerence announced and stepped back leaving Greyson and Matt standing alone on the platform.

Greyson cleared his throat. "I would like to first give you all an update on the condition of my wife. I know that many of you have been inquiring about her. She is doing well and expected to make a full recovery." Cheers and clapping filled the room, and Greyson raised his hand to silence the crowd. "According to my Beta, both packs want the trials of Queen Alice's attackers to be held immediately. I am more than willing for that to happen. However, I am unable to sit as judge at their trials." Murmuring started up, but Greyson pushed on. "Beta Matthew and I are too personally involved with the three of them, and as a result, cannot be impartial judges. I will randomly select six members from each pack to sit on a council to judge in my stead."

Greyson gave a nod to his men standing along the walls and they began moving through the crowd of people. Five minutes later, twelve individuals sat with Lawerence at a table in front of the platform facing the crowd. Greyson and Matt took up their seats on the platform to watch the proceedings. The room quieted down as Cain was brought into the room escorted by John and Phil and chained to the floor where Greyson had been chained. John and Phil assumed their positions flanking the prisoner.

"What is your name?" Lawerence asked as he stood.

"Cain Michaels." Cain said as he stood tall.

"Cain Michaels, you are here to be judged by your peers for breaking the terms of a formal challenge issued by Beta Matthew of the First Moon Pack, murder, kidnapping, and attacking Alice Hunt. How do you plead?" Lawerence asked.

Cain sputtered for several moments before finding his voice. "Murder? Kidnapping? Who is Alice Hunt? What are you talking about?"

"Very well." Lawerence took his seat. "The council can now begin their questioning."

Greyson listened as the members of the council asked Cain multiple questions. Cain kept denying killing or kidnapping anyone. Greyson ground his teeth in an attempt to control his rising anger. Finally, a man at the end of the council table stood.

"You do realize that ordering the command to have two elderly people killed in their home and having their grandchildren taken to a remote cabin is considered murder and kidnapping, don't you?" Greyson realized that the man was Bear.

"Bradley was the one to suggest it. He said those kids were important to Alison, and I needed leverage." Cain shot back at Bear before snapping his mouth shut and glaring.

"So, you did have the Finns killed, their home burned, and their four grandkids taken?" Bear asked.

"There were only three." Cain growled.

"Ah, yes. Three grandkids kidnapped so that you could blackmail Alice Hunt?" Bear continued.

Greyson was impressed with Bear. Cain had practically admitted to everything and implicated Bradley as well. Cain did not say anything.

After several minutes of silence, Lawerence led the council from the room to deliberate on what everyone thought of Cain. Ten minutes later they returned. The council retook their seats, but Lawerence remained standing.

"Cain Michaels, this council has found you guilty of breaking the laws of a challenge, murder, kidnapping, attacking the royal family, and blackmail." Cain pulled at his chains, but Lawerence continued. "You are hereby sentenced to life in prison. You will remain within the Howling Meadows Pack until arrangements can be made to transport you to the First Moon Pack prison where you will live for the rest of your life."

Cain tried to pull the chains free as he yelled and threatened the council members and Greyson. "Alison is mine! She will be mine!" He roared.

Greyson stood and pushed his Alpha presence on Cain. Heads bowed and Cain stopped fighting. "You chose the wrong woman to try to claim, Cain." Greyson removed his Alpha presence so that Cain could look up at him. "Do you know why?" he asked while holding Cain's glare.

"Because Beta Matthew is her brother, Alpha King?" Cain sneered.

"No, because Alice is *my* wife." Greyson growled out and Cain's mouth fell open in surprise.

John and Phil took the opportunity to drag Cain from the room. Greyson retook his seat and let out a tense breath. He would have loved to rip Cain's throat out. He was glad that Cain wouldn't be able to hurt Alice anymore and that the council seemed to be working together to see justice done. If it had been up to him, Greyson would have probably challenged Cain to a death match, and he would have enjoyed every second of it.

The crowd, once again, fell into silence as a woman walked gracefully with John and Phil flanking her. Once she got to the ring in the floor, Phil chained her to it and took a step back. The woman was tall with obsidian black hair and eyes just as black. She had a long nose and flawless skin. She looked exactly the same as the day Greyson had first seen her at the orphanage.

"What is your name?" Lawerence stood as he asked.

"Sasha Barnett."

"Sasha Barnett, you are here to be judged by this council for…" Lawerence was cut off as Sasha laughed airily.

"Oh, certainly I have done nothing wrong. I was merely just standing there, and your men arrested me." Sasha smiled at the council.

"You can plead your case once I am finished informing you of what you are accused of." Lawerence said evenly.

"Very well. What is it that I am being wrongfully accused of?" Sasha's smile tightened slightly.

Lawerence narrowed his eyes as he stared at her. "Sasha Barnett, you are standing trial for mass murder, slave trade, multiple kidnappings, multiple counts of torturing children, and attacking the royal family. How do you plead?"

Greyson watched as Sasha's smile pulled down into a thin straight line. "I want to speak with my son." Sasha demanded.

"Your son will be on trial next. Depending on the outcome of both trials, you might be able to speak with him." Lawerence retook his seat.

"Not Bradley. I want to speak with Greyson." Sasha raised her eyes and looked straight at Greyson.

"I am not your son." Greyson said coolly.

"All you boys are my sons." Sasha smiled sweetly. "Including you, Matthew."

"You lied on the adoption forms, took us to Arlania, and had the older boys beat us until we learned to defend ourselves!" Matt yelled. "We are not your sons." Stunned silence filled the room.

"I did you both a favor." Sasha's sweetness melted into coldness as she spoke. "Look where you are now, Greyson. You are in a place of power. You could not ask for anything better."

"I didn't ask for or want to be Alpha King." Greyson stood. "And doing us a favor. I was four when you took me and forced me to learn to fight, to kill. Matt and I did what we had to in order to survive. What about the boys who did not learn quickly enough?"

Sasha laughed. "You know very well what happened to those boys who were not cut out for the work we needed done."

"What happened to the boys?" A woman on the council asked.

"They were...removed from the program." Sasha stated.

"You claim to be Bradley Barnett's, Grayson Hunt's, and Matthew Hunt's mother." Bear said.

"I am." Sasha nodded.

"You look to be their same age. How old are you?" Bear asked.

Sasha laughed. "Hasn't your mother taught you that it is impolite to ask a woman's age?"

"She is at least one hundred and twenty years old." An older woman in the crowd spoke. The crowd parted and Greyson smiled at Alice's great grandmother. She was standing next to Lord Mason and the rest of Alice's family.

"My, my, my. Is that little Anna?" Sasha sneered. "You look old."

"Who are you?" Lawerence asked.

"My name is Lady Anna Caverton. I have known Sasha for nearly eighty years." Anna said as she and Mason made their way towards the front of the room.

"How is that possible?" Bear asked, obviously confused since Anna looked to be nearly eighty herself and Sasha looked like she was in her late twenties at the most.

"Might I tell you all a story? I promise it will explain my connection to Sasha and give you an understanding of who she is." Anna directed her question towards Lawerence.

"I am quite curious to hear what you have to say, Lady Caverton. But it is up to the council if they will hear your story." When everyone agreed, Lawerence smiled at Anna. "Please continue."

"Have you heard of the Guardians?" Anna asked.

Lawerence nodded his head. "They are descendants of the first Alpha King and Queen. We have been taught that they held powers."

"That is one way of describing it, we call them gifts." Anna smiled. "Some Guardians had the gift of talking with animals or controlling elements. Others saw visions of the future while some could heal. We lived in a castle in Arlania near the border of Valencia. I was raised from a very young age by a woman named Miranda. Miranda was in her forties when she took me in. She was the Matron of the Guardians and had the belief that with these gifts, Guardians were meant to aid Shifters and humans in living in peace."

"Miranda was a fool." Sasha spat. "Shifters and humans could never live in peace."

Anna continued as if Sasha had not interrupted. "Miranda's sister, Sasha, held different views. She thought Guardians were superior to both Shifters and humans. We had knowledge of a sacred stone that would grant the owner the ability to control Shifters. Sasha wanted to use the Stone and have the Guardians rise to power. When Miranda refused, Sasha left the castle. Years later she returned. I was barely eighteen when the castle was attacked."

"The nearby townspeople were manipulated into thinking that the occupants of the castle were dangerous to the community by a man and his wife. They gathered as many as they could and attacked the castle. The townspeople were under the assumption that justice would fall upon those at the castle for their crimes. The women that lived within the castle were gathered up and burned alive within a lower room of the castle." Mason took up the story.

"How do you know this?" A man on the council asked.

"I was there. I was one of the many townsmen that was taken in by the woman's passionate speeches. Once I realized what was actually happening, it was too late, and I was unable to stop the massacre." A haunted look crossed Mason's face as he remembered that night.

"Do not believe his innocent look. This man just admitted to helping kill thirty innocent women." Sasha yelled. "He should be the one on trial."

"Let me get this straight, you two are claiming that this woman," Bear pointed at Sasha. "Was there when you were young?"

"I'm sorry, young man. Let me clarify something. Sasha is a Guardian with the gift of being young." Anna looked over at Bear with a smile.

"Eternal youth, little Anna. I have the gift of eternal youth." Sasha said, clearly annoyed.

"And what of the kidnapping charge?" A woman from the council asked.

"She kidnapped me twenty years ago and has been trying to capture me and then my daughter ever since I escaped." Greyson smiled as Lady Kyrie stepped to stand by Anna.

"And you are?" Lawerence asked, raising his brow.

"My name is Lady Kyrie Talford. I am a Guardian as well. I have the gift of visions. Sasha and her son, Teddy Barnett, captured me in hopes that my visions would lead them to the Guardian's Stone." Kyrie explained.

"You clearly did not matter much. I only tried to find you again in order to avenge my Teddy." Sasha glared at Kyrie with pure hatred.

"I think we have enough to discuss Sasha Barnett's case." Lawerence stood and the rest of the council followed suit. They exited the room again and low voices hummed as those gathered began to talk.

Greyson met Sir Lance's eye and he gave Greyson a nod and smile. How had they known where to come? Then Greyson saw Isaac standing next to Rowan. No wonder no one had seen Isaac since he reported that Alice was safe. He must have flown back to the Talford's to bring them here to see Alice. The door opened and the council filed back in. They were gone for less time than with Cain.

"Sasha Barnett, you have been found guilty on all counts: mass murder of the Guardians, working with the slave trade by trafficking children, multiple kidnappings of children from orphanages, multiple counts of torturing those children, and attacking the royal family." Lawerence paused and looked up. He kept eye contact with Sasha as he continued. "You have been deemed too dangerous of a person and have been sentenced to death. You will be taken back to your cell until your sentence can be carried out."

"Please, take pity on my Bradley." Sasha begged. "He was so distraught seeing his father killed. He only wanted to avenge his father." Tears filled Sasha's eyes, but her voice remained strong. "As Alpha Maddox's firstborn son, he, by right, should be the next Alpha of this pack."

Greyson felt like someone had punched him in the gut. Bradley was Alpha Maddox's son? That made him Greyson's brother. Greyson glanced over at Matt to see the shocked look on his face, too. Lawerence called for the guards to take Sasha away and to bring the next prisoner. Greyson swallowed. Could Bradley really be his brother?

Lawerence approached Greyson and Matthew on the platform while they waited for Bradley to be brought in. *"Was she telling the truth?"* Greyson asked through the mind-link, opening it up to Matt as well.

Lawerence took a deep breath and let it out slowly. *"Isabel had written to me shortly after your oldest sister was born. A woman came to Maddox claiming her one year old son was his. Maddox sent her away and Isabel figured that was the end of it. But seventeen years later, Maddox went on a trip and came back angry. He got drunk and ranted about one woman only being able to bare females and the other a worthless human."*

The door at the end of the room opened and Bradley was dragged into the room by Phil and John. Greyson studied him more carefully. Bradley had Maddox's black hair and many of his facial features. Now that he thought about it, the resemblance between father and son was definitely there.

Lawerence stepped back to his place at the table and closed his mind to Greyson. Bradley fought as they chained him to the floor and spat in John's face. To John's credit, he just wiped the spit off his cheek and stepped back to his place.

"What is your name?" Lawerence asked.

"Bradley Barnett." Bradley said as he turned from glaring at John to face Lawerence. The moment Bradley saw Greyson, his face turned purple with rage. "You little cockroach!" He roared. "How many times do I have to kill you for you to stay dead?!" He lunged for Greyson, but the chains pulled tight. "If only I had followed through with strangling you when you were six and lied to me. And you!" His eyes flicked to Matt. "You were always doing what that piece of trash asked you to do. You should have been killed on that mission, but he just had to interfere, didn't he? I won't make the same mistake twice; I will kill you myself instead of expecting others to do it for me."

Matt and Greyson stood as they glared at Bradley. But Bradley continued his tirade. "You have always thought yourself better than me. First, when you refused to submit to me in the ring and those barbarians from the north took you for a few years and then again when you saved your precious shadow. How did you like the Pit? Did you enjoy all those creatures down there? I should have been there with George and the others as they showed you what happens to those who do not follow orders. I wouldn't have let you live like they did." Bradley strained against the chains again. "You think you are all big and powerful because you found you carry Alpha Maddox's blood in your veins, well guess what? So do I. You are nothing special. How does it feel knowing that your own parents sent you to an orphanage instead of keeping you?"

Bear rose from his chair, took three steps and punched Bradley in the face with such force that he landed on his back. He groaned but did not get up. "I think we have enough information to discuss this vermin's case as well." Bear didn't wait for anyone, and he left the room. The rest of the council stood slowly, eyeing Bradley, and followed after Bear. While they were gone, Bradley regained his awareness.

Greyson remained standing as Bradley struggled to get to his feet. When he finally stood and faced Greyson, Greyson crossed his arms over his chest. "How does it feel, Bradley, to be punched when you can't defend yourself?"

Bradley growled and lunged again. The chains pulled tight, and Bradley fell to the ground again. The side door opened, and the council reentered. None of them sat as they faced Bradley.

"Bradley Barnett, you have been found guilty on all counts: murder, attempted murder, child abuse, slave trade, kidnapping, and attacking the royal family. You have been deemed too dangerous and have been sentenced to death. You will be returned to your cell where you will wait for your sentence to be carried out." Lawerence said with no emotion in his voice. "Take him away." John and Phil dragged Bradley from the room as he continued to yell at Greyson and Matt.

When the doors closed behind him, silence filled the room. Greyson retook his seat feeling exhausted. "Alpha?" One of the men from the council stood before Greyson. Greyson nodded for him to continue. "We understand that you did not wish to judge due to your history with them. However, as Alpha King you are required to carry out their sentence." The man gave him an apologetic look. "The council wishes it to be done as quickly as possible so that the pack can feel safer knowing the threats have been eliminated.

Greyson looked over at Matt who looked just as unsure as Greyson felt before looking back at the man. "Very well. I will speak with my advisors, and we will get this taken care of today." Greyson stood and sent a mind-link to Lawerence, Drake, Luther, Bear, and Matt to meet him in the council room in twenty minutes.

Chapter 28

Alice tried not to show her anxiousness as she and Isabel walked with the kids to the garden. Their guards, Linus and Jonah, weren't happy that Alice insisted on going to the garden, but they relented when she put her hands on her hips and glared at them.

Isabel said that she had used her Alpha presence on them, which made Alice feel a little bad. Once Isabel opened the door to the garden, the kids stepped inside with wide eyes. Asher took off across the grass, chasing birds while Isabel and Alisha wandered off to the shade of some trees. Alice repositioned Avery on her hip and turned to her guards.

"I'm sorry." she said and lowered her eyes.

"What for, Queen Alice?" Linus asked in surprise.

"I didn't realize I had used my Alpha presence to get you to agree to bring us here." Alice looked back up at her guards' faces. "I shouldn't have, and I am sorry."

Both looked a bit taken aback by her apology before smiling at her. "You are our Queen." Jonah bowed. "We will protect you no matter where you wish to be."

"If it makes you feel better, the garden has the same protection that Queen Isabel's rooms have on them." Alice smiled back at them, and they laughed. Linus gestured for her to go farther into the garden. They stayed near the door as they watched over them.

Alice found the tree she had read Greyson's letter under and laid out the blanket she had brought with her. She put Avery down to play while she turned to watch Asher run across the grass and smiled. He had so much energy. Alice's smile faded.

Where was Greyson? She had awoken to find him gone and his side of the bed cold. She had tried to mind-link him, but he didn't respond. When she asked Isabel, she had said that he and Matt had pack business that required them, even though Greyson had tried to get out of it.

Apparently, they had left hours before Alice had even woken up. She spent the next several hours playing with the kids and trying to distract herself from Greyson's continued absence. But the longer he was gone, the more her anxiety grew. It did not help that poor Asher felt cooped up and was practically jumping off the walls.

Alice let out a tense breath as she scanned the garden again. Alisha was reading the book Alice had bought for her at the market with Isabel sitting several feet away. Asher was hanging off a low branch of a tree. Avery was playing with some baby blocks that Isabel had found in a box.

Alice jumped as arms circled her from behind. She whirled around to see who grabbed her. Greyson stood there with a tired smile on his lips. "You scared me." Alice accused him as she tried to slow her racing heart.

"I am sorry, Love. I didn't mean to scare you." Greyson leaned down and kissed her. When he pulled back, she could see exhaustion in every feature.

"Would you like to sit with me?" Alice asked, motioning to the blanket.

"Dad!" Asher yelled as he raced towards them. Greyson let go of her and scooped Asher up and kissed his cheek. "Come play with me." he demanded as he wiggled to get down.

"Your dad needs to talk with your mom for a few minutes, but I would love to play with you." Matt crouched down to Asher's level. "After all, I need to solidify my title as favorite uncle."

"You are my uncle?" Asher asked, amazed.

"I am your dad's brother." Matt glanced up at Alice and winked. "Would you like to play with me?" Asher nodded enthusiastically. "Do you want me as a wolf or how I am now?"

"You can shift to a wolf?" Asher was practically vibrating with excitement. Matt jogged away and shifted to his wolf. He turned around and did a playful bow, tail wagging. Asher squealed as he chased after Matt.

Greyson sat on the blanket and looked up at her. She smiled and sat next to him. He immediately wrapped his arms around her middle. He pressed a kiss to her neck. "I thought you were supposed to be resting." He said quietly.

"I am resting." Alice turned and leaned more comfortably against him. "Now, will you tell me what happened at the field and why you have been gone all day?"

Greyson took a deep breath and leaned his head back against the tree. "I pinned Maddox, but he would not submit. I mind-linked him and told him to give it up. He told me to kill him because he wasn't going to stop. I mind-linked Lawerence and he said there was no other way to end the challenge if Maddox was not willing to submit."

"I'm so sorry, Greyson. I know how you feel about ending a life." Alice wrapped her arms over his and squeezed.

"Then you were in front of me as a gunshot went off. You fell and that's when I saw the blood." Greyson's arms tightened and he lowered his head so that it rested on her shoulder. "Never do that again." He begged. "Please, Love. I thought I would die right there along with you."

Alice turned slightly so she could see him. Greyson looked so beaten down. She had never seen him look so broken. Not even in her visions of him as a kid being beat, or while he was a prisoner. She pressed a kiss to his cheek, and he closed his eyes. He took a deep breath before opening them again.

"The pack quickly got Cain and the others involved. Matt saw to their placement in the dungeon while I stayed with you. Your heart stopped, Alice, before the doctor even got there. You were not even breathing. When the doctor was checking for a pulse, he said he felt a single beat but then lost it again. I commanded him to perform the surgery. I know he thought I was crazy. Your heart literally only beat once every two minutes, and you were barely breathing." Alice could feel his desperation and panic flowing through the mate bond.

Alice didn't know what to say so she just leaned more heavily against him and held tighter to his arms. She felt him take several more deep breaths. He cleared his throat. "The packs wanted the trials for the attackers to be done as soon as possible. That is where I have been all day. Cain has been sentenced to life in prison while Sasha and Bradley were sentenced to death." Greyson said in a tired voice.

Alice gasped and turned in his arms to face him. She put her hands on his cheeks as she studied his face. "Sasha and Bradley were here?"

Greyson moved his hands to her hips. "Bradley is the one that shot you. Sasha was with him and Cain. I didn't feel like I could be impartial in judging them, so I appointed a temporary council. However, as Alpha King, I was required to carry out their sentences." Alice saw pain in his eyes. "We are free from them now. You do not have to live in hiding anymore, Princess."

Tears filled Alice's eyes as the meaning of his words hit her. They were safe. They did not have to live in fear anymore. The relief that filled her was accompanied by the realization of what Greyson had said about their sentences. "You had to...?" Alice asked as a tear slipped out onto her cheek.

Greyson wiped it away and pressed a quick kiss to her lips. "I had the doctor administer a lethal dose of a medication that slows the heart. Once they were both confirmed as dead, the council set up a place to burn their bodies. Drake and Lawerence are overseeing that right now."

"I love you." Alice whispered as she laid her head on Greyson's shoulder.

He put his arms back around her and laughed softly. "I love you too, Alice."

Avery crawled over to them and climbed on Greyson's legs as she hit Alice's leg with her hand and smiled. A scream and growling had Greyson setting Avery in Alice's lap and jumping to his feet. Alice quickly stood as well, as she looked across the garden. Asher was sprinting back towards them with his face pale.

Greyson immediately shifted and took off in the direction Asher had come from. Asher crashed into her legs, almost causing her to fall, as she watched three wolves fighting on the far side of the garden.

Two wolves were attacking Matt, while two others raced toward them from the other side of the garden. Greyson jumped into the fray. As soon as Greyson's wolf got there, the other five wolves stopped and dropped to their bellies and whined. Alice slowly approached with Avery on her hip and Asher walking behind her, clinging to her leg.

Matt shifted back to human. He was breathing hard but seemed unharmed. Greyson turned his big head to the dark grey and brown wolf. They shifted back to human, and Alice gasped. Her father and brother stood there looking sheepish.

Greyson shifted and crossed his arms over his chest. "Sorry, Matt. We didn't realize it was you. All we saw was a wolf attacking a child." Rowan said. "When did you shift?"

"On my birthday." Matt laughed as he stepped up to Rowan and gave him a brotherly hug. "It's good to see you, again."

"It's good to see you too, Greyson. Man, you are intense as a wolf now." Rowan laughed.

"Alice? Who are these little ones." Lance asked, stepping up to her slowly.

Alice gave her father a side hug. "I missed you, dad." She said with a smile. She watched as Greyson picked up Asher who shyly laid his head on Greyson's shoulder. "This is Avery and that is Asher. Alisha is over there with Queen Isabel." Alice turned and pointed across the garden to where Alisha was now standing, watching them.

"Alice!" Alice turned to see her mother rushing towards her. Greyson lifted Avery from her arms and settled her against his other shoulder. Alice gave him an appreciative smile as her mother pulled her into a hug. "You are in so much trouble, young lady. I cannot believe you ran away and didn't tell anyone where you were going! We have been so worried." Kyrie scolded Alice while crushing her in a tight embrace.

"Mom, I'm sorry I made you worry but I had to go, and you wouldn't have let me." Alice explained stepping back and moving to give Rowan a hug.

"You look like you are doing better." Rowan commented as he hugged her tightly. "Like seriously, you looked like a minute away from death when you left."

"Thanks, Rowan. You are always so kind." Alice said dryly.

Alice realized that not only were her parents and brother there, but her great grandparents, Uncle Marcus and Aunt Sam, and Luke with a pretty blonde were there too. She greeted everyone and learned that the blonde was Luke's wife. She was so happy to see everyone that she had not noticed Alisha and Isabel crossing over to them. Alisha moved to Greyson's side.

"It is good to see you in such good health, Greyson." Kyrie said with a smile. "Who do you have there?"

"This is Alisha, Asher, and the baby is Avery." Greyson introduced the kids. Avery was asleep on his shoulder and Asher was still shyly laying on his other shoulder while Alisha half hid behind him. Alice moved to Greyson's side and lifted Avery from his arms. She woke for a second before settling back to sleep on Alice's shoulder.

"I didn't get to tell you before, but I sent some men over to the Finns to confirm what the kids had told us." Greyson sent her a mind-link. "Mr. and Mrs. Finn were both killed, and the store was burned to the ground. Dante's body was found behind the shed." Alice blinked back tears. "My men said they only found Midnight and are taking him to the First Moon pack. I don't know what happened to Prince."

"I had to sell him when I came to Valencia." Alice told him.

"Where? And I will see if our men can find him." Alice told him what pack she had sold him in and knew he had sent someone to go look for her horse. His attention focused back on her. "I also sent someone to Miss Mary's. Since the kids are considered orphans, I am having her put together adoption papers so that we can legally adopt all three kids. She said she should have the paperwork here in the morning."

"Don't mind them." Matt laughed. "They are mind-linking."

"They are what?" Rowan asked and Alice turned around to face her family.

"Since Greyson is now the Alpha King, he is able to mind-link with his pack members. Mind-linking is like having a conversation with a person but through just the mind so no one can overhear you." Matt explained.

"How fascinating." Anna clapped her hands. "So, what are you two discussing?"

"It is something that we can talk about later." Alice said as she glanced at Isabel. "This is Queen Isabel, of the Howling Meadows Pack, and Greyson's mother."

"She's my mother too." Matt whined.

"It is so good to meet all of you." Isabel smiled kindly. "I will let you all catch up and make sure that dinner will be ready for all of us in the dining hall."

Alice watched her go before turning back to Greyson. "We should probably get the kids upstairs for their naps." Greyson nodded. "It was good to see everyone. Matt can show you to your rooms and we will see you at dinner."

"Look at you, Alice. Queen of the castle." Rowan teased.

"Queen Alice's castle is bigger." A deep voice caused the group to turn to face the newcomer. Drake stood there with a serious expression. "And the lands that surround it are much bigger than Howling Meadows." He winked at Alice before turning his attention to Greyson. "Alpha, it is finished."

"Thank you, Drake. You and your family are invited to dinner in the dining hall tonight. Let Luther and Bear know as well." Greyson gave him a quick nod.

"Yes, sir." Drake turned and left as quickly as he had come.

"We will see you all at dinner." Alice said again before walking with Alisha and Greyson back up to their rooms.

Once there, Greyson settled Asher in their bed while Alice put Avery in Queen Isabel's. Greyson and Alice settled on the couch with Alisha sitting across from them.

Greyson explained that his men had found the burned down building and that her grandparents had been buried at the cemetery near their home by the locals. He went on to explain that as orphans, the three of them would usually be sent to an orphanage. Alisha looked upset at the prospect and Alice motioned for her to come sit by them on the couch.

"You could always stay with us like I mentioned earlier. However, we would love to adopt you." Greyson said once Alisha was settled next to Alice.

"But only if you want us to. If not, you can choose to go to the orphanage, or we can help you find any family you have left."

"No." Alisha sat up straight. "I want you to adopt us." She turned and looked at them. "Asher already calls you dad and Avery calls you da-da." She looked at Greyson. Turning to Alice, her eyes filled with tears. "I want to stay with you. You are like a mom to me."

Alice hugged Alisha close, and Greyson's arms came around both of them. They talked for a while more until Asher and Avery awoke. Greyson helped get the kids ready and they went down to dinner as a family.

During dinner, Greyson had Alice announce that they were adopting Alisha, Avery, and Asher in the morning, to their friends and family. Congratulations were extended and the kids were introduced more to Alice's family.

Asher sat between Rowan and Matt during the meal. The two of them were trying to convince the five-year-old who was the better uncle. Alice smiled at all those gathered, feeling happy and at peace. She looked over at Greyson and caught him watching her. He leaned close and kissed her gently, which caused her parents to beam at them.

Epilogue

Ten Months Later

Greyson opened the door to his and Alice's room to find her sitting up in bed. She looked up and smiled when she saw him. "Where are the kids?" She asked.

"Alisha is with her tutor. Avery is taking a nap with her nanny keeping watch. Asher just finished his riding lesson and is with Matthew." Greyson sat on the bed beside her and kissed her cheek. "How is our little Mason doing?" Greyson touched the little head of their son.

"He is doing better now that he has a full belly." Alice laughed.

"I am sure he is." Greyson kissed the top of the baby's head. "I have asked his grandmother to come up and watch him while we go out for an excursion." Greyson smiled at Alice.

"I don't know, Grey. Mason is only a month old. What if he wakes up?" Alice protested.

Greyson lifted the sleeping infant from Alice's arms and walked to the cradle. He laid his son carefully down, tucking the blanket snuggly around him. He had Alice's dark brown hair and Greyson's amber eyes. A perfect combination of his parents.

Alice came to stand next to Greyson and he wrapped his arms around her. She leaned into him with a sigh. "We will only be gone for an hour, Love. Then we will be back in time to eat dinner with the kids and put them to bed." Greyson pulled Alice towards the door.

He opened it to find Isabel standing in the hall with a smile on her face. "I'm glad you were able to come visit after seeing Faith."

"Of course, Grey. I'm just sad that I wasn't here when the baby was born." Isabel gave both Alice and Greyson a quick hug.

"Kyrie and Lance were here, and everything went smoothly." Greyson gave his mother a quick kiss on the cheek before pulling Alice from their room.

"Thank you again for watching Mason for us." Greyson called over his shoulder as they continued down the hall.

Alice laughed when Greyson didn't stop, even though several people tried to speak to them. She heard his mind-link to the pack, declaring him and Alice as unavailable for the next hour and all issues were to be directed to Beta Matthew.

At first Alice had thought they were going for a ride. They had found Prince and got him back not long after they returned to the First Moon Pack, but Greyson pulled Alice to a slightly overgrown path. He slowed his pace, and his smile grew. He continued to hold her hand as he led her through a dense part of the forest. He stopped and turned to her.

"Okay, close your eyes." Greyson said. He couldn't stop the huge grin that spread across his face. Once Alice closed her eyes, Greyson stood behind her and wrapped his arms around her waist. He helped guide her forward and around a bend before stopping again. He rested his chin on her shoulder. "You can open them now." He whispered.

Alice gasped as she took in what was in front of her. They were standing on a small strip of beach that had large rocks going from the thick forest to the water on both sides. The beach looked to be a mile long and fifty feet from the water's edge to the forest. The sand was clear of debris and the surf was calm. She leaned back against Greyson as she took in the scene.

"It's beautiful." She breathed.

Greyson pressed a kiss to her cheek before letting her go. He stepped around her and walked towards the water. Halfway there he turned around and gave her his crooked grin.

Walking backwards he pulled his shirt off, winked and then ran into the water. He dove under a wave and when he came back up, he looked back to where Alice had been. She was no longer there. His smile slipped before she surfaced next to him. She wrapped her arms around his neck and pressed a kiss to his lips.

"Thank you for bringing me here." She said with a smile.

Greyson put his arms around her waist. "Any time, Love. I have made this our private beach. Only you, me, and the kids are allowed here." He watched as Alice's face lit up with happiness and he grinned at her.

"Have I told you lately how much I love you?" Alice said with a sweet smile.

Greyson's grin widened. "I'm not sure you have."

Alice's smile widened just before she shoved off his chest as a wave broke over his head. He came up sputtering and saw Alice as she reached the beach, laughing and pulling her soaked shirt off. Greyson let out a playful growl as he chased after her. She screamed as he caught her.

"Please, Grey. Go easy on me. I just gave birth to your son." Alice pleaded.

"Mason was born a month ago and to your mother's disbelief, you were completely healed from the ordeal within 24 hours." Greyson laughed.

"Fine. Go easy on me because you love me." Alice changed her plea though her eyes sparkled with laughter.

"I do love you." Greyson said as he walked along the beach while keeping her pinned to him. He started kissing her neck causing her to squirm and laugh. "And I know you well enough to know when you are trying to manipulate me." And with that Greyson threw her into an incoming wave before diving in after her.

Greyson stood back up and shook the water from his face. Alice laughed and wrapped her arms around his neck. Greyson carried Alice back to shore and laid them on the warm sand. Alice rested her head on his shoulder as she continued to laugh. She let out a contented sigh as she looked up into his face.

"I love you, Grey."

"I love you too, my Queen." He said as he kissed her forehead.

THE END

The Hunter Guardian Series

The Hunted Guardian
The Stone's Keeper
The Stone's Secret

Other books by this author:

Left Broken

Upcoming Books

Prey of the Corrupted Alpha
Embracing Dove
Enforcer's Mark
Hoodwinked

www.ingramcontent.com/pod-product-compliance
Lightning Source LLC
LaVergne TN
LVHW012016060526
838201LV00061B/4330